PLATFORMED

A NOVEL

KELSEY JOSUND

Platformed

Copyright © 2021 by Kelsey Josund

Publisher's Cataloging-in-Publication data
Names: Josund, Kelsey, 1993-, author.
Title: Platformed : a novel / by Kelsey Josund.
Description: Seattle, WA: All She Wrote Productions, 2021.
Identifiers: LCCN: 2021936309 | ISBN: 978-0-9968993-3-8 (hardcover) | 978-0-9968993-5-2 (paperback) | 978-0-9968993-4-5 (ebook)
Subjects: LCSH Computer software developers–Fiction. | Climatic changes–Fiction. | Conglomerate corporations–Fiction. | Dystopian fiction. | Science fiction. | BISAC FICTION / Science Fiction / General | FICTION / Dystopian | FICTION / Feminist
Classification: LCC PS3610.O78 P43 2021 | DDC 813.6–dc23

FIRST EDITION
Written by Kelsey Josund
Edited by Thea Chard, All She Wrote Productions

Jacket design by Thea Chard & Andrew Wilshere
Book design by Thea Chard & Vicky Haygood

Published by All She Wrote Productions, Seattle, WA
www.allshewroteproductions.com
Join us on Instagram: @AllSheWroteProductions

Join the ASW Book Fam: Post a photo of yourself enjoying this book on Instagram (tag @AllSheWroteProductions & @KelseyJosund) for inclusion in future special sneak previews, freebies & other bookish goodies!

"'THERE IS GRANDEUR IN THIS VIEW,' SCOLDS A QUOTE FROM DARWIN hanging over my dad's desk at his lab. The words are written in looping brown calligraphy, enclosed in a varnished wooden frame. The quote comes from the last sentence of *On the Origin of Species*. It is Darwin's sweet nothing, his apology for deflating the world of its God, his promise that there is grandeur—if you look hard enough, you'll find it. But sometimes it felt like an accusation. If you can't see it, shame on you."

– Lulu Miller, *Why Fish Don't Exist*

1

IF THIS WENT AS SHE HOPED, SARA WOULD SOON BE INVISIBLE.

The little building was low and unassuming; starkly human amid so much nature, all smooth concrete and black glass, it sat upon the dunes like a barnacle. No familiar logo in sight and nothing like the corporate campus Sara had driven past a thousand times, but it could only be the entry to her new life.

It made sense that it was so simple. They wouldn't want it associated with their brand if things went wrong inside.

She followed her friends from the car along a path cut into the landscape, their footprints falling apart in the rain-damp sand behind them. Green lichen and red succulents and twisted salt bushes swept across the hills. In the distance, waves rolled silver and constant under the cloudy sky, beating against the shore like her heart on her ribs and her feet on the sand.

She wondered what would happen to her rickety old car, left alone in the empty parking lot. She pictured it swallowed by the dunes, buried by the hungry sand, unnoticed by anyone who might come after.

How strange that the parking lot was empty, she thought. Their choice to come quickly had been wise, it seemed—before a tide of fleeing people tried to do the same.

Or maybe no one else was coming. Maybe they were fools, falling for something rather than cleverly getting out ahead of the masses who saw through it.

Sara lingered on the edge of her new life, searching the empty highway for her sister's car, hoping that, somehow, she had caught up to them in time.

They reached the building. Zach held the door in some semblance of chivalry that part of her hated and another part loved. She watched him stand in the rain as she let the other three women enter before her, not minding the rain dripping down her nose. A few more moments to breathe fresh air and smell the sea.

The air inside the building was dry and cool, with too much air conditioning for a drizzly winter day. She expected books on shelves and racks of t-shirts and hoodies scattered about, all the signifiers of the company that so many wore as badges of honor, but instead it was empty. Their footsteps echoed off brushed cement walls and bare wood. Skylights let in the day from above.

In the center of the room, a youngish woman with gray-streaked blonde hair stood behind a counter, smiling blandly. Her expression was almost robotic, giving the impression that she had been standing there alone and smiling for hours.

Sara glanced at Beatrice beside her, who smiled slightly—reassuringly. Sara looked away.

This had been Bea's idea. They all waited for her to act.

She stepped forward and Sara fixated on her red-purple dyed hair, how familiar it was amid so much strangeness. Sara would never have followed anyone else into this unknown future.

"Is this the screening center?" Bea asked. "Maps said we had arrived, but…"

The woman nodded and her smile stretched wider. "Yes, you're in the right place! I'll help each of you, just line up."

Bea glanced back at her friends, asking a silent question.

"Entry is an individual process," the woman went on. "But it'll go quickly, don't worry. Just wait right there." She gestured at a sign that said *Please Wait* in sans-serif font, dark gray on cool blue. Calming colors.

Sara did not feel calm, and she did not feel like waiting.

Bea approached the counter. Sara noticed that the others—Priya and Cleo who she had met just weeks before and Zach who she had lived with for years—hung back. She stepped forward, second in line.

The woman spoke to Bea in soft tones and Bea replied in a murmur. Sara made out occasional words, but nothing consequential. The woman spun a tablet to face out and Bea glanced at it, flipping through the pages, then clicked, signed, and smiled awkwardly over her shoulder at them, apologetic and encouraging.

Bea followed the woman to the back of the room and disappeared through a set of swinging black doors. Sara swallowed, took a deep breath, and approached the counter as the woman returned to her station.

"Your friend tells me you fled the fires up north," the woman said pleasantly.

Sara nodded.

"You must reply verbally."

"Yes."

"Okay," the woman said. Her eyes flicked almost imperceptibly from side to side. Sara turned as if to follow her gaze but saw nothing that should have caught her attention. "What do you know about what we do here?"

Sara shrugged. "Not a lot." She paused, thought. "It's one of the intentional communities."

"Good, good. We like you to come in without preconceptions. Your friend, well, she had a lot of ideas…"

"Will that…" Sara's voice cut off and she had to clear her throat before proceeding. Why was she so nervous? Job interviews never bothered her, especially after all the practice she had in the last year. "Will that be a problem for her?"

The woman smiled again. "I just do the initial screening," she said, as if that was an answer.

She seemed to expect a reply, so Sara said, "Okay."

"Anything else we should know about you?"

Sara blinked. What could possibly qualify? "Um…no?"

"Lovely!" the woman said. "Just great." She typed a few things into the tablet, biting her lip, then nodded decisively and turned it to face Sara. "Just fill this out, read the disclaimer, and sign at the bottom."

A little note at the top of the page read 1/24. Sara couldn't believe how quickly Bea had worked through the document—unless she'd had a shorter one. What did it mean if they were given different forms? Had one of them been rejected already?

The words swam before her eyes and Sara realized she was on the verge of tears. She told herself not to be silly. This was no reason to cry. She was making the right choice.

The first page was a very standard intake form like at a doctor's office— name, age, address. *Do you have any of the following medical conditions? Do you have any allergies? Have you traveled outside the United States in the past twelve months, or to the Southeast or Hawaii where tropical diseases are a concern?*

The next several pages seemed to be a personality test, a long list of statements that she had to rate on a scale from Agree to Disagree.

I am an anxious person.

Being around people recharges me.

I am very organized.

I lose things often.

She quickly forgot everything about herself as she clicked down the page.

Didn't they already know everything about her? She'd used their platform for fifteen years, their servers watching her every click, purchase and comment. She imagined they knew her better than she knew herself.

Pages six through eleven were a long list of puzzles. An IQ test?

Sara assumed that she failed it because by that point she was panicking.

She felt acutely aware of her friends standing behind her, waiting for a turn, while she lurked over the glowing screen and stared into its void. No way Bea had had the same never-ending survey; she would have still been taking it.

The next few pages were easier, asking her to fill in her education and employment history. It wasn't long—high school, college, a few short-term roles and one long job before her recent year of unemployment.

She assumed most people who came here had that last element in their work history, so it didn't bother her to note it down. Much.

14/24. What else could they possibly want to know?

With a sigh, she flipped the page and was faced with a solid block of text, smaller than on the previous pages, written in dense legalese.

This was the sort of terms and conditions she knew she should thoroughly read, and she did try—but after detailing shortcomings in her personality, intelligence and career, and with people waiting behind her, and with the knowledge that Bea *certainly* had not read anything like this in the scant minute she'd looked at the tablet, Sara couldn't bear another glance.

She almost made it through the first page before losing the ability to comprehend a single word. Feeling like a failure once again, she clicked through to the end and signed with her finger on the screen, then handed the tablet back to the woman, feeling drained.

"Welcome," the woman said, and her artificial smile stretched even wider.

2

SHE FOLLOWED THE WOMAN THROUGH THE DOORS IN A DAZE, FOOL-ishly expecting to see Bea waiting for her on the other side. The hall she entered was wide, with crisp right angles and concrete walls so smooth they looked soft. The floor sloped slightly downward and the overhead lights hurt her eyes.

Another woman greeted her with a now-familiar empty smile, wearing the same tight bun and simple blue cotton clothes as the first—the most stylish scrubs Sara had ever seen. They could have been the same person, in fact, except that this woman had warm brown skin and much darker hair.

The blonde woman returned to the entry hall without a look over her shoulder. Sara caught one last glimpse out as the door swung closed. She looked through the windows to the horizon instead of seeking out Zach's face, avoiding his searching gaze and instead trying to burn the vast expanse of cool coastline into her mind. She could not see the ocean from where she stood, but from the curl of the clouds and sweep of the salt grass on the sand, she knew it was there.

"Welcome to the processing center," the woman said. She put her hand on Sara's arm. "I'll be taking care of you today."

The place looked like some kind of clinic. Which would make sense, she thought. They'd want to understand your health before admittance.

Sara decided that it all made sense.

She was in no position to protest, anyway, and far too tired to wonder.

The woman asked Sara to step inside and remove her clothes, motioning toward a gown.

"What should I do with my things?" Sara asked, approaching the room. "Is there a locker?"

"Just leave them there. They'll be donated. We'll provide you with everything you need."

Sara balked at the idea of not carrying a bag with her.

Ever since college she'd carried her backpack whenever she left the house—phone, wallet, laptop, water bottle, snacks, tampons.

"But..."

The woman's smile broadened. Of course it did. "Don't worry. We'll provide you with everything you need."

Her expression took on a note of performative caring, but her eyebrows drew together with a sense of unnerving urgency. Sara offered her own tepid smile in response.

The tears that had threatened to spill out of her eyes made another move, and this time she couldn't fight them back. She blinked mascara down her cheeks.

The woman pretended not to notice.

"In here, now." Her tone was calm and steady, but Sara heard the command.

She crossed the threshold into a room that might have been any dressing room in any department store anywhere and dutifully peeled off her clothes, damp from the rain and still smelling of smoke from the fire. That scent had come to be a perverse comfort.

The gown was barely more than what was typically provided at a doctor's office, but again she reminded herself that it all made sense. This all made sense. She pulled it on and realized just how cool the air felt against her skin.

She knelt and looked through each of the pockets of her backpack as if she might select a few items to keep. She wanted to remember each of these things.

The solar charger for her phone.

A crushed granola bar she meant to eat that morning but had forgotten.

The old water bottle that she had carried daily for years.

An almost finished tube of lip balm.

A half-chewed pack of gum.

Keys to the apartment that had burned to the ground.

The detritus of a life she no longer lived.

3

THE WOMAN LED HER DOWN A HALL AND INTO A ROOM THAT RESEMbled a hospital room, with a large bed surrounded by machines, a screen on one wall, and a call button beside the door. It had a tiny attached bathroom. Everything was exactly as she would have imagined it—clean, white and full of empty spaces where she would not have known what details to include. Sparse, but not spartan.

"You'll be here for a few days," the woman said, still smiling serenely, and left.

Sara stood shivering by the door for a moment, trying to process what had happened. Were they just going to leave her there? Why had they taken all of her belongings?

She thought of her backpack, sitting alone in that room. It had contained a book that she hadn't finished reading and a sweatshirt balled up in the bottom that she really could have used just then.

Upon emerging from the changing room, she had clutched her phone out of some desperate hope that they would not take it from her, but the woman had just shaken her head and pried it from Sara's fingers, tucking it away out of sight. The phone felt like an extension of herself. It was bizarre for it to be gone.

They even took the hair ties from around her wrist; her hair hung stringy and limp around her face. She hated it. At least they let her keep her emergency-kit glasses, though they took the case and cleaning cloth.

She stood shivering long enough to realize how ridiculous she was being. The room had a bed and blankets. She could at the very least warm up.

Feeling like maybe she could be dreaming and vaguely hoping that she was, Sara walked across to the bed, peeled back the comforter, and retrieved a synthetic woven blanket to drape around her shoulders. Never trust a hotel comforter.

If she was dreaming, when had it started?

Maybe the fire, tearing through the hills. Maybe when her parents called to say they, too, had fled—a different fire, flames bearing down on San Francisco Bay from all directions. Maybe when Bea convinced them all, even Zach, to give themselves over to the Community.

Or earlier? When the startup folded. When it became clear it would fail, a full year before the fire took their home.

She was not dreaming. Her life was not a nightmare.

It seemed odd that they had not given her anything to do. Was this some kind of test? See if you could withstand boredom?

She knew how boredom worked. It did not faze her.

But the lack of information was unnerving. She had refused to imagine what life would be like in this place before they arrived, but being left alone for hours in an apparently normal hospital room was too absurd to have occurred to her even if she had.

Unless they were testing hospital equipment?

She sat on the floor wrapped in the blanket and stared into space.

A few years before, when things were what she still thought of as normal, she went to an escape room with Zach and Bea and a few other people whose faces she couldn't recall. Friends who apparently didn't matter. The sort of casual weekend activity sandwiched between brunch and cocktails that had filled so many years of her life.

It was a haunted asylum, or something like that. Cursed, maybe. Padded walls, hidden doors, and they had had to escape. She couldn't remember now how they did it, or even if they did.

Maybe this was also an escape room.

But that seemed unlikely. The door was obvious, to start. And she had thought she would be testing products here. They weren't testing *her*.

Right?

She wondered if asylums were actually like that. Did they still lock up the crazies in rooms covered in pillows? That didn't seem half bad, though it would get lonely and boring.

Rather like this.

She pushed to her feet, keeping her hands tucked inside the blanket, wondering why they kept the place so cold and why they shared so little information.

Bea would hate this so much.

It seemed like exploring the room was the thing to do, so she did, taking stock.

Walls: white.

Floor: concrete (cold).

Bed: twin sized.

Table: rather like that in an Apple Store.

The door had the kind of handle you would sooner find in an office than a home and a window cut into it, covered with paper from the outside. So they hadn't thought of everything when they first designed this place.

Speaking of windows—how strange that the room did not have one. No wonder the walls felt claustrophobic.

The screen mounted on one wall, high and large and empty, might have acted like a window if she could turn it on. But she tried all the wake words she could think of to no avail.

How much time had passed? She had no idea.

The lights didn't seem controllable either, which was frustrating. She was so cold and so bored that sleep would be a good solution. It had been days since she slept well; she was confident that now she could. This place was unsettling, but at least she felt safe. But the damn lights.

Maybe she was testing an I-want-to-sleep sensor. She climbed into bed and snuggled into the blankets—plush, fresh, all those bedding words. The mattress probably came in a box.

Maybe she was testing bedding.

The lights did dim eventually, but she was pretty sure she laid there cradled by the fancy mattress for at least an hour before they reacted, so she assumed it had nothing to do with her trying to sleep. But maybe the AI was just really bad at predicting human sleep desires.

She spent that hour trying as hard as possible not to think. Repeating *nothing nothing nothing empty empty empty* over and over and over.

4

Nine years before the Community

"GOT YOU SOME BOBA," BEATRICE SAID, PLOPPING DOWN ON THE bench across from her.

Sara looked up from her laptop, acknowledged her friend and the drink with a smile, then turned her attention back to the screen. "You changed your hair again."

Bea tossed her head and flashed a grin, then took a sip from the giant boba straw. "Like it?"

It was straightened to within an inch of its life and dyed a shade of rather sickening green, but Sara wasn't about to tell Bea just how much she hated it. "It looks like it took a lot of effort."

Bea snorted. "You think it's ugly."

"I liked the blue better."

"Yeah, but the blue was a bitch." Bea leaned forward, craning her neck to see Sara's screen. "How can you work in the sun like this?"

Sara tipped the screen back to give Bea a look. "We don't all have ancient computers, Bea. There's a filter so I can see."

"You gonna try the tea?"

Sara sighed and picked up the blue-gray drink. It had sweated all over the picnic table. "Earl Grey?"

"I knew you'd want caffeine."

"Thank."

"Welc," Bea giggled, never able to keep a straight face.

Sara smiled, though her bad mood from earlier lingered even with her friend trying to cheer her up.

"Why're you working on this beautiful Friday afternoon, you nerd?" Bea asked.

"I have something due at midnight," Sara explained.

"On a Friday? Gross!"

Sara shrugged. "If it was easy, everyone would do it."

"Everyone *is* doing it," Bea pointed out, since computer science was by far the most popular major. She chewed a tapioca ball dramatically.

"Close your mouth when you chew. Were you raised in a cave?"

Bea waggled her eyebrows. "You *know* I was."

Sara laughed. "Anyway, tonight. I'll come out with you guys after I get this turned in."

"You better!"

"I will, I promise," Sara assured her, repositioning the laptop screen as if she were going to return to work.

The sound of raised voices echoed across the quad and they both looked toward it but didn't see anything. Probably some a cappella group performing or something.

"Anyway, this is like all I have to do this weekend. Well, and internship apps."

"You'll have a hard time getting an internship looking like that."

Sara looked across at her sharply. "What do you mean?"

Bea was the one with hideous green hair and a nose ring.

But then, in Silicon Valley that was fairly acceptable.

Bea gestured at Sara with her bubble tea, now almost empty. "You look like a fucking cheerleader or something. Way too blonde for the startup boys."

Sara relaxed. "I thought you were calling me ugly or something."

"That'll never be your problem, my love."

Sara rolled her eyes. "Whatever. Now fuck off, my build is failing."

"I'm proud to say that I don't know what that means," Bea said. "But aren't you going to ask me how *I'm* doing?"

The voices were getting louder, more obtrusive, and Sara fought to keep them from distracting her. Much as she loved Bea, she really did have a lot to do before midnight.

Sara took a long sip of her tea, making Bea wait, then said, "Will you go away after I ask?"

Bea shrugged. "Only one way to find out, isn't there?"

"Fine, then. How are you doing, friend?"

Bea leapt up and pointed dramatically at a building to their left, startling Sara so much she almost dropped her tea. "You know what happened there in the '70s?"

Sara shook her head. "Is that the history building? Anthro?"

"Psychology," Bea said, with dramatic flair. She waited to see if that would trigger recognition in Sara's eyes, but she had no idea what was special about the psych building.

Bea sat down again and slurped up the last of her tea before continuing. "They did this super unethical experiment, recruited a bunch of students here and told half of them they were prison guards and the other half convicted criminals."

"Was ethics just not a thing in the '70s?"

Bea shrugged. "I think they invented morals sometime around when people realized the Vietnam War was a disaster."

Sara shook her head. "Pretty sure that's wrong."

Bea grinned. "Anyway, you know what happened?"

Sara could guess, but she knew Bea wanted to tell her. "What happened?"

"The dudes embraced it! Like the prisoners were groveling or rebellious, the guards got abusive—they had to call it off early."

"Wild."

"*Right?*"

Sara shrugged. "I mean, I don't really see the big deal."

"What?" Bea looked shocked.

Before she could elaborate, though, the shouting voices they'd heard went drastically up in volume. "*Divest the rest!*"

Sara put her hands over her ears, though it wasn't really *that* loud. "Guess they got the microphone to work."

A crowd of about a dozen students marched past, holding handmade cardboard signs and shouting. Sara couldn't even make out for certain what they were advocating.

They rounded the end of the quad and continued on toward the university president's office, their ruckus fading. The girls watched them go.

When they'd thoroughly passed, Sara sighed. "What do they think is gonna happen?"

Bea had a quizzical expression on her face. "I should protest more."

Sara snorted before realizing her friend was serious. "That's what that made you think?"

"Yeah, I mean, they're doing something! What're we doing?"

"I figure once I get my tech job, I can donate to the Sierra Club or the ACLU," Sara replied. "I can't do anything now."

"But they are!"

Sara scrunched up her nose. The crowd had congregated around the president's office and stood there, clapping their hands and wearing out their voices. They had no audience. "Are they?"

Bea stared at her for a moment, looking disappointed, if anything. Then her usual chipper expression returned.

"You were going to add something about the prison experiment?" she said.

Sara shrugged. "I don't remember, was I?"

Then an alarm went off on Sara's phone and she swore.

"What's that?"

"My timer—I need to go put my laundry in if it's gonna be done before dinner, and then I'll have time to get this all done by midnight and—"

"You need to lighten up, is what you need," Bea said, shaking a finger in mock warning. "I'll see you at midnight, my little reverse Cinderella lovely!"

Sara folded up her computer and held it in one hand, the last of her warming tea in the other. She waved awkwardly with the hand holding the tea. "See you tonight!"

She went off to do her laundry and didn't see Bea wander toward the protesters and join their chant.

5

SOMETIME LATER THE LIGHTS RETURNED, AND NOT LONG AFTER that the door opened. Based on how well-rested she felt, she figured an entire night could have passed. Without a clock, she couldn't be sure. She couldn't remember the last time she didn't have a clock.

She expected to see a person, felt her pulse quicken at the prospect of mental stimulation, but it was just a delivery cart. Her pulse calmed down, but her stomach perked up at the prospect of something even better than human interaction: food.

The door closed and the tray sat there, metal cover over something that smelled good and which she really hoped was warm because damn if it wasn't still cold in there. She rose from the bed with the blanket around her shoulders and padded across to the food, thinking that breakfast was usually the only meal she ate without shoes on, but they hadn't given her any shoes, so this was going to be all meals now.

She sat at the plain table on a minimalist metal stool so high her feet didn't touch the ground, and stared at the metal cover, building up to the big reveal.

In a room this empty, food could transform everything. It would be foolish to rush into it.

She ran her fingers over the curves of the cover—brushed steel, so smooth she could barely feel the ridges. So perfect. Someone's career involved designing this thing. Imagine that being your life.

The smell barely escaped, but she thought there was coffee and maybe maple syrup and she hoped there were pancakes. They hadn't given her dinner the night before so she could really appreciate a good breakfast, the kind she used to have as a kid on Saturday mornings, that made you feel a little unwell in the best possible way and left you full until evening.

She'd waited long enough, she decided. With no way to meter out the seconds she had no idea how long it had been except *long enough*.

She was not disappointed.

Coffee, black and opaque in a white ceramic mug, with little cups of cream and soy milk and oat milk and who needed so many options? She poured a little of each into the coffee, watched them whirl through the darkness.

Two pancakes with butter and syrup that tasted real, none of that corn syrup crap, plus apple sauce with chunks of actual apples and yogurt that was maybe the slightest bit vanilla but mostly just tart and delicious.

She was very hungry, it turned out.

Zach loved pancakes. She hoped he had the same meal she did.

Though the thought made her feel more than a bit ridiculous, she thought it nonetheless: just this meal made coming here worth it.

But soon enough the food was gone, and she was left with sticky syrup fingers and dirty dishes and unknown hours laid out before her.

Feeling that delicious post-carb discomfort she had longed for, the tray back by the door, the blanket around her shoulders, she took to walking in slow circles, her footsteps tracing close to the wall and around the bed, weaving in and out of the center of the room.

Left a few laps, then right a few laps.

Like a caged animal.

She stopped, considering the implications, not wanting to be like that poor, sad tiger at the zoo who loped around with its tongue hanging out. But understanding how it must feel.

And after less than a day, too.

She resumed pacing. It didn't hurt her to admit that it felt good to move, even if it was in steady circles. It was pleasant to hear her bare feet on the concrete, the blanket trailing behind her like the cape of a king surveying a lonely kingdom.

When cooped up, animals sometimes hurt themselves to fight the feeling of nothing. Wasn't that why depressed kids cut their arms, too? She'd never been sure, but that sounded right. Pain was better than nothing.

It would be very easy to stub her toe.

She decided she hadn't reached that point yet.

There must be a reason for all of this, she thought, because it cost them something. The bed was comfortable and the food delicious and the light as precisely engineered as the edges of a new laptop. Modern and clean and healthy. The room was not cheap.

The point, she decided, had to be control. Not controlling her, though that also, but controlling a trial. They were testing things. They needed to reset her standards, make people the same in some way, level them. Feed them the same great food and keep them in comfortable and bland rooms for days. Days? Days.

She'd forgotten that the woman had said *days*.

Okay, so maybe it was quarantine, then. That also made sense. The people in here were in a controlled setting. There's that word again. They would not want to introduce illness if they did not have to, and of course they didn't have to, because they could keep anyone new locked up like this.

Quarantine was only fourteen days back during the pandemic. Before that, historically, it used to be forty days. This had better not last forty days.

But that had been, what, Europe and the Black Plague? She tried to remember a high school history class that she had most likely slept through or else blocked from her memory. That wasn't how things worked now, with germ theory and antibiotics and genome sequencing.

She wondered if Emily had arrived yet. Maybe Emily wasn't far away at all, just behind a series of locked doors, eating the same meals as Sara and thinking the same flat, traumatized thoughts. She hated the idea of her little sister alone out in the burnt landscape in her cheap car. Other people said they looked alike, but Sara had always thought Emily just looked vulnerable.

The delivery bot returned and retrieved her dishes. She waved to it.

Was it sequencing her microbiome right now? Probably, she hoped. Maybe then it would declare her fit to join the actual Community soon.

She laughed at herself then. As if the delivery bot was the one keeping her there, not people somewhere watching or herself signing away her freedom without even reading the terms of service.

6

THE NEXT MORNING WHEN THE DOOR OPENED IT WASN'T THE DELIVERY bot, but rather a man in a white doctor's coat.

Yesterday the robot had brought a salad of fresh vegetables, including the most flavorful tomatoes she'd had in years, and a creamy risotto studded with mushrooms, and a soup that was maybe butternut squash, and crunchy, warm garlic bread. She felt immense relief that the pancakes had not been a fluke.

"Sara?" the man asked.

She sat up in bed and nodded.

"I'll be your doctor today," he said.

She expected to be asked to verify her birthday, to scan her thumbprint, to be told his name, but there was none of that. He just stood in the doorway waiting for her.

She stood reluctantly, leaving the comfort of her blanket bunched up with the sheets. "Dressed like this?" she asked.

He smiled, that same patronizing smile she was starting to hate. "I see we didn't give you socks!"

She didn't notice him do anything, but moments later the delivery bot arrived with freshly folded clothes where the food normally was.

"Um," she said, retrieving the clothes. Warm from a dryer.

He nodded and stepped away, letting the door close. She wondered what the point of privacy even was. Of course they were watching her. But there were some things you really needed to pretend in order to feel human.

She shook out the clothes and draped them on the bed. The material was very similar—dull blue-gray and slightly stiff—but they did provide her socks and underwear and shoes that were basically slippers. The dress was slightly more substantial than the last one. And, *thank God*, a sweatshirt.

When she emerged into the hall to find the waiting doctor, she was in a much better mood.

He smiled, an expression that felt slightly more real than the ones before, and set off down the hall with her following. Not making any of the small talk she expected.

The hallway sloped down, enough that had she been in a wheelchair she would have rolled away. The mental image made her smile.

Were all these rooms occupied by people like her? Waiting?

She didn't ask.

They turned left, then right, always down. How big was this place?

"Just in here, now."

The room was small and square with a doctor's table in the middle and many instruments she didn't recognize mounted on the walls and ceiling. She sat dutifully.

"I hope you're doing well, Sara," the doctor said, rolling up on a stool.

"Sure," she said, not knowing how else to reply.

"We're going to start with a physical," he said. "I have your chart here." He tapped through screens on a tablet. "Your last physical was…three years ago?"

She shrugged. "That sounds right."

"Great, great," he said, still reading.

She had never heard a doctor say it was great how infrequently she got checkups.

He retrieved one of the devices hanging from the ceiling—large and sleek and metallic. With earbuds attached.

"We'll start with a hearing test. I want you to raise your left or right hand when you hear something in that ear."

A sequence of beeps, a sequence of raised hands. The doctor nodded.

He inclined his head for a moment as if thinking, then nodded decisively and pushed the device back up. "And your eyes now."

The same procedure, but with goggles placed over her eyes and tiny flashes of light.

"Good news!" he said brightly. "Your eyes and ears and reaction times are all great."

"I'm wearing glasses," she pointed out.

He seemed unbothered by this. "We care about your corrected vision."

The rest of the appointment involved a scale and a heart rate monitor and a stethoscope listening to her lungs, then a long silence in which he mostly just looked at her.

She thought maybe it was a staring contest, though that would be even more absurd. Obligingly, she tried not to blink.

Finally, he got to his feet and opened the door. "Thanks, Sara," he said. "It was great to meet you."

Apparently the appointment was over.

"Aren't you going to walk me back?" she asked.

"Just follow the…" he started, then laughed slightly. "Of course. I'll show you."

She decided not to waste time trying to figure out what he had almost said and followed. How quickly she was becoming complacent.

7

THE APPOINTMENT HAD BEEN A WELCOME RESPITE FROM HER LACK of routine, but it had made her miss breakfast. To her great relief, two trays awaited her outside the room—breakfast and lunch at once.

She unveiled the trays and picked just the best parts from each: the coffee, which was somehow still warm; a bowl of berries; perfectly roasted brussels sprouts; lasagna with crispy cheese.

She left the oatmeal, gone cold and thick with the hours.

The Community was advertised as an experiment in the future of living. People with stellar credentials and no better prospects could join and be coddled the way only the most elite engineers once were, within a tech giant's corporate wonderland, testing their new products and avoiding the worst of the newly broken seasons. It was a job, though a strange one.

This part had to end soon.

She had many hours still before her and nothing more to do with them than the day before. There had to be a way to turn on the screen: it couldn't be there just for the aesthetic.

She ran her fingers along its edges, feeling for anything that might be a button. Nothing.

She scrutinized the perimeters of the bed and the chair and the trim around the walls. Maybe she would find a light switch while she was at it.

Nothing.

Sometime before dinner she gave up and sat on the edge of the bed, tapping one foot, trying to tell herself a story. She'd never been good at that kind of thing, but surely a story would come to her, given enough empty time. Think pieces constantly lamented the end of boredom and what that meant for Western creativity. Well, she was bored now.

Once upon a time there was.

Beginning, middle.

The hero's journey.

The end.

8

THE NEXT MORNING SHE HOPED THE DOOR WOULD OPEN TO REVEAL
a human again, but it was just breakfast, and, inexplicably, eye drops.

She couldn't bring herself to feel excited about food this time.

Maybe this was all an exercise in lengthening attention spans? Corporate
MKUltra for the twenty-first century. Can we reset humanity?

Man, that would suck.

She ate toast and an omelet like it was an obligation, which it was.

She was *obligated* to keep herself fueled, to keep herself alive. On a genetic
level, her body demanded she keep going—you have not reproduced so you
cannot relax.

Funny she was thinking that, because when a person appeared at the
door in the early afternoon (after she failed to finish tomato soup and grilled
cheese, buttery and delicious but also somehow infantilizing) it was a woman
who interrogated her about birth control.

She was young and chipper and wore a doctor's coat. Did not introduce
herself. She led Sara to an OBGYN's office complete with stirrups.

Why not?

"We don't have a pap smear in your files," the woman said. "We don't want
you to get cervical cancer."

As if checking for cancer stopped it from appearing. Schrodinger's can-
cerous cells that always fell away into nothing if you looked often enough?

After the pap smear she explained that everyone who entered the Community had to be on long term birth control. "It's just so much easier," she
said, while prepping a T-shaped metal object that Sara understood would
soon take up residence inside her.

"Even the men?" Sara asked.

Last she heard, men's birth control spiraled the drain and never hit
the market.

The woman grimaced and tried to pass it off as a smile. "It's like
herd immunity."

Which was funny, since a lack of that had been part of the problem.

What had Bea said—what's the point of feminism while the world burns?

Sara desperately wanted to talk to Bea about all of this. She couldn't quite
figure out how she felt without talking through her ideas with Bea, like a

strange emotional barometer.

The procedure was more painful than she'd expected but less painful than she'd feared, and over quickly.

"You'll be crampy and spotty for a week or so," the woman said, patting her on the hand and passing her a bag containing pads and pain meds.

Sara nodded and clenched her teeth. The cramps started almost immediately.

"Ready to go back to your room?"

As if she had a choice.

9

THE NEXT DAY NO ONE CAME TO HER ROOM TO GET HER, BUT SHE didn't mind. They sent her a chocolatey breakfast and indulgent macaroni and cheese lunch and rich stew for dinner and she wished for distraction but was also perfectly okay to not be forced out of bed.

The day after that, a short man with dark hair knocked on the door when she expected dinner. It had been almost two days since she'd done anything besides eat and sleep and was quite ready for whatever kind of examination this might be.

"Everything going well so far?" he asked as they set off down the hall. He had some kind of accent she couldn't place.

"As well as can be expected."

He smiled like this was funny. "Well, today's an exciting day for you!"

"Is it?" She found it hard to summon emotions of any kind. So many days with so little stimulation had deadened whatever emotional range she still had.

"Just in here," he said, practically bowing as he gestured into yet another clinic room. She thought she knew the drill by now, but she did not recognize the machine that took up most of the room. An MRI, maybe?

He noticed her hesitation and gently guided her towards it, his hand on her shoulder.

"What…?"

Instead of answering, he thrust a glass of water and a white pill toward her. Her eyes wide, his smile wider. Was it reassuring?

"A mild sedative."

No one here liked to explain what was going on.

"Why?" she demanded.

"The laser moves quickly," he said. "It stops if you move, so it's much easier if you're relaxed."

Her eyes darted around the room. Her heart pounded.

"Laser eye surgery, right?" she asked, hoping she was right.

"Of course!" he said, laughing now.

Relief flooded her and she didn't know what she'd been worried about, but was glad not to have to confront it. She swallowed the pill, climbed into the chair and settled in, waiting to feel something. He chattered on about the machine and what she would feel and smell—*smell!*—and how quickly it would be over.

Her eyes were forced open and something numbing dropped in, which stung for a moment. Both eyes were suddenly so dry. She thought to ask if that was normal, but then the man stepped away and the machine whirred to life.

She did indeed smell it for just a moment and hear it for just a moment and then it was over. And the world was already so much clearer!

Lights like starbursts mounted in the ceiling, but she could read the *Wash your hands* sign on the other side of the room.

"Now go rest," he instructed her, the words falling around her as she blinked slowly, awed. "Don't rub your eyes."

The pancakes had not made this place worth it, she decided. But this did.

10

Eight years before the Community

SARA SAT CRAMMED INTO THE VERY BACK SEAT OF ERIC'S NEW RANGE Rover with Beatrice and another girl—Ella was her name, maybe? They'd just met that evening. Eric's latest girlfriend. She figured she didn't need to spend much time getting to know her since anyone Eric dated wouldn't last long.

Eric had the music cranked loud, playing some awful Top 40 song that seemed incongruously poppy compared to the concert they were headed into the city to see.

There was no use trying to make conversation, but Bea tried anyway. "Are you excited?" she whisper-shouted.

"Excited to get out of this car!"

Bea laughed and, as if to punctuate their comments, Eric swung wildly across several lanes, throwing them against each other. Sara felt a little ill.

She craned her neck, trying to see out the window or over the heads of the three guys in the middle row—on the crew team with Eric, all indistinguishable jocks in Sara's eyes—to look out the windshield. The car in front of them grew bigger much too quickly and she tensed, wishing Eric would please hit the brakes.

Instead he swerved into the next lane, passing the car they'd almost hit at twenty over the speed limit. Maybe more.

"I'm never riding with Eric again," she muttered, probably too quiet for even Bea to hear.

Out the window, the wide 280 freeway glowed like a miracle as it dove through the hills in the golden hour light, cut smooth and precise across the landscape. A perfect ribbon of black pavement against rolling green springtime that stretched from San Francisco out to indistinguishable suburbs. She could appreciate the contrast.

The brilliant silver of the narrow peninsula lakes in the distance calmed her in spite of Eric's horrific driving. She tried to focus on it.

All too soon, the freeway split into its constituent parts and vomited them into the city, the hills and water long-forgotten memories. The sunset turned into a foggy gray sky and the view became constrained by overpasses and abandoned construction projects.

Eric pounded on the steering wheel and turned the music down. "All right, so who's paying for parking?" he said, looking back at them with an exuberant grin as they rolled to a stop at a red light.

Sara averted her gaze; Eric's dad was the billionaire, not hers. If it had been up to her, they'd have taken the train.

David, sitting in the passenger seat, punched Eric in the arm as the light turned green. The car rolled forward.

They bumped through the city as night fell. At least Eric wasn't running lights. Finally, the car dove underground into a new parking garage, all eco-friendly permeable pavement and LEDs. The radio faded to fuzz. A robotic attendant guided the flow of concert-goers efficiently to open spots and they all spilled out of the car.

Eric looked like he was having trouble staying calm, like at any moment he might start jumping up and down. He descended on his new girlfriend and practically tossed her into the air.

That would have made Sara slap him if he'd done it to her, but Ella seemed to find it hilarious.

Bea rolled her eyes. "I give it two weeks."

David paid for parking and the group wandered up to the street, heading in search of a quick dinner and a liquor store before the show. They stepped around multiple people stretched out asleep on the sidewalk, featureless and run-down on their cardboard beds. Sara looked away.

It smelled of cigarettes and urine and rotting garbage, making the sizzling onions at a street corner hotdog stand entirely unappetizing.

"Does anyone even smoke tobacco anymore?" Sara asked as they waited for a traffic light to change.

Bea scuffed at a cigarette butt with her toe. "Evidently."

One of Eric's teammates pulled an e-cig from a pocket and twirled it in his fingers, grinning at Sara.

"But that's weed, right?" she asked.

He shrugged, took a hit, and put it away. It definitely was.

It was thoroughly dark by the time they sat on a curb eating food truck tacos and drinking out of the cheapest bottle of wine they could find in a 7-Eleven. She'd adjusted to the stink of the city, or maybe just gotten hungry enough not to care.

Bea flipped through a hookup app on her phone, her face illuminated in the glow of the screen. Sara looked over her shoulder.

"Anyone good?"

Beatrice shrugged. "Everyone showing up has the same bio—I like hiking and brunch and dogs."

Sara laughed. "But you also like hiking and brunch and dogs."

"Not enough to sleep with someone about it."

"Come on guys, eat up!" Eric cried, crumpling his taco wrapper and throwing it at a No Parking sign. It missed, but he seemed not to care.

David offered the last swig of the wine to Sara as they all got up. She demurred.

"He likes you, you know," Bea whispered, once he'd turned away.

Sara squinted at his back where he walked in front of them. "But does he like hiking and brunch and dogs?"

The concert was more a mass of writhing college students and a lot of noise than a real show. Sara had been to much better concerts that cost a lot less.

"Do they think having a good enough light show means you can have a shit sound system?" she shouted over the music.

"You're just not drunk enough!" one of Eric's friends shouted back, offering a flask.

She smiled, thinking he was definitely right, and took a swig. "How'd you get this in here?"

He just grinned. Maybe he hadn't heard her.

The crowd danced on around her and Sara tried to enjoy it. The music, when she could hear it, was energetic and fun, and at least here she didn't feel conspicuously whole, the way she had out on the street. The city was in such disarray that her lack of decay felt out of place. Here she was among her peers—young, healthy, full of possibility.

But she couldn't get the image of one particular homeless man out of her mind, propped against the facade of the convention center, looking as dead as alive. Staring at the revelers with empty eyes. Not even trying to ask for change, because who carried change anymore?

"Hey, you want anything?" David shouted in her ear.

She blinked up at him, confused.

"A drink?" he tried again.

"Yeah, sure," she shouted back.

Bea elbowed her. "Are you gonna sleep with him?"

Sara just shrugged.

As it turned out, she didn't sleep with him that night—everyone was too tired after the concert and the long, terrifying drive back in Eric's Range Rover—but several months later, in the depths of finals week, she ran into him on the way back from the library. It was probably two in the morning and they were exhausted in a very different way than after a concert, but it was the kind of exhaustion perfectly healed by french fries and awkward, quiet sex while his roommate slept in the adjoining room.

Nothing like college to sap you of your appreciation for sleep and privacy.

The sex wasn't great, but it also wasn't terrible, and Sara didn't know enough guys to feel like she had any right to be picky.

She would have hooked up with him again, but then it was summer, and then he studied abroad in Madrid, and then they'd just changed too much and she really didn't care. And wasn't that how it always went?

There was a reason Sara fell half-heartedly into and out of relationships, after all. She had much more important things on her mind, too much ambition to be quashed in deference to some generic boyfriend. It was why she liked hanging out with Eric so much: they had a mutual understanding that neither one could ever be interested in the other, and they each appreciated the permanence of a friendship over a flickering romance. He wasn't a very nice person, and hardly a caring friend, but she had Bea for that.

11

THE NEXT DAY THE SCREEN ON THE WALL STARTED TO WORK.

Calming music played out from all sides in the room when she returned from the surgery, a pleasant surprise, and stopped when she verbally requested silence. It was comforting to be back in a room that heard her when she spoke.

In the morning, wondering if the music had been a dream, she asked the room to resume it. Instead, an image of waves appeared on the screen, fresh and blue and expansive.

With her new perfect eyes, watching the waves was the closest thing to a religious experience she had ever had.

She had never noticed before how each wave was unique. Like a snowflake or a fingerprint. Or a tongue.

The waves melted over the course of an hour from deep blue to gray and on toward black, tinged silver where they reflected a light she could not see. Was the sun setting somewhere?

It moved her in a way she could not attach to words. The slowness and transience, the fact that each moment the water formed a new shape that she would miss if she looked away.

If they're trying to lengthen my attention span, she thought, they have succeeded.

12

THE MAN SAID THAT HER EYES WOULD TAKE A COUPLE WEEKS TO heal, so she resigned herself to staying in the little room at least that long. It had begun to feel like home.

The days became one, which made sense given that no daylight reached her. She recalled reading that people actually had an imperfectly calibrated circadian rhythm; in a world without light it would drift, disconnected from all conceptions of day or night.

While eating lunch she considered that it could be midnight and she would never know.

For perhaps the thousandth time she wondered if her companions were living the strange, lonely, medical vacation she was. The complex was clearly massive, though she'd never seen any other patients. Guests?

Prisoners?

Sometimes she was certain Bea had been rejected; other times she tried to convince herself that she misremembered the difference in the forms they'd been given, or that it really didn't matter, or other such lies. Bea was not a perfect candidate for a place like this—too much of a free-thinker, too wild. All the things Sara strived to be but never was.

She tried to hope Zach had been admitted so that she could see him again. She knew she should—she was a terrible girlfriend for letting him go so easily—but in truth the relationship had ended long before.

Priya and Cleo she barely knew, but she had no trouble at all hoping to see them again. They were the kind of bright and funny kindred spirits she'd spent her decade of adulthood searching for, now that she wasn't restricted to friends delivered to her by random chance of geography. The kind of people she'd discovered were very rare.

Mostly she thought of her sister. Emily was an adult, able to take care of herself, but Sara had never been able to think of her that way. She wanted to protect her, keep her close, shelter her from the world or, at the very least, be assured that someone was doing so.

How stupid she had been not to text her before they took away her phone. But it had all happened so fast. How could she have known when she entered the building that she would so shortly be unreachable? She didn't know anyone inside the Community, but it had not occurred to her that they would cut off all outside communication. Communication was such a huge part of the company's business!

She never let herself worry for long. What could come of it? There was no way to know what had become of any of them until she made it through this part of the experience. She could drive herself crazy asking questions for which answers would not come.

But she was increasingly wondering if there *was* an end to this. She knew admittees signed up for a five-year stint—yes, she knew that much—but what else did she really know? What if none of the Community and nature and future that she'd read about on their website actually existed? What if all she'd signed up for was this?

After several of the imperceptibly different days alone in her room with a luxurious bed and delicious food and a cramping abdomen and perfect eyesight, there was another knock at the door.

It was a dark-haired woman with Southeast Asian features. Before she could say anything, Sara held up a hand, her comfort with the place giving her confidence. "Let me guess—a dentist?"

There was really no part of her left to treat besides her teeth, so she wasn't surprised that she had guessed correctly. Such a simple pleasure, knowing something without being told.

Maybe now, after this, she would be deemed whole at last and freed.

13

AFTER SEVERAL FOLLOW-UP EYE APPOINTMENTS, ANOTHER KNOCK came at her door.

She was met by a chipper woman with a high, blonde ponytail, smiling broadly and positively bouncing with excitement.

So they do let people have hair ties.

Compared to the staid and almost robotic doctors, she appeared childlike. This was the kind of woman who had been a cheerleader in high school. A welcome contrast.

"Get excited!" the woman said, grinning wide enough to show off her perfectly white teeth. "It's time for you to enter the Community!"

Sara shifted uncomfortably. A wave of unexpected trepidation washed over her. She wanted this, of course—companionship, other people, a little variety in her days. Sunlight. A purpose.

But the hospital room felt safe now. She had a routine she understood, if one characterized by tedium. She knew the cadence of the days and the quirks of the shower and what to expect with each meal.

"Now?" she asked.

The woman pressed forward onto her toes. "Now!"

With a single glance over her shoulder at the room, Sara followed someone down that familiar hall for the last time. It felt strange to just walk away from where she'd been living without bringing anything with her, but she had nothing to bring. Not a single thing marked that room as belonging to her instead of someone else.

They proceeded down the hall for a longer distance than Sara thought she'd ever gone before, down into the earth. The woman didn't say anything, but Sara was used to silence. It felt more natural than small talk would have.

The end of the hallway appeared in the distance after they turned a corner, and a flat gray wall stood several hundred feet in front of them. Sara watched it grow larger as they approached, wondering where there was to go after that.

They reached the wall and the woman said, "Touch it for good luck!" before opening a door Sara hadn't noticed that took them into a stairwell going up.

As instructed, Sara pressed her palm against the smooth cement of the wall, feeling how cool it was. She didn't see how a wall could give her good luck and wasn't sure why she needed it.

Then they started up the stairs, back and forth and ever upward toward a light so pure and white Sara thought it must be from the sun. Their footsteps echoed against the concrete and steel. Her breath came heavy. Was she really so out of shape?

The woman bounded up the stairs easily. Sara fought to keep up and almost succeeded.

Finally, after several flights—four, maybe?—without pause, the woman came to a halt and opened a door out into a cool, sunny morning.

Sara drew a delicious breath of fresh air, relishing how it felt in her lungs. She hadn't noticed the staleness of the indoor air until freed of it. The scent of plants and moist soil wafting on the breeze and the light rushing sound of wind in leaves made the air more real, more nourishing. In that moment, she felt like she could live off such air.

The woman allowed her to stand there just breathing for a moment as if she understood. Probably she'd been in Sara's place before.

They stood atop a tall dune, overlooking a valley that had once been farm-land and was now developed into modular buildings with tidy modern fin-ishes—textured siding, solar panels, green walls of clinging plants. Narrow pedestrian streets cut between the mid-rise buildings, people in dark clothing moving about along them. Fresh ocean air washed across it all. This fit the description of the Community she'd been given.

A building as simple and commercial as the one they'd just left stood directly beside her on the bluff. Clouds whipped across a mostly clear sky and the ocean sparkled along the horizon.

"Let's get you set up now," the woman said after a comfortable pause.

Sara nodded and followed her into the other hilltop building, drawing a final gulping breath of winter air before stepping inside. The constant in-bound breeze from the ocean kept out the toxic smoke that sank heavily over the bay to the north, or maybe it had just been long enough that the wildfires had faded into memory.

The room they entered had shelves along each wall, piled with fabric that Sara quickly realized was clothes, and stocked with boxes that she soon saw contained the supplies of life—toothbrushes, mugs, and, what a relief, hair ties. The woman retrieved a black duffel bag and began filling it with clothes so quickly Sara could barely keep track of what she grabbed.

"We know your size, of course," the woman explained, holding up a gray t-shirt and checking the tag. It went into the bag along with a sweatshirt and several pairs of pants, all in shades of gray and black. "Pick out your sundries."

Sara smiled at the old-fashioned word but approached the shelves, search-ing through the boxes. The woman moved with such urgency and efficiency that she felt she had to as well.

It all seemed a bit culty to her. Everyone dressed in the same colors and fabrics, with no personal items that everyone else didn't also have. Like 1950s America's idea of communism.

But they were there at the behest of a massive corporation the likes of which could only emerge in an unfettered capitalist wonderland, so that was ridiculous.

"You know how to put in contacts?" the woman asked.

Sara looked up from what she was doing. "They corrected my vision."

The woman brandished a box. "These aren't for correction. You'll need them."

Sara frowned but accepted the box, which was white cardboard and unlabeled.

"You can go in there to get changed," the woman said, nodding to a curtain-enclosed dressing room in the corner.

Sara stepped inside and pulled on a pair of black yoga pants and a gray t-shirt and tied her hair up in a loose bun the way she so often had in her old life. Looking at her reflection in the mirror as she slid the contacts onto her eyes, she felt more like herself than she had since arriving.

She could almost have been lounging around her apartment on a Saturday afternoon, dressed like this. Without makeup she would have to be at home. In her old life, she would have gone out to buy another box of hair dye; blonde roots were beginning to show through the brown. But she looked well rested, if a bit pale. Skin unblemished and eyes bright. Not half bad, all things considered.

The contacts were imperceptible on her eyes and didn't make any apparent difference to her vision, just as the woman had said. As she put them in, she wondered if they would change her eye color, but she couldn't see them any more than she could feel them.

Just another mystery of this place.

14

SARA EMERGED WITH THE SCRUBS IN HER ARMS AND HELD THEM UP in question. "What should I…?"

"Just leave them," the woman said. "Follow me."

Dropping the clothes on the floor felt uncomfortably like littering, but she did as she was told. They stepped into an elevator and lurched briefly downward, then entered a room that looked like a classroom, complete with desks in rows and bland nature photos on the walls.

A few people were already there, young men and women who all looked as bewildered as Sara felt. The woman who had retrieved her handed over the duffel bag, nodded once, and then retreated back down the hall, leaving Sara in the silent strangers' company.

Sara stood in the doorway, looking around the room. The front hosted a blank wall that she imagined would become a screen. The desks, much like those she remembered from high school, were mostly unpopulated; there were enough for a couple dozen people. Along one wall stretched a table with tea and coffee and water and fruit.

There were three men and two women, some seated in the desks, others hovering by the refreshments, no one talking to anyone else. Everyone in simple black and gray outfits and holding identical black duffel bags. Everyone well rested and unadorned.

Just like Sara.

Breaking the silence seemed daunting and perhaps unwise, so instead Sara crossed to the coffee, her movements careful and controlled, not wanting to draw attention to herself or bother anyone. She realized there were no cups set out and blinked in confusion before remembering the mug in her bag. How eco-friendly to reuse mugs. Of course.

Wrapping her hands around a warm drink seemed to pulse life into her even before she took a sip. A pleasant chill went down her spine.

Someone else moved toward the coffee and she lurched away before they could ask her to move, bag in one hand and coffee in the other. Picked the nearest open seat and sank into the plastic chair. Tapped the wooden table, careful to use the pads of her fingers instead of the nails so as not to bother anyone with the sound.

They waited. Waiting was easy now.

Had all these people been there as long as Sara? Surely so many people hadn't arrived on the same day?

And where were her friends?

"You guys excited, or what?" a male voice said.

Everyone turned to look, eyes wide and anxious. Why were they all so nervous? Sara was just picking up on the energy in the room.

A guy with sand colored hair and a slightly goofy smile sat sprawled in the back row, assuming the posture of a cocky, well-liked, powerful man that she identified immediately. That kind of personality had always bothered her a little, but it was reassuring to see it present in a place like this. Unbroken, unchastened.

His words broke the tension enough to get the rest of them murmuring to each other, *hello*s and *can you believe this*es and "I always wanted to work for this company, but I never imagined it would be like this!"

After some amount of time that Sara didn't even try to guess, another woman and then another man were delivered to the room by the smiling blonde one at a time, and then she strode to the front of the room and clapped her hands.

"Welcome, everyone!" Her elation seemed genuine. "Welcome to the *future!*"

The eight of them glanced around at each other, inclining heads, declining her excitement.

Still no sign of her friends.

"Our acceptance criteria are quite selective, and you have all been *chosen,*" she said. "You should be very pleased with yourselves! We sure are!"

Sara didn't think the enthusiasm actually made sense.

"Now we're going to go around and introduce ourselves, then go over some rules and policies, then you all can start your exciting new lives! I'm so excited for you!"

Sara fought the urge to roll her eyes. Anyone who mentioned excitement this much had to be acting, at least a little bit.

"Please just tell us your name and where you are from originally, and, umm…what your favorite meal was in the past few weeks, shall we?" She grinned out at them and widened her eyes.

Sara noticed what they were not sharing—what they did or where they went to college or even what brought them here. All the usual ways to categorize people.

Names and hometowns and food preferences washed over her without meaning. She did not make any attempt to remember.

She said her favorite meal was the pancakes from the first day, because by the time it was her turn to speak everything else she could remember had already been said.

"Fantastic!" the woman said. "You'll all get to know each other very well here! My best friends are all from my orientation group, so look around and get to know one another!"

Sara wasn't opposed to the idea of new friends, but what she really wanted was to find the ones she already had.

"Now, you all know your purpose here—contributing to the future. It's important work, but it can be fun, too! Every experiment you'll take part in is carefully controlled, even if you can't see how. Don't worry too much about the details! Just remember that we are all in this together and that the system is important, so follow the process and do your part and we'll all have a great time."

Sara wasn't sure what any of that meant.

"There aren't many rules, but they are important ones. Follow instructions, of course—you'll know when you get them. Sometimes there will be enrichment activities, for team building or other purposes. When you are summoned to one, you are expected to participate.

"You will not have access to any outside news or communications channels, but if you look hard enough, you'll find ways to contact your family and friends. But don't worry too much about that! We encourage you to embrace your new life, and not dwell in the past.

"And remember that you can leave at any time, but you can't just walk away—if you do leave, you cannot come back, so think hard before disengaging! This is a *community* and we don't want to lose *anyone*. We will work with you if you work with us, but we will relocate people who can't play along. But, like I said, all of you have been chosen. The Community won't work for just anyone, but I'm confident it will be perfect for each of you."

She smiled out at the group and eight blank faces stared back.

"Great!" she said, clapping again. "Some day-to-day, now. You'll each have a roommate, someone not from your orientation group, so you can meet other people. You're encouraged to get a job, if you like; there are many in the Community. But you don't have to—so much better than the outside world, am I right?"

She winked and laughed conspiratorially.

"We want you to take care of yourself, so we have lots of opportunities for socializing and exercising. If you're not taking care of yourself, expect to be talked to.

"And remember why you're here! There will be many things you've never seen before and you're encouraged to test out everything. Don't worry about breaking things; that's what you're here for! It'll be fun, I promise. Now—any questions?"

They were silent for a long minute, and Sara feared no one would say anything. She knew she had a question, but she didn't want to be the only one asking anything.

"Do we need to report anything?" asked a girl with red hair in an asymmetrical cut.

The woman beamed. "Great question! No, you don't. We'll keep an eye on everything and track how you're doing with our test devices. Don't worry about anything."

"Is there, um, privacy anywhere?" someone asked. Sara looked around to see who, but everyone's expressions were equally curious.

The woman laughed. "We're not voyeurs here, don't worry. You'll soon forget that anyone's watching. And there are so many Community members that most of the time nobody is!"

Sara noticed that she didn't answer the question.

"Anything else?" the woman asked.

No one seemed about to say anything. Sara's heart pounded; her throat tightened. She had to ask. "My friends who I arrived with. Where are they?"

The woman shrugged and looked utterly unsympathetic. "I don't know about any particular entrants. The day you enter the adjustment center and the day you enter the Community are not necessarily correlated, though, so maybe they're already inside, or soon will be. Just keep an eye out for them!"

And that was it.

15

Seven years before the Community

SARA AND BEA CLAMBERED UP THE STAIRS OUT OF THE BART STATION
into the fog of a San Francisco morning, two among thousands traipsing
through the city that day. The streets had been blocked off and police cars
were parked every few blocks, lights flashing but sirens silent. Like this was
some kind of parade instead of the protest it purported to be.

Maybe that's what made their presence feel so ineffective and useless. If
the authorities sanctioned a protest, was it really a protest?

Something about the whole endeavor felt a little masturbatory, throngs of
angry people wearing North Face jackets and expensive tennis shoes, shouting slogans about caring for the planet and defeating the policies their parents had championed.

How many of them had arrived in gas-burning cars?

Bea handed her a piece of cardboard on which she'd drawn a globe with
a thermometer sticking out at a jaunty angle. The planet is sick, get it? And
we're the virus.

Sara dutifully lifted the sign above her head and fell in with the marchers,
stepping through puddles up Market Street, shouting and singing. It really
was like a festival—a festival of probably doomed maybe-optimists.

If this many people were protesting, this many hundreds of thousands in
every major city around the world, taking to the street with signs and pleas,
why was nothing being done?

Bea was grinning broadly, positively dancing, singing along to songs Sara
didn't know. Sara wished she could feel the contagious energy that had so
clearly infected her friend. On the train ride up Bea had been ranting, angry
at the failed accords that would've been their last chance to stave off the very
worst, fuming at the idiocy of politicians and the selfishness of big business
and *how could they not see?* How lucky they were that they would not have to
live through the hell world of their own creation!

But now she was dancing, apparently full of hope.

The city stank of human bodies crushed together and the air echoed with raised voices, but didn't it always?

Sara shouted along, but she did not really feel the words she was saying or believe in the power of their chants. She knew—like everyone there had to, on some level—that it was already too late.

16

AS SOON AS THE WOMAN DISMISSED THEM FROM THE INTRODUCTORY class, the purpose of the contacts in their eyes became clear.

A yellow line appeared on the ground so suddenly it startled everyone but the woman leading the orientation, who laughed in response to their jumps. Sara assumed, at least, that the others saw the same thing she did.

"Go on, then," the woman said. "Make like Dorothy and follow the yellow brick road!"

Sara and her new companions exchanged looks, then set off along the line. They followed it into the hall and to an elevator, moving in a clump as if for protection against the strangeness of it all.

No sooner did someone say, "What now?" than −3 appeared in the air before them. Sara pressed the down button and the doors slid open immediately, and they descended smoothly and emerged blinking into the daylight in the complex of modern buildings she had seen from above.

People walked about, laughing and talking, some holding cups of coffee, some hand in hand. No one paid them any mind. No one looked at a phone. There were no phones—or screens, for that matter—as far as Sara could see, anywhere.

Sara's yellow line stretched out before her, across a wide expanse of pavement and planters, between a row of mid-height buildings, and then curved toward the coast. At first, she thought the whole group would continue with her, but as soon as they crossed the courtyard and reached the first of the buildings two people turned right instead of continuing.

"Are you guys not coming in?" one of them, a tall woman with dark hair and a slightly pinched face, asked. She sounded mildly distressed.

Hurried shaking of heads and whispers of confusion.

"I'm going here," said the blond guy who had been so brash earlier.

The tall woman did not look comforted by this. She waved at the others forlornly while they continued on.

The group continued to thin as they proceeded through the town. Sara struggled to take it all in, rows of shops and apartments, neat paving stones and charming lights, trees and flowers and birds. It reminded her a little of the pedestrian-friendly cities in Europe that she'd seen in photos but never visited, with narrow lanes and balconies and buildings only a few stories tall.

Like that, except shiny and new.

She scanned the faces they passed, searching for anyone familiar. If her friends weren't entering with her, maybe they already had. Bea would stand out with her vibrant hair. Emily would be less obvious; she was short enough to hide in a crowd. Conversely, Zach was tall enough that she couldn't possibly miss him.

People peeled off to the left and right, entering buildings and murmuring goodbyes. As ever fewer people plodded on, Sara began to worry that there had been some mistake. When would it be her turn?

The duffel felt heavy on her shoulder. Her hands grew cold in the sea air. Following the line started to feel ridiculous.

She passed side streets and pocket parks, cafes spilling out onto the sidewalk, a broad promenade along the coast with sweeping views out into infinity. It was lovely, and charming, and safe, if lacking character. But where was her home?

The empty green hill at the other end of the bay reared up before her, trees growing over a neighborhood that had been abandoned, an old State Park extending its reach into the city. She had to be reaching the edge of the Community by now. The last of her companions had stepped away at least ten minutes ago, she thought, though she really couldn't trust her perception of time.

A light rain began to fall, the kind that you could barely feel as it collected on your hair and eyelashes. She shivered.

At last, *finally*, the line ducked into a building. Sara passed through the glass door gratefully and set down her bag in the warm lobby. The line continued down a hall, but she wanted to consider this place for a moment, learn the contours of her new home.

The carpet was thin and marbled blue-gray, like she would expect in a school, and the walls a bland gray that seemed vaguely industrial. The ceilings were high and gave the place an expansive feel. Blue-tinted windows made up one entire wall.

The light that filled the place began to throb urgently, as if before a concert. Criticizing her for hesitating. With a sigh, she picked up her bag and set off down the hall, suddenly exhausted.

After days of nothing, so much novelty overwhelmed her.

The line ended at the third door down the hall, a heavy-looking thing made of gray-washed wood. It didn't have a room number or names written on it, and it didn't have a lock or even a doorknob.

She paused before it for a confused moment and then it swung open slowly, a speaker somewhere playing a pleasant whooshing sound.

"Hello!"

A young woman looked up from her seat at a desk on the other end of the room, smiling.

Sara crossed the threshold and cleared the door and it swung closed again. The yellow line disappeared.

The girl had thick dark hair and the soft face of a child, though Sara knew she had to be at least nineteen to join the Community. She didn't get up from her desk but turned around entirely in the chair and introduced herself as Alexa Huang.

"Alexa? That's unfortunate," Sara said, trying to make a joke that she only realized was perhaps ill-advised after it had passed her lips.

But Alexa smiled good-naturedly. "And my sister's name is Siri, believe it or not."

Sara wasn't sure how to react to that.

"Your parents big fans of virtual assistants?"

She shrugged. "My mom worked at Amazon and my dad at Apple. Their friends thought it was hilarious."

"I'm Sara." She'd been worried at the prospect of a roommate; she hadn't lived with anyone besides Zach since college and had not liked her roommates much when she had them. But Alexa seemed friendly and normal. Which was really all you could ask for, right?

She reminded herself that this living situation was a compromise, but it was also a good decision. Not the only choice: that would be too restrictive. There were other options; she had not been forced into this. But this was the *best* choice.

She turned in a slow circle, studying the room. It was basically a studio apartment, with a tiny strip of kitchen—mini fridge, tiny postage-stamp counter, but no clear way to cook a meal—a door that presumably led to a bathroom, and a set of beds and desks along two walls. The walls were a rich turquoise, much homier than the gray of the hall. A wide window that reached most of the way from the floor to the ceiling looked out on the coastal promenade.

She could see the ocean from her bed.

She knew immediately which bed belonged to her. Alexa's side was already decorated with block printed paintings and delicate string lights and a multicolored pastel-hued bedspread. Something about the decor looked slightly off, but Sara could not put her finger on what it was. It seemed flimsier than she would have expected, not quite solid.

"When did you get here?" she asked, still standing in the middle of the room.

"About a week ago," Alexa said.

"You look so settled in!"

She shrugged. "Not a lot else to do. And it's good to make it feel like home."

The cadence of her voice and the words she chose reminded Sara of her sister. Or maybe it was just the prospect of living with a younger girl.

The thought of not seeing her sister for five whole years was almost more than she could bear. Being separated from her parents was bad enough, but she'd been able to accept that after thinking about it enough. No matter what she did, she would eventually have to live without them. Her sister, though...

"What're you thinking about?" Alexa asked.

Maybe she'd seen the worry on Sara's face. "Just wondering about the people I hoped to join with. I haven't seen any of them."

"You arrived with friends?" Alexa asked, looking surprised and maybe awed by the idea. "What a power move!"

"What?"

"Just, like, I dunno," she said, shrugging. "Trying to mess with their plan like that."

"What do you mean?" Sara said slowly.

"They shuffle us around, you know. They want *mixing*. Showing up with friends, though, wow. I know it happens, but..."

Sara wasn't sure she followed. "So you came here alone?"

Alexa nodded. "Yeah. It's a great way to meet people, you know."

Sara sat on her bed. White sheets, white blanket, white towel folded at the foot. "Right."

She studied the decorations on Alexa's side of the room again, comparing them to the solidity of her own basics. They were no more real than the yellow line had been. The realization sent a shiver down her spine.

"It'll be fine, though, I think these are all just rumors, you know?" Alexa went on. Sara had no idea what she was talking about. "Your friends must be here somewhere. They won't, like, actively keep them from you."

"You're talking like it's a social experiment."

"Well, isn't it?" Alexa said. "We're testing things, sure, but they need to get us into the right situations for that. I'm sure there's a lot that's not random."

"How do you know all this?" Sara asked, yawning. She was even more tired now than she had been. She wanted answers, felt like this conversation was valuable, but she also just really wanted to sleep.

"Oh, you'll see," Alexa said. "Everybody knows. But you look wiped. Take a nap. I'll wake you up for dinner!"

Sara nodded and slid under the neat white covers.

17

THAT EVENING, ALEXA ANNOUNCED THAT THEY WOULDN'T BE GOING to dinner after all. There was a party at the museum! A soiree! A gala!

Sara had no idea what that could mean in a place like this, but followed Alexa's instructions. Alexa was excited and it sounded like the kind of fancy event she never would have gone to in her old life. And she hardly had a choice. It probably wasn't technically required—why would it be?—but she was afraid of leaving Alexa's side. She didn't know how to navigate this place at all.

Alexa led the way out into the darkness. The rain had stopped—recently, if the sparkling puddles were any indication—and the town was aglow with twinkling lights reflecting off the water. It was just on the edge of cold.

"My friends will meet us on the corner," Alexa said as they stepped out into the evening, and Sara could see two young women waiting under a streetlight who waved at their approach.

"How'd they know to wait for you?"

Sara was used to constant communication and coordination, but didn't have any idea how to contact anyone here.

"We meet up every day," Alexa replied. "It's like the '80s or something."

Sara nodded, Alexa introduced her, and she promptly forgot their names.

The other three chatted idly about their days, this party, the weather. Nothing in their conversation was deep or joking or flowing the way Sara was used to with her own friends, but she understood that they'd only known each other for a week. Relationships would come.

Sara drifted along just behind them through the streets, which grew ever more crowded with people headed in the same direction. Restaurants and shops that had been buzzing earlier were shuttered now. This was an event for nearly everyone, it seemed.

An opportunity to spot her friends?

The museum was a low, curving, glass-walled building that jutted out over the water like a flying saucer crashed to Earth—how people fifty years ago imagined the future. The windows glowed out into the night, singing of warmth and light and humanity, and even if the concept was an assumed identity and the role she was supposed to play was unclear, Sara felt drawn in.

She imagined that the ground beneath her feet shifted slightly, rolling, bobbing.

Or maybe she didn't imagine.

"Are we floating?" she asked.

Alexa and her friends laughed, but not in a mocking way. "It's high tide!"

And Sara remembered that this town had been abandoned when the ocean swallowed the shoreline, when the dunes were no longer enough to protect the old cannery and new hotels, when tsunami escape routes became high tide escape routes. Of course they were floating.

She turned her head slowly, trying to see how it worked. Amid all the buildings, she could not see any tethers or pontoons; the whole place looked utterly normal. But the motion beneath her feet could not be denied.

"Wow," she said. "That's…"

"Cool, right?" Alexa asked. "Innovation. What our company's known for!"

Our company. The way she said it, with such ownership that Sara did not feel—and would not feel a week from now either, she was sure.

Bea had been set on the Community, out of all the options they had to choose from, because the company was the least evil of the tech giants—focused on true invention and bright new ideas, at least some of the time, rather than just an ever-greater market cap. Sara had let Bea do all the research and draw all the conclusions. Until the fire, she had never felt desperate enough to consider a place like this.

"It's going to rain again," one of the friends said. "I keep forgetting to pick up an umbrella."

They entered the building and were swallowed by the crowd. As she stepped up inside, she realized that the museum was not afloat, but rather mounted solidly on a pier. Its floor, still and solid beneath her feet, was the reprieve she needed.

The atmosphere felt uncomfortably familiar for a place Sara had never been. Walls hung heavy with art that she didn't understand, warm light bulbs spotlit tables and sculptures, people swirled around holding champagne flutes, laughter rose over light music that she could barely make out. It looked like a fundraiser scene in a movie, except that the people wore inexpensive athletic clothes instead of dresses and tuxedos.

"You good?" Alexa asked her, clearly wanting to disappear into the room.

Sara nodded mutely. It had been a very long day.

She watched Alexa and her friends flit off, filled with a sense of possibility she remembered from her own teen years. A night felt like an eternity then. Most of the time she didn't feel terribly old—college wasn't that far away—but around Alexa she did.

As she watched people drift around her, she felt an urge to laugh. It was all so absurd.

Here they were pretending to be fancy at a museum, fundraising or cel-ebrating, when in reality they were low-paid test workers stuck in long term contracts with no control over their lives, drinking what couldn't possibly be real champagne as the evening faded into night.

A waiter passed by and she snagged a glass, feeling more and more like a heroine in a movie that was going sideways by the moment, and dramatically downed the amber liquid like she had seen actors do so many times. Didn't she read somewhere that they used apple juice when filming?

Not only was it not fancy champagne but also not even wine, she guessed after tasting it.

Which made sense, now that she considered it for even a moment. Hun-dreds of people—a thousand?—were crammed together in this small town for years. Bored people would need only the smallest amount of alcohol poured into them to spark a fight.

Nevertheless, it tasted *fine*. And everyone else was acting, so why not act too?

But how did they decide who had to play the servers instead of the high rollers? How did people here know what role they were supposed to assume? Did it change by the day? It could not be dictated by who you were before; that was central to the sales pitch. Your old life no longer mattered.

So did they rotate roles, sharing parts evenly like in preschool? Or were they placed in the roles that were optimized for them, taking the need for choice away? Such optimization would have to be based on underlying abil-ity, not experience, or else everyone would end up doing what they had done before. She wasn't such a fool—or such a Silicon Valley true believer, which amounted to the same thing—as to think everyone maximized their talents in the real world.

She set her champagne flute on a table beside an ugly sculpture and walked into the crowd, scanning for Bea and Emily and Zach. They had to be there.

Laughter and words floated past her in the air, snippets of conversation that lacked context.

And then we sat by the water for a few hours, it was glorious!
I'm so ready to learn to swim in VR.
Did you hear that she's thinking of leaving? Biological clock hitting hard.
He's a baker or something, so eighteenth century.
I want to leave tomorrow.
I never want to leave.

She'd never seen such a perfectly gender-balanced crowd. After years in tech, her mind was calibrated to expect more men in a group and it took her a moment to realize that there weren't actually more women. An equal number made sense, though; if they could control for it, of course they would.

The crowd shifted, and she spotted several girls in a cluster across the room, wearing bright red dresses and full faces of makeup. Utterly different from the rest of the crowd.

She felt a pang of jealousy she couldn't explain.

She watched them, moving among the people, standing out as more beautiful and compelling than everyone else. What odd power a little makeup could provide; how strange that was. How unfair.

If Alexa had been there Sara would have asked who they were, but she was alone among the laughing crowd with no one to talk to. The enigmatic girls disappeared and reappeared behind the drifting crowd, and she watched them, rapt.

A man leaned against a cocktail table near her, his gaze trained the same direction as her own, but it seemed wrong to ask a stranger a question to which she feared she knew the answer.

Her curiosity won out.

"Who are they?"

The man turned to her, startled, expression slipping. "Are you new here?"

She nodded, not wanting to be the focus.

He looked back towards the girls, still in a cluster, still looking so different. Given what this event was supposed to be, they were the only ones dressed appropriately.

"They were rejected during admissions," he said, "but are still allowed in."

"Because..."

He looked at her, eyebrows raised, lips smiling. She understood.

That jealousy did not go away, no matter how much she told herself to feel luckier than them. She had been chosen. She did not have to do anything. She had been *chosen*.

"Not enough women here?" she asked, adding a layer of derision to her tone that in her old life she would have hidden.

The man shrugged, downed his drink, which was something brown and swirling poured low over an ice cube like whiskey. Sara wondered if some alcohol, too, had been rejected but allowed in. "They're just not desperate enough."

Sara walked away, no part of her interested in continuing that conversation. Details like intentionally *desperate* women made the Community feel oddly like the dream of men like Zach, which she realized, with some disappointment, it probably was. Who else ran the company but the same people who had always run Silicon Valley?

Desperation was not what separated those women from everyone else in the Community, though, and she knew it.

18

Six years before the Community

"CONGRATULATIONS, MY GIRL!" HER FATHER EXCLAIMED, CLAPPING her on the back.

Sara smiled, though she was sweating heavily under her black graduation gown and eager to get back indoors.

"One more picture!" her mother said, arranging the cap on her head at a different angle.

"I think the tassel's wrong," Sara said, reaching up to switch which side it hung from.

"Hurry up now," her dad said. "We all want to get inside."

Her mom shot him a look. "Be patient. Your daughter's only going to graduate college once!"

"But we could take these pictures inside," Emily pointed out. She was sitting in the shade in a wispy white minidress and strappy sandals, fanning herself with a Commencement program and sipping an iced coffee. By all appearances she was much more comfortable than the rest of them, posing in the sun with the classic Spanish architecture of the Main Quad behind them.

Sara met her eyes over their mother's shoulder and mouthed "soon." Her sister rolled her eyes and leaned back dramatically, like she might take a nap.

"Hold this again," her mother said, thrusting Sara's diploma into her hands.

Sara dutifully struck a pose, then another and another, while the sweat collected in the small of her back and under the cap on her head. At least the gown was loose; a breeze tossed it around, refreshing around her ankles. She wondered how it would look in the pictures but couldn't really bring herself to care.

How hot was it—110? More?

The wind blowing on her face felt like it had passed through an oven.

Finally, her mother declared them done with the photo shoot, and they all sighed in relief. Sara peeled the gown off immediately and tossed it to her dad to carry, leading the way to the waiting car in her tiny black athletic shorts and sports bra.

"We should've taken your pictures in that outfit," Emily said, catching up to her.

"Oh yeah, for the computer science pinup calendar?"

Emily grinned. "Not sure you're hot enough for that."

Sara elbowed her and they both dissolved in giggles, a bit giddy from the heat. They had never gotten along this well when they lived together at home, but in the four years since she'd moved out, she and her sister had grown much closer.

"Excited for your own graduation next week?" Sara asked while they stood in the shade of a tree waiting for their parents. Their dad had run into someone he knew, apparently, and had paused to chat as if the heat was nothing.

"Oh please, like high school means anything."

"It means adulthood!"

Emily scoffed. "No, it doesn't. *You're* still a child, after all."

"You're in fine form today," Sara replied.

"I'd rather not talk about it."

Emily had gotten into her top choice college but decided not to go because it would be prohibitively expensive. She was headed to a community college in the fall and very bitter about it.

Before Sara could make any assurances—like reminding her sister of the $300,000 in debt hanging over her own head, for example—someone called her name.

Emily squinted into the sun and Sara shaded her eyes with her diploma, hoping it would have other uses besides this one, as they tried to make out the identity of the figure jogging toward them in a rumpled, ill-fitting suit.

David arrived, panting, his forehead glimmering with sweat.

"Hey," Sara greeted him. She hadn't said goodbye to him yet, though she didn't much care, either, since they hadn't really been friends since they'd slept together sophomore year.

"Who's this?" Emily whispered, loud enough for David to hear.

"David," Sara said, nodding toward him. She gestured toward Emily. "My little sister."

Emily looked delighted to be meeting him. Sara supposed he was pretty cute, but more likely Emily was just looking for something she could tease her sister about.

"So, Sara, I was…could I talk to you for a sec?"

Sara frowned. "Uh, sure?"

"Over here?"

He led the way deeper into the trees and lowered his voice. "I've been thinking, you know, about college, the past four years…"

"Get on with it, David, I want to get out of the heat. It's been a long morning."

"Of course, sorry." He looked uncomfortable. "Anyway, just, um, regrets. I was a dick to you."

"What?" She didn't remember it that way.

"We had a lot of fun, didn't we? Freshman, sophomore years?"

"I guess?"

"Anyway, I wish I'd been more forward, had my shit together more."

"David, what are you talking about?"

"We should have dated, is what I'm saying."

She laughed. "Great, glad you, uh, think so."

He looked confused and barreled on with his apparently rehearsed speech. "But now I'm off to New York, and you're—what, working at a startup?"

She nodded, though she hadn't actually accepted a job yet.

"Anyway. Too little, too late."

She smiled and patted him awkwardly on the arm. "Take care of yourself, David. Good seeing you."

And she walked back to her waiting family, leaving David standing in the trees. They'd already gotten into the car and had the air conditioning mercifully cranked. She sank gratefully into the cool air.

"What was that all about?" her mom asked.

"Just a guy I used to be friends with," Sara said, buckling her seat belt. "This AC feels amazing."

It was probably still ninety degrees in the car, but the temperature was rapidly falling. She felt so much better.

"Modern day miracle, huh?" her dad said as the car reversed itself onto the street.

"I think AC's been around for like a hundred years," Emily pointed out.

Their father grunted in reply. "So, speaking of AC, I heard that the university is closing for the summer quarter for the first time ever."

"Yeah, I think I heard something about that," Sara said. Her mind was dulling in the relief of the air conditioning and she kind of just wanted to sit there, watching the palm trees go by out the window without talking.

"Too hot?" her mother asked.

"Yeah," her dad said. "They're retrofitting all the old buildings with AC, so they'll be usable again next year."

"They had to cancel classes a few times this spring and last," Sara said. "Deemed a safety hazard to make us leave the air-conditioned dorms."

"Crazy," her mom said. "You know when we were here, I don't think the dorms even had AC?"

"Ancient history," her dad said.

Emily turned to look fully out the window. Sara wondered just how angry her expression was in that moment.

"They're installing solar panels, too," Sara said, trying to steer the conversation away from how everyone but Emily got the elite education, even though it had been entirely Emily's choice. "On the buildings that don't already have them."

"A full micro-grid, I heard," her mom said.

Sara nodded. "It's fascinating, actually. I learned about it in my engineering elective."

"Can we not?" Emily said suddenly.

They all fell silent and their mom turned to look at her daughters in the back seat. "Of course."

Their father turned the dial on the stereo, streaming some weird, experimental music he'd found. The family fell silent.

19

THE ROOM BEGAN TO FEEL OVERCROWDED AND WARM. SO MANY DAYS in the cold, stuffy medical wing meant Sara now wanted to seek out as much fresh air as she could.

It seemed wrong somehow to leave the party entirely. Far too early for that. But if she could find a patio or something, some way to feel like she was not retiring for the night but still escape and feel the ocean breeze on her face...

She made a slow lap around the periphery of the room, eyes toward the floor, listening and trying not to seem like she was. Ever aware of the door she had entered through, searching for another exit.

Since all the exterior walls were bare glass, stretching floor to ceiling, doors and windows blended into each other: all a way out of some kind, but as elusive as they were ever-present.

Finally, at the end of a short hall that extended away from the gallery toward a bathroom and a drinking fountain, she found a door out onto the dock and eagerly stepped through it. The air was cold, more so than she had expected, but it felt the way water tasted after a long run.

The dock only extended a few feet before giving way to the waves, gently lapping at the wood. Things had calmed while she was inside.

The building glowed behind her, obscuring any stars she might have seen, but light from the moon overpowered light from humanity and cast a white slice across the waves, stretching like a finger into the distance. She almost felt she could walk out along it, and almost wanted to.

She'd been here once before. Many years ago, before the town yielded to the ocean, before the ocean encroached onto the land, she had come down with her parents and sister. The drive, which she knew now to be just a few hours, had felt impossibly long in the distorted perception of a child.

They had stayed in a little apartment and played on the beach, shrieking as they chased the waves in and out, sand between their toes and rotting seaweed stinking up the air. How different it seemed than the rocky beaches near her parents' house. Like a whole different ocean.

Over meals of sourdough and clam chowder they had all laughed. She never suspected that their vacations, like that one, were far more modest than those of some. They felt utterly sufficient.

Most incredible, though, had been stepping into the dark gloom of the underwater aquarium, gazing up at thirty feet of kelp forests, adrift with hiding fish and wheeling sharks, the water glowing iridescent blue from sunlight above. A flash of silver, the pulse of a jellyfish. Magic.

Such wildness and strength held at bay by nothing more than glass, so fragile and yet so immense. It didn't seem possible. A tangible image of human control over nature, pressing back against the power of the ocean with those massive tanks perched so delicately atop a pier.

She had been entranced and never wanted to leave, but eventually her father had pulled her away from the aquarium, hoisted her onto his shoulders in a motion that reminded her that she was as small as the massive tank made her feel. They climbed into the car and began the long drive north toward home, then settled back into their regular lives of school and work. But, in a way imperceptible at the time, she was forever changed.

20

SHE LINGERED OUTSIDE UNTIL THE COLD DROVE HER BACK INDOORS, then loitered near the door until she noticed other people begin to wander off toward bed. There were no clocks here, either, but she could guess at the time. It was that point where some people decry the lateness of the hour and others feel the night has just begun.

For her part, Sara had always been the girl on the edge of the party, so this was a familiar role. Perhaps, she thought as she began to walk through the resumed drizzle, that's all this event had been—everyone assuming their preferred roles, whether they knew it or not.

Alexa did not return with her, but she hadn't expected her to.

Sara fell asleep in her new pajamas in her new bed with the window cracked open to let in the cold sea breeze. She'd always dreamed of a seaside home.

The next morning, Alexa still had not returned.

Some part of her thought maybe she should be worried, but she dismissed the idea. This place was so thoroughly watched and controlled that Alexa could not possibly have come to any harm she didn't actively seek out. Begrudging her of aspired danger wasn't Sara's role. Alexa wasn't *actually* her little sister.

Sharing a room with anyone was not something Sara had expected, but she did not let herself chafe against it. This was a free home, and a luxurious one in so many ways. A roommate may have been something she thought she left behind years before, but she could adjust.

Sara realized with a start that she had forgotten to remove the contacts the night before, something she knew from her days of wearing regular contacts could be very bad for the eyes. But her eyes did not protest with the dry sting of overnight wear she remembered. And they hadn't given her a case for them, anyway.

She opened the blackout curtains to reveal a stunning day, the world washed clean by the rain of the night before, and the pull of the sun along with a sudden realization of her own hunger drew her out into the town. Her dinner the night before had been a strange assortment of snacks from the waiters; nothing substantial.

But she didn't know how things worked here. No one had given her any money or explained how she was meant to procure what she needed. Would there be rations? Food deliveries? Would she be unable to feed herself until she found a job?

That last idea, at least, she realized she could strike down. The introductory instructor had said no one had to work, so there must be some provision system.

But she would work, Sara decided. Not right away, probably, but she couldn't imagine a life without a job. She'd mowed lawns and watched her neighbors' pets as a child, then graduated to a restaurant and then a teacher's assistant in college before embarking on a career. Work was a part of life, and a rather large one.

Which was why the last year had been so degrading.

She pulled on the pants and sweatshirt from the night before and headed out into the sunlight, blinking and wishing for sunglasses. Hoping she would figure out how this place worked soon.

She set her course toward the commercial district she recalled from her walk into the Community, crossing the promenade. She passed a handful of early morning joggers and very few others.

Sara caught herself searching for Bea even though a part of her knew Bea had not been accepted. What else could the difference in their intake forms presage than that? Bea would be noticeable, with her brightly dyed hair and loud demeanor. Bea stood out of every crowd. If she had been there the night before, Sara would have found her.

It was the kind of scene where she expected to see people walking their dogs or playing with their children, but both pets and kids were not permitted here. It made the space feel oddly dead, unnaturally calm and adult.

Something that might appeal to other people, but which, to Sara, cast a one-dimensional and empty feeling over the environment. She had always appreciated a little chaos.

A seagull swooped and cried above her, plaintive and annoying all at once. She wanted it to stop. The sound was grating; she hated to hear an animal in distress.

The sky overhead was so much bluer than she was used to. Just the blush of sunlight after a rainstorm, or something more? She tried to guess if they could somehow enhance the outdoors, then decided they probably didn't need to. The ocean brightened every vista.

She continued toward the town, enjoying that she had a bit of a commute to reach the areas that thronged with people. Most of the apartments were right over the shops. How had they known that she would prefer to be at a distance? She worried that the people who constructed this place knew her too well.

The streets grew more crowded as the minutes passed and she neared the center of town. Even after the party last night, she had not realized just how many people there were. Far more than she would have guessed. Where had they all come from? What brought them here?

She'd had to sink to the lowest point in her life to be willing to give up the freedom of the open world for the security of this place. Had so many people really had their lives similarly collapse? Or did they require less incentive than she had?

Watching people laugh with their friends, she felt somehow removed. She caught herself judging them for having made the same decisions she did. Who could let their lives come to this?

Who could feel so content with it?

And if everyone else here was so much happier with this life, if they took to it fluidly where she struggled, why had she been accepted? She did not deserve it; she did not fit in here. These were not her people.

Speaking of which…

Where *were* her people?

The street she walked had a dozen cafes, each with a dozen customers. None of their faces were familiar.

"Sara!"

She whirled around at the voice.

Not one she recognized.

"It's Sara, isn't it?"

A woman approached her—thirtyish and round, with a terribly unflattering haircut but a pleasant face. She was slightly out of breath. Sara had no idea who she was.

"Yes, I'm Sara," she said cautiously.

"Oh, I'm so glad to see you!" the woman said, blowing her brown hair out of her eyes. "There are so many people here and no one I know. It's exhausting, right?"

She must be from the intro class, Sara decided.

"I'm sorry, I can't remember your name."

"Oh, don't worry about it," she said. "I'm, like, awkwardly good with names sometimes. I'm Drew."

Sara smiled, genuinely, for the first time since arriving there. "Great to meet you. I know what you mean about overwhelming."

Drew laughed, evidently as relieved as Sara felt. "Want to get breakfast? I was just in search of a smoothie."

"Breakfast sounds great," Sara said, following as Drew started to walk down the street. "But do you know how…?"

She trailed off, unsure how to phrase her question.

Drew, to her relief, nodded vigorously. "My roommate took me out to eat last night," she said. "You just look at the camera."

Sara snorted. "Right, of course."

There had been stores that worked like that for a decade. It should have been obvious to her that it would work that way here, too: the tech giants all had everyone's faces connected to payment information, so your identity could be your wallet. She compulsively worried about her dwindling bank account, but that had been another point in the Community's favor—you would not have to touch your own money during your five years there, and they would deal with any reasonable creditors. For Sara, buried under so much debt, that was a dream.

"What did you do for dinner yesterday, if you haven't seen how the shops work yet?"

"I didn't, really," Sara said. They paused in front of a cafe, skimming the chalkboard menu out front, and wordlessly agreed to move on. "We went to this party at the museum."

Drew nodded as if this was familiar to her. "My roommate said it would be a waste of time."

Sara shrugged. "It was, sort of."

"Everything here is pretty spectacular, though," Drew went on. "I have trouble seeing any of it as a waste of time."

"Really?" Sara asked. "Time is, well, time. You know. Precious. Whatever." Her point had sounded better in her head.

"Let's go here," Drew said, indicating a cafe with a line out the door. "It smells good."

The scent of fruit wafted out as if intentionally broadcast. Sara had to admit it did smell great, and expensive. The kind of costly, almost-healthy breakfast she'd avoided even when she had plenty of money.

"Is there a limit?" Sara asked. "Of what we can, you know, spend?"

"Not as far as I know," Drew replied. "I assume if you went off the deep end being wasteful they'd talk to you, but, well, who's going to do that?"

Most people Sara knew were plenty wasteful, but she didn't say that.

In a bid to make conversation, she said, "So, you like smoothies?"

The dumbest thing she could have said.

Drew laughed again. "I like everything, girl. I just feel like today's a fruit smoothie kind of day, you know? Beautiful, sunny, new start."

"Right," Sara said. "I totally agree."

Drew shook her head, grinning ear to ear. "You're really uncomfortable with all this, huh?"

"What?"

"Look," she said as the line inched forward. "I don't know you. But you're so on edge, even I can see it. It's okay!"

Sara forced herself to laugh a little. Because really, Drew was right. It *was* okay.

"This is our new life! And it's awesome!"

"Thanks," Sara said. "It's just all a bit much, you know?"

Drew nodded. "Oh, I know."

They reached the front of the line and ordered. The girl behind the counter was in a better mood than any service worker Sara had ever seen, exuding the kind of gleeful cheer that really did go quite well with fresh orange juice or pomegranate smoothies, but which seemed odd coming from someone who stood behind a counter all day.

They stepped out of the way to await their drinks and continue their conversation.

"I was a teacher before," Drew was saying. "Middle school English."

"I hated middle school English," Sara said. "No offense."

Drew laughed again. "I hated middle school in general, so none taken!"

"And you went back to teach it?"

"Only way to conquer it, you know?"

Sara laughed for real at that.

"How about you?" Drew asked.

Sara felt suddenly uncomfortable admitting her previous role amid the technological elite. But she didn't want to start a friendship with a lie. "I was a software engineer."

"Ooh, wow! What're you doing in here with us losers, then?"

Drew's tone was joking, but the words felt real to Sara. Back in college, she had believed she would rise above the masses by studying computer science, but it had not been the escape she had sought. No degree or career choice was a ticket away from struggle, not in the world she knew.

She tried not to overreact when she replied. "It's not all billion-dollar valuations and ping pong games, you know."

Drew nodded sharply, realizing immediately that she'd touched a nerve. "Understood." Give that to teachers, Sara thought. They were good at reading people.

"Anyway, we're here now," Sara said.

Drew stepped forward to claim their brilliantly colored smoothies and handed Sara's over. "That we are, girl. That we are."

Sara took a sip through the paper straw, then lifted the smoothie aloft. "Cheers to that."

21

Five years before the Community

SARA'S OWN APARTMENT WAS NICE ENOUGH, BUT ERIC'S PLACE WAS downright palatial—much grander and more plush than any single twenty-something really deserved, but who could be surprised? This had always been Eric. The place was just his personality made material.

And material it was. Every gadget she'd ever heard of was tucked away somewhere, including a pile of discarded electronics in the closet, because, as he said, he didn't want to be wasteful. As if collecting things he would never use didn't count as waste.

"It's like ghosts of CES past in here," Sara said to Emily, who she'd brought along, as Eric led the way back from the closet to the rest of the apartment. Sweeping views to the Bay spun out before them, the city sparkling below.

What floor were they on? Very high, though she couldn't say for sure. Eric had made a mocking comment about the *surface dwellers* far below, something he clearly intended to be synonymous with service workers and didn't seem to realize included Sara, too.

He lived there alone, except for the frequent app-sourced girls who stayed the night or friends who crashed on the couch or in the guest room or sprawled out on the thick living room carpet after a wild night out. As often a Tuesday as a Saturday, or so he made it sound.

He was bragging, but Sara really wasn't impressed. In fact, she felt a little sorry for him.

There was no way he could afford this place on the vague job he'd acquired. It was not the intense kind of finance gig with hundred-hour workweeks, but instead the sort only rich kids got that mostly involved laughing at the water cooler and getting drunk with clients. It surely paid well, but nothing paid *that* well.

So that meant Mommy and Daddy were paying the bills, and how sad was that? She would feel like a failure if she were still dependent on her parents at this point in her life. Independence was huge, wasn't it? The American way.

Of course, she could never say that to Emily, who was still limping through a low-cost degree of pieced together community college and online classes, living at home and working as a barista at the same coffee shop as in high school.

But that was different, because Emily was trying. Eric was not trying, as far as Sara could tell.

They sat on his multi-thousand-dollar leather couches, bare feet buried in thick carpet, sipping cocktails he'd made out of expensive liquor. At least he knew how to mix a good drink.

Eric lounged across an entire couch, legs sprawled, head thrown back. Like a king or something. He left the other couch to the four girls—Sara, Emily, Eric's latest conquest, Christina, and Emily's friend X from college, who Sara belatedly realized was not, in fact, a girl.

Christina fiddled with her long black hair while Eric droned on. Sara stared out the window, watching the white lights on the Bay Bridge twinkle and swish, like waves rolling across the ropes and wires that held it there, suspended, reflecting on the water below, bringing it alive.

As long as she could remember, people had talked about how that bridge was due to collapse, how some Chinese steel had ruined everything, or a greedy engineering firm, or something. She hoped it wouldn't, selfishly not wanting to lose such a perfect piece of industrial art, and also because it could kill people and would certainly snarl traffic throughout the Bay Area.

Funny how beauty makes you value something.

She noticed Emily shifting beside her—bored? Uncomfortable?—and looked up to find Eric's eyes on her sister, taking in the brightness of her twenty-one-year-old green eyes, her perfect blonde hair, as blonde as Sara's had ever been and much better cared for. Freckles across her nose. Giant ironic glasses that she made look cute instead of silly.

Sara shot him a look, caught his eye, shook her head. He raised an eyebrow and smirked as if to protest his innocence, but she knew what he'd been thinking.

"Let's play a board game," Christina said, getting up. Apparently, she'd spent enough time in Eric's apartment to know where he would keep something like that, though Sara hadn't seen any games.

She returned with some game Sara had never heard of and launched into a lengthy explanation. X seemed more interested than the rest of them, and when they broke into two teams, they and Christina each led one. As the game developed it became increasingly apparent that it was really X versus Christina, with the others almost spectators.

"Ooh, that was clever!" Christina said, grimacing and laughing at the same time as X made some move that Sara didn't quite understand.

The game was somewhere between poker and charades, with some randomness thrown in via an electronic die that had a thousand different possible outcomes. Sara wasn't really paying attention, still hypnotized by the lights on the water, as lovely and calming as watching a campfire. Alcohol always made her tired.

"I have a good teacher," X replied.

"Are you sure you haven't played before?"

Eric got to his feet. "Anyone want another drink?"

A chorus of yeses, so Sara nodded too. The bridge danced and flickered. She noted to herself that she should look into hanging a painting of it on her wall.

Then the lights went out.

Sara blinked, her vision so myopically focused on the bridge that for a strange moment she didn't realize the power in the apartment had disappeared too. The hum of the fridge fell silent. The city below vanished into the black night, the flow of car headlights along the streets suddenly standing out like blood cells coursing through veins.

"What the hell?" Christina asked, saying what they were all thinking.

It wasn't stormy. There was no reason for power lines to fall and no cause for the utility to preventatively shut things down, like they might in high winds to stave off a fire.

"It'll be back," Eric said. He sounded utterly unconcerned.

Almost as soon as he said it, the background noise of a living home resumed and the lights warmed back on, as if on a dimmer switch, gradual and comforting.

But the bridge stayed dark, the buildings low and high stretching to the water hidden in the night.

"What's happening?" Sara asked.

Eric shrugged, grinned. "The building has backup power. Like a hospital."

"Why?" X asked.

His grin spread even wider. "Why not?"

Emily leaned toward Sara and whispered, "Only the best for those who can pay for it."

X noticed that she'd said something and inclined their head, curious.

Emily said, louder, "It's not really fair, is it?"

Eric, from the kitchen, called, "Capitalism, baby!"

Christina rolled her eyes. "He's obnoxious, huh?"

X snorted. "You're the one dating him."

Christina just shrugged. Like always, Sara figured they wouldn't last, but this time she had a feeling Eric would be the one getting dumped.

"What do you think happened?" Sara asked.

X and Christina both walked over to the window, and Sara and Emily joined them shortly after. Looking out into the darkness.

"It's even in the East Bay, look," Emily said. Where their parents were.

"I assume BART's not running," Sara commented. How would Emily get home?

X shivered. "Imagine people stuck in the tunnel."

Sara didn't want to, but she couldn't help it. Stuck in a crowded train car beneath the Bay, crammed in with strangers, plunged into darkness as if the water had dropped down into the tunnel. Trapped by a decades-old pretense at modernity.

Sara had the oddest sense that they were floating in a bubble, hovering over the real world, looking down upon it.

Reality had divorced from her life in that moment, held off by a fragile glass windowpane and hundreds of feet of open air.

Reality was so far away.

Was this how Eric always felt?

He delivered their drinks, making some suave comment, hitting on each of them, but they ignored him, captivated by the beautiful strangeness of the traffic slowed to a crawl by the blackout. Flowing more slowly, even more like blood now that it stopped and started at each intersection, pulsing through endless rows of four-way stops. A city still living. But for how long?

22

THE DAY PASSED IN A DAZE. SHE WANDERED THE STREETS WITH Drew, chatting idly without saying much. They had salads for lunch that were every bit as delicious as the meals in the hospital room—and much more pleasant for the company and fresh air.

Sara tried unsuccessfully to narrate her experience in her mind, put to words the crispness of the brickwork and the precision of the plantings, the perfect greenness and blueness and overbearing sense of clean. She seemed to move through a rendering of the world: too perfect and new to be fully real.

Everything, from the width of the pedestrian avenues to the density of the crowd to the temperature in the air, was exceedingly pleasant.

Surely no one could control the weather?

Somehow the hours melted away, the way they did on vacation, slipping by languidly and without note. People laughed, the water rose and fell and lifted the city onto its back, the air heated slightly then cooled slightly as the Earth turned, and it was evening when Sara felt it should still have been morning.

Sometime in the late afternoon Drew excused herself for a nap. Sara accompanied her back to her apartment and tried to remember its location, but all of the little streets were eerily the same in their manufactured charm. She doubted she would even find it again, should she ever look, but also felt unbothered by the thought. Drew was just one person among so many here.

Hours earlier, Sara had noticed something she wanted to examine further—like a light pole, perhaps, or a blue emergency station on a college campus. Taller than a person, with a screen on the side, as much brushed steel and smooth edges as everything else but utterly unfamiliar.

Drew hadn't seemed to notice it; Sara hadn't pointed it out. Drew was nice enough, and funny, but Sara felt none of the indescribable connection that had singled Bea out of the college-freshman chaos so many years before. Drew was in some unnameable sense *boring*, with potential to be a second-tier friend at best.

In a life as thoroughly surveilled as this one, Sara wanted the illusion of privacy, so she returned to the strange pole only after Drew had left.

A camera watched her, certainly, but she had spent the day searching for them and failed to spot a single telltale dome. The prickle down her back of being watched had started to fade. How quickly she forgot it was ever there. She did not need Drew's eyes to augment the distant ones.

As darkness fell, she regressed. Away from the shops, away from the noises of cutlery on ceramic and voices over dinner, away even from the streetlights: the evening stillness propelled her backward into childhood, where being out alone was a thrill and transgression. She felt she should not be there.

The pillar was back by the water, not so far as her apartment on the edge of town but in the same direction. She would pass it on the walk home.

No rule had been communicated so no rule was being broken, but she felt too alone for this possibly to be allowed. She crept on tiptoes through the descending chill, shivering but restraining her teeth from chattering.

The pillar stood in a wide courtyard, near a planter with white flowers folded in on themselves against the night. As she had imagined it would, it glowed with the blue light of modernity. Not a warning but also not a call.

She approached. How strange that no one else was around. How strange that something as clearly designed to be used as this could be so utterly ignored.

Silver, columnar, solid, with details somehow reminiscent of any familiar consumer tech, though it was on a much more imposing scale. She imagined the large size was more for effect than necessity, since nothing needed to be so big anymore.

She blinked and the blank metallic surface revealed itself to be a screen. After so many years of voice interfaces she found herself expecting a verbal exchange but was relieved when it remained silent—in the hush of the plaza, silent dark buildings and shushing thrum of waves, she doubted she would have been able to speak.

What appeared before her, almost inexplicably, was the familiar image of her contact list. An alphabetically ordered listing of every person she knew.

She reached toward the list and was mildly surprised to realize that it had appeared through the contacts in her eyes, a fact revealed through the way the light bent around her hand. The image distorted and then stabilized.

A smile appeared on her face unbidden. The column forced her to communicate out in the open where anyone might see, but the contents were restricted to her contacts: an incongruously public display of privacy.

She assumed someone would read her messages, or at least that an algorithm would parse them for intent and emotion. How else could they assess the utility of such a device? But the anonymous watcher grew less and less important by the minute.

Without having to touch anything, she flicked her fingers and the display spun by. Too quickly at first, then slower—a blur of everyone she had ever known.

When had she last looked through this list? Phone numbers and emails and social media handles tucked behind names, or nicknames, or descriptions that made sense to her when she'd added them. A heart beside the entry for each of her parents. A listing for her grandmother who had died years before. The chance to contact someone she worked with on a project in college, an old classmate from high school, a childhood friend.

She selected her mother's name, half expecting a phone to start ringing. Instead, a keyboard.

Was this a text? An email?

What were the protocols for communicating via screen projected upon a giant pillar?

Hi, Mom,
Sorry you've been worried. I have no idea how long it's been.

Hi, Mom,
Tell Dad hello.

She should write to him also.

New message, to both of them:

Hi,
I've been accepted. I guess I'm always accepted, huh? School and jobs and now this. I'm a very selectable person.

That was a long-running joke in her family, how Sara was admitted to everything she applied to. It had ceased to be true in recent years, with jobs harder and harder to find as the economy collapsed, and had a biting note now that it never had when she was growing up.

Hi—
I miss you and I hope you are okay.

They had fled their home just days after Sara had fled hers. She couldn't bring herself to ask if her childhood house still stood.

She just wanted to see her mother's face, hear her father's voice. If she did, she would know what to say.

The empty screen stared back at her, taunting. Her fingers hovered, unsure what to say or how to say it.

Miss you, love you, hope all's well. Sorry if you've been worried. I think I'm happy here. Is Emily coming?

Send.

23

THE NEXT MORNING SARA AWOKE TO AN ALARM FOR THE FIRST TIME since beginning her new life.

It took her a blundering moment to understand what the noise was, and once she did, her confusion did not abate. She hadn't set an alarm and saw no clear way to turn it off.

When she sat up, it fell silent.

She looked around the room urgently, heart pounding, for some reason afraid. Alexa stirred, rolled over, fell back asleep.

A message resolved in the air before Sara's eyes. She blinked a few times and shook her head, trying to bring it into focus, but the confusion of the carpet and shelves and window made it too difficult to read. Feeling like an idiot for not thinking of it sooner, she flopped back and stared up at the plain white of the ceiling.

The alarm resumed its sounding and she groaned, rolling out of bed. But not before reading the message:

Community-building enrichment activity in one hour. Follow directions.

Evidently, Alexa was not expected to join.

Sara moved blearily through the dark room, searching out her shoes and jacket while trying to close the message. It blocked her vision enough to be annoying.

The light was still low outside, though the sun seemed to have risen. Just how early was it?

Some combination of rubbing her eyes and blinking finally swiveled the message away, and to her surprise and wonder a small, unobtrusive clock appeared at the edge of her visual field. It vanished when her startled eyes flickered toward it directly, but reappeared when she focused elsewhere. 7:03 a.m.

"Sweet," she whispered.

Shoes located, she stepped out into the hall, expecting to find others there waiting or moving, half asleep, toward wherever they would be led. The hall was empty, and so was the courtyard when she went outside.

The sea, like the sky, was a dull gray. Wind whipped through the town, tossing dried leaves forward and tugging at her hair until she managed to wrestle it back into a tight bun that she hoped would hold.

Nothing was projected before her eyes yet, but she assumed her destination would be back toward the main town. She would follow any directions they gave her, but no one could hold it against her if the directions never arrived, right?

Along the promenade she walked. No one was out yet, not even the early morning joggers she had come to expect. As she neared the more crowded buildings of the village, she could see on the corner a pair of women wrapped in jackets against the cold, seemingly more bothered by it than she was, staring toward her as if waiting.

Nothing but the sound of the wind and her footsteps on damp pavement.

"We have just one more," one of them called.

She frowned. "What?"

"You're Sara, right?" the woman asked, her voice lower now as Sara reached them. "We're supposed to wait for one more person."

"A guy named Zander," the other woman clarified. She stomped her feet against the ground like it was cold.

Sara nodded, considered asking their names and then didn't.

After barely a minute, not even long enough for her to feel bored in the waiting, a thirty-something with a beard and a face that seemed to be missing glasses walked up.

"Morning, ladies," he said. "We're to walk along the shore for a mile and meet up with another two."

They all looked familiar to Sara, she now noticed.

"We all started together, yeah?" she asked as they began to walk.

Nods all around. Probably all remembering that they were supposed to be best friends but realizing that they didn't know each other at all.

She hadn't walked this stretch of the shore yet, where buildings jutted up right to the coast and a narrow sidewalk bent in and out over the water. The waves washed right up to the edge and then ducked beneath, carrying the platform on their backs; the wind assaulted them. The mile felt interminable.

The other two turned out to be another four—the entirety of their introductory class.

Sara exchanged good mornings with the group and moved to stand closer to Drew. She noted with a pulse of annoyance that the talkative blond man from the first day was trying to be the center of attention and succeeding, making everyone laugh and guess their goal and rally in one direction or another.

"Seems like some people have been given a piece of instructions," Drew said. "But no one knows much."

"Him either?" Sara asked, nodding toward the loud man.

Drew snorted. "I hope they don't encourage him."

To Sara's great relief, they didn't.

As their self-appointed leader railed on about how the whole point of this was obviously to get them all to talk more, awareness of a different message rippled through the little crowd. Sara couldn't tell with whom it originated; it arrived to her in waves from both sides.

They were to climb the dunes.

Someone said they should climb the dunes!

"The dunes?" the loudmouth asked skeptically. "Why would they ask us to do that?"

A small, slight man with dark hair and a forgettable face raised his voice. "I have a message! We are supposed to find a trail through the dunes!"

Loudmouth begrudgingly gave in and followed, still joking but less effectively now. The small man dissolved back into the group as soon as his message had been delivered.

Drew whispered to Sara that the loudmouth had once been a very successful salesman, which explained why he was so annoying. Sara laughed softly.

The dunes were near, roaring up mountainous along the side of the town. Looming, Sara thought. The group moved cautiously along the edge of the tamed land, looking for anything that might have been a trail, and found it with only minimal difficulty in the form of driftwood stairs that held back the forever sand.

A shared groan and reluctant climb, collective heavy breathing and murmurs of annoyance. But Sara honestly didn't mind: exertion felt good and her cold muscles warmed to the ascent, quickly settling into their new role.

Words filled her line of sight. She almost stumbled as they obscured the steps before her.

You'll soon enter the competition. Your objective: evade.

She fought the urge to laugh. What was this, a reality show?

Actually, she wouldn't be entirely surprised if it was. She hadn't exactly read the intake form with care. And wouldn't they try anything to ring any profit out of the people here?

But, rationally, she doubted it. Putting on a reality show would do nothing but dilute the company's brand. No, this was more likely what they said it was: an exercise. They realized that people locked away to test products quickly became too bored to be useful.

Enrichment, like raw meat in a tire for a captive tiger.

She blinked the message away, somewhat surprised that they let it vanish without her reading it aloud. But maybe that was part of the activity.

Who knew how many of these people had received messages they hadn't shared?

They neared the top of the hill and the clock in her peripheral vision neared 8 a.m. Whatever this was, it would begin soon.

Before she could muster the will to share her revelation, an Asian man who had been lingering near the back of the group said, "We're against a smaller, more experienced team! What does that mean?"

Incredulity rolled through the group and Sara fought to be heard. "We—hey!—let me!"

Drew cleared her throat and shouted, "Shut up!"

It took some effort on Sara's part not to laugh. "It's a competition and we are supposed to, and I quote, *evade*."

"Like *tag*?" Drew asked.

"Is this gym class?" someone asked.

"I loved gym class!"

Sara had hated gym class.

"Evade a more experienced enemy?" loudmouth said. "This is *not* fair!"

"Anyone else got anything?" asked the tall woman who split from the group first after the introductory class.

Silence.

Then Drew's voice: "We win if anyone is left standing."

Chaos erupted.

"Obviously, then, we all go at once."

"Leave a few people to distract—"

"Like bait?"

"Like sacrifices?"

"We should be civilized people!"

"Oh, come *on*, let's be adults."

"Well, if video games have taught me anything—"

Sara turned to the long-haired woman, who Sara saw was actually young enough to be barely out of high school. "You want a hair tie?"

The woman smirked, accepted it, and pulled her hair up in a high ponytail. Something about that hairstyle meant business and Sara thought back to a thousand games growing up, her muscles readying for an attack, eyes suddenly more alert. She'd hated gym but loved sports after school.

She watched the clock tick forward. One hour from the alarm.

As her teammates continued yelling at each other, Sara took off running across the sand.

24

THE COMMOTION FELL AWAY BEHIND HER. OTHERS WERE RUNNING, she thought, but she didn't turn or slow to watch them. This was about her now, just her and her feet against the sand, her lungs against the salt air. It had been so long since she had run like this, free and wild, not an obligatory suburban jog or careful track-based sprint. No, Sara ran like a child, as fast as she could, across uneven terrain without a goal besides escape.

She had to concentrate to keep her feet beneath her on the loose sand, only taking the time to assess her surroundings when she paused to catch her breath. Military maybe, too old and decrepit to be from the city that had been here just a few years before. Concrete with collapsed roofs and graffiti, with something of a skate park or jungle gym vibe. Sloping down a hill toward old farmland turning now to wildness, sand becoming grass beneath her feet.

Behind her, the sound of conflict. Shrieks—of laughter? Of fear? A body hitting the sand, the oof of breath knocked out of lungs. Protestations and celebrations.

She ducked, sliding around what in her wildest imagination was once a bunker. Paused for a breath, as hidden as she could be while still so exposed. She could still get away if someone approached. Breathing heavily but trying to be as quiet as possible.

The soft *shush, shush, shush* of footsteps on sandy ground. An enemy or an ally? Either way, Sara did not want to be found.

She held her breath, waiting for them to walk away. A pause, a muffled voice, a retreat, and then she was running again, blood pumping and mind calculating—like a predator more than like prey, so aware of everything— eyes racing to keep up with her body's progress. Stumbling and recovering and not stopping. Not even sure if anyone was following.

Why did this feel so real? The fear she felt was not imaginary. Someone hunted her and she didn't know why.

They hadn't even laid out any stakes. What happened if she was caught?

She had to get away, and so she would.

Her feet pounded across the terrain, more deft than she expected, zig-zagging around the concrete and steel structures, crunching over bushes and avoiding trees weathered by the coastal breeze. The cold air was so bright in her face.

How long had it been?

She had not run far—had crossed back and forth over the dunes—had darted from the buildings to the swamped farmland, now too saline to grow anything useful. A startled family of ducks burst into the sky. She plunged up to her ankle in a puddle but did not slow down, then scraped her arm through brambles enough to bleed.

The sun began to burn through the clouds. She hadn't seen any of her teammates in a while. Could it be that she was the last one left?

Ahead, a hill. More dramatic than the dunes: sharp and stark, with large boulders suspended in loose sandstone, sea-ravaged roots of dead trees snarling through the soil, reddish bushes clinging up the side. So many places to hide, and such a vantage point. How could she not climb?

Her heart pounded as she raced across the field that separated her from her goal, each step surely her last. She was certain someone would see her, someone would be waiting. She would fall and it would all be over.

Instead, she reached the base and began to climb. Perhaps no one noticed or perhaps no one cared. Maybe no one had ever chased her at all.

Finding a way up was not trivial. The ground dissolved beneath her feet; in order to make progress she had to rely as much on her arms as her legs, gripping the exposed roots and pulling herself up. Ready to catch herself when, inevitably, she lost her footing.

Her hands raw from the effort, her muscles straining, the wind prickling at her eyes and with leaves in her hair, Sara hauled herself upward. She felt feral; her body coursed with the desire to get away. Take the high ground and *get away*.

From who?

She tore her way upward. If someone sought to follow, they would know exactly where she had gone—she left a scar through the vegetation as she plowed on.

Uncaring, like humans always were.

The end was above her now; the air became refreshing instead of punishing. She tried to stop for breath but found her excitement too great for that. Much as her lungs protested, she could not pause so close to the goal. Something great awaited her.

Pushing through the branches, she broke free to the limitless sky.

At some point the clouds had melted away entirely. Seated there atop the hill, she turned her face to the sky and let the sun wash over her, her eyes closed against its brightness and mouth open to taste the wind.

Then, once she had revived and calmed her furious heart, she turned toward the tableau below her and opened her eyes.

Her team sat on a bench, all seven in a row. A caricature of defeat with hung heads and folded hands.

Three people paced around them, talking animatedly in voices she could not hear. They hadn't spotted her yet, which seemed impossible after her mad scramble up the hill.

She turned outward then, her interest in the scene fading quickly. She realized belatedly that her plan had been to disappear down the other side of the embankment but saw that such a feat would be more dangerous than she wanted to attempt. Perhaps in her frenzied fleeing she might have tried it, but not anymore.

None of it mattered. Her bleeding hands were absurd.

The hill dropped to the sea far below, almost a cliff. A strip of gray beach curved away from her, hidden from any vantage point but this, and rugged greenery raced inland like slow-growing vegetal waves. It was inviting and sent a thrill through her, something primeval.

But again, the cliff. Edging closer was a terrible idea, descending even worse. She would not try it. At least not today.

A pair of birds swept through the blue sky above her, darting toward each other and then away again in a three-dimensional dance. How freeing it must be to move through all the world's dimensions, she thought, and to exist on a plane apart from the land that sank and shrank. They were too small and high for her to identify, but she wanted to call them swallows.

A sound below, a raised voice. Too far away for her to understand the words, but she knew what it meant.

Her eyes turned from the birds lazily, directing her gaze back to the other people. They looked as small and inconsequential as the birds soaring above her.

One of their three enemies had stepped away from the group, moving determinedly toward the hill she now thought of as hers. Not in a hurry, but making his intentions clear.

She might have gotten away still, had she wanted. Dove sideways, dared to risk the plummet toward the waves, gambled upon roots that didn't look reliable, thought a little harder to come up with a better escape plan.

But while the ocean rolled and the birds danced, how could she bother with something as useless as that?

She watched him clamber up the hill and didn't run, both of their faces expressionless, pretending not to notice how stupid all this was. His ascent was slow, but she was patient.

And when he reached her, they stood awkwardly, since tag didn't make any sense when no one was running and you were both adults. The urgency, the heart-pounding fear, had gone out of the moment. They faced each other and instead of tagging her arm or tackling her as they had her teammates, he extended a hand to shake. She smiled at the ridiculousness, but that counted. His team had won.

"Everest," he said.

She figured that was his name, not some weird comment on the immensity of the hill. "Sara."

He had a kind face, nondescript. By which she meant she wouldn't have been able to describe it. Brown skin, brown hair, brown eyes.

They descended the hill together, all semblance of teams evaporated.

25

Four and a half years before the Community

AFTER GRADUATION, SARA WORKED A MINIMUM WAGE INTERNSHIP at a startup that folded shortly after she left and then a six-month quality assurance contract at a tech giant, both of which were tedious and frustrating adventures in being underestimated and navigating bureaucracy. So when she got the offer for a software engineer position at One, a well-funded startup, she was very excited.

One had a dozen employees and she was the first female engineer, but there were a couple women on the business side, so she wasn't entirely alone. They were just starting to scale, rolling out into new markets beyond Silicon Valley and supporting products besides the few things they'd started with—expanding from the potato chips and paper clips of their slogan to trickier things like matches and sewing needles.

The idea was simple and, in Sara's mind, genius: how often did you need just one of something that only came in large packages? Especially if you were a college student or a young professional living alone, you didn't need a twelve pack of light bulbs, but you did want the discounts that came from buying in bulk. Or what if you were on a diet but really craved french fries? It was just wasteful to throw away most of your order.

The way she saw it, this solved a problem she actually had, and could only become more successful and useful as it became more popular. With more users, they could apply ever greater economies of scale and get their customers better deals. They were *helping* people.

It was the end of her first week on the job and she had finally been assigned a ticket that required writing actual code. Since she didn't have any Friday night plans, she figured she'd just plug away at it, navigating the code base and searching for the best way to implement the simple fix she'd been assigned. Why not make a good impression by finishing her first week strong?

She sat at her desk with her earbuds in as the rest of the company trickled away for the weekend, studying her two monitors and stepping through the code in a debugger. It got dark outside, but she didn't have a long walk home, so she didn't care.

Sometime after 8 p.m. she felt someone tap her on the shoulder, and looked up with wide eyes to see the CEO standing over her, grinning. His name was Zach, but it felt odd to call her boss by a name so casual.

He was tall and muscular, but also carried a few extra pounds around the middle, like a college football player after a few years at a desk job. Very blond but very tan in a way that only seemed to come from Hawaii. Maybe a surfer?

"Hi!" she said, trying to keep her voice from squeaking.

"Why're you still here?" he asked.

Was she in trouble? "Um, just trying to…"

"I'm headed out for the night," he said, interrupting her. "Want to join me for sushi?"

She didn't know what the right answer was, career-wise, but she was hungry, and sushi sounded delicious. "Sure," she said, after considering for just a moment.

They walked out into the evening and over to his car, which was low and sporty and curvy. And tiny. Just the slightest promise of spring was discernible in the chilly air.

"Is this…" she started to ask.

But again, he cut her off. "Original Tesla Roadster!"

"That's gotta be thirty years old!"

"But drives like brand new," he said. "You'll see."

They sped out of the parking lot and down El Camino into downtown Palo Alto, the acceleration plastering her to her seat. All electric cars were like that, but in her experience, only Tesla owners drove so obnoxiously.

It felt good to be back near Stanford. After almost a year working remotely from her parents' sleepy town, middle class suburbia nipping at the heels of Napa, she had been itching for some of the energy of Silicon Valley.

"So how was your first week?" he asked as they parked.

She smiled. "Fantastic! Everyone's very nice."

"And good engineers," he said.

"Yeah," she said, feeling like she'd been chastised. "That, too."

"Have you been here before?" he asked, nodding toward the restaurant they were entering.

She shook her head. "I didn't go out a lot in college."

He laughed. "Seems like that's all I did. I lived more in Palo Alto than on campus."

She raised her eyebrows. She hadn't realized he went to Stanford, too. "What year did you graduate?"

She had a lot of older friends; maybe they had overlapped. How old could he be, thirty? Younger?

"Oh, I didn't," he said. He pulled out her chair for her and then walked around to the other side of the table. "Dropped out before junior year."

"A startup?"

"Yeah, a flash-in-the-pan neural network thing. Didn't last."

"Serial entrepreneur, then?" she asked.

"Only until I hit it big," he replied with a conspiratorial grin. "And let me tell you—I think this is the *One*."

She laughed, since it was clear she was supposed to. Eating dinner with her boss felt uncomfortable, especially when he learned she'd never had sake and insisted on ordering a full selection. Getting drunk with her boss felt even stranger.

But then sushi turned to gelato at a shop a block away and gelato turned to a nightcap of his favorite Japanese whisky on his living room couch.

If dinner and sake had been a minor transgression, this was definitely crossing a line. Sara may not have been the most socially savvy person on the planet, but even she could tell where he was trying to direct the evening, and she was a bit shocked to find herself in such a stereotypical position.

New young software engineer hit on by her boss? Just what everyone had warned her to avoid.

But he wasn't *not* cute, and he sure was tall, and she was pretty drunk, and hadn't gotten laid in a year, so when he kissed her, she didn't push him away, and when she woke up in his bed the next morning, she wasn't embarrassed at all.

But she resolved not to tell anyone in the office on Monday.

26

THE SUN BURNED OFF THE LAST OF THE CLOUDS AS THE MORNING stretched toward its end and Everest and Sara returned to the group, dusty, scratched and in much better moods than the crew who awaited them on the bench.

Sara's teammates looked sour and bored, though her escapade had drawn out the prospect of their entire team's success much longer than any of them had managed. Everest's two partners appeared impatient and far less appreciative than she thought he deserved. He had ended the game in their favor, after all.

They all regrouped, commingling with their recent enemies, lines between them dissolving almost immediately, though no one seemed eager to chat with their opponents. No one seemed terribly chatty with their own group, either.

She wondered if there had been a way for her team to win at this game. She wondered why there were only three in the group opposing them. She wondered what the point of it all had been.

They traipsed back through the concrete ruins, starkly gray against the blue sky. People moved in irregular clumps through the remnants of a shattered human landscape.

"What do you think this all was?" Sara asked, though she wasn't really curious enough to care. It was just something to say when something so clearly needed to be said. The air was too fraught to be hanging around eleven people who had no reason not to be friends.

Before speaking, she had carefully varied her pace to walk between Everest's two companions, a man and a woman, both tall, both strong looking. Perhaps siblings, she thought. But Everest was not their sibling; he looked nothing like them.

Neither replied to her, but she hadn't really expected them to. It had been more a gesture of good will, speaking so calmly to two people whose posture made it clear they had no interest in making friends.

Someone from her own group said, "Dunno," in a flat voice. The conversation died.

Sara let her pace slow, falling behind the two as they left the structures behind. The dunes sloped upward now, gradual at first but growing steeper.

It was the kind of landscape that discouraged conversation, but Sara did not want to give up without at least a few more attempts at alleviating the tension.

This whole endeavor had been billed as a team building exercise, hadn't it?

If that had been the goal, she feared it had failed. She didn't know the people from her introductory class any better than when they met for the first time; she hadn't even exchanged real hellos with the remaining two.

"What do you suppose this was supposed to test?" she asked into the air, hoping someone would understand what she was trying to do. Hating herself for using the word *suppose* twice in one sentence.

Nothing but the sound of feet on sand and heavy breathing.

She let her hope deflate. What did it matter if they walked in silence? This was a very small number of people compared to the thousands in the community; they didn't have to be friends. Getting a conversation off the ground was not a test she was failing.

But then, Everest's voice: "I find it's better not to ask questions like that."

He was behind her by several people, had heard her speak thanks to the wind and was almost shouting so she could hear him now. She looked over her shoulder, back down the hill, and couldn't suppress her grin. "Why not?"

Something about his stance seemed to invite conversation. She stepped aside to let a few people pass, falling toward the very back of the group to match steps with him.

"No real reason beyond superstition, I guess," he said. "It feels like it would break the spell."

She snorted.

"What, you don't think of it like that?"

"You mean you're trying to maintain the illusion that this is all normal, right?" she asked. "Or is there some magic I'm missing?"

"It's not an illusion," he said. "It *is* normal."

"None of this is normal!"

He laughed lightly, and she got the impression he was laughing at her. "I can't speak for you, but I consider myself a normal person."

She laughed and it came out jagged from the exertion of the climb. Bringing back fond memories of strenuous hikes and good friends. "And what does that matter?"

He smiled. His teeth looked very white against his brown skin. "I'm a normal person and this is my life. Therefore, this is all normal."

She didn't think that was a very good argument, but she couldn't find the words to explain why, so she didn't try. "It's just different, that's all."

"I'm not even sure that's true," he said. "For the past twenty years every product we interacted with was an experiment, wasn't it?"

She paused, the idea hitting her hard enough to halt her feet for a moment. It should have been obvious. In her old job, they pushed alternate versions of their app out to randomized users all the time. But somehow being experimented on in the physical world felt more intrusive.

"Touché," she said.

"You don't have to agree with me."

She shrugged and increased her pace, suddenly anxious to get away. "I do when you're right."

The conversation felt too easy, too familiar, to be held with someone she had just met. The irony was not lost on her that this was exactly what she had wanted, to progress past the pleasantries to something of substance and ideas, but it happened too quickly with Everest.

Perhaps there was a reason to stick to small talk with practical strangers. Even such a brief exchange left her feeling exposed and alone when it delved past the surface.

27

A STORM BLEW IN FROM THE COAST BEFORE SARA MADE IT BACK TO her apartment, drenching her by the time she reached the densest part of town. Puddles materialized on pavement she had thought was flat and rivulets poured neatly off the corners of buildings. Her companions melted back into the town without so much as a goodbye.

She ducked her head against the onslaught, but it didn't much matter. Water soaked quickly through her sweatshirt and tennis shoes, poured into her eyes and down the back of her shirt and off the end of her nose.

For the first few minutes it was miserable, but once thoroughly soaked she didn't care anymore. Walking past the buildings along empty sidewalks didn't feel like drudgery but rather an adventure, the town made strange by the flowing water, silvered with wet and brown with mud that wasn't there before. Some of its perfection was lost in the storm. She liked it better this way.

Even in a perfect built environment, all sharp edges and precision, it almost felt like one good storm could reset everything.

Still, she stepped gratefully into the warmth of the lobby when she reached her building and hurried, dripping, down the hall. A trail of water on the carpet behind her showed just who would be so crazy as to go out in such a storm.

At some point she had started shivering, but she didn't notice until enveloped in the dry indoors.

Her sodden clothes fought to stay put as she peeled them off and then stood naked alone in her room while the water steamed off her damp skin. She felt warmer already. She wondered where Alexa had gone but didn't much care, glad that she was somewhere else.

The room lacked a mirror, and she wasn't sure that she would have looked in one if it had been an option. She thought she would look uncomfortably pale and annoyingly flabby, and decided she didn't need to see it. For years she'd rarely seen her own face without makeup and didn't care to be reminded of that, either. Her nose would be red and runny from the rain, her cheeks blotchy from the cold.

She draped her wet clothes over the shower curtain rod and put her pajamas back on. What now?

In her old life she would have had a library book, either a physical copy before they closed the branch near her apartment or an e-book once down-loading was the only practical option. She would have been streaming music, some massive playlist on shuffle, each song a novelty.

Back before One folded, every spare moment was spent working. Es-pecially once she lived with Zach, who worked even more hours than she did. In the end, no amount of weekends at the office or date nights with their laptops out—side by side at the kitchen table with a bottle of wine and code that needed debugging—had been enough to save the company, or their relationship.

And before that, she'd been at home with her parents, never bored be-cause her mom always wanted to chat, or her dad always had a chore to assign. Or in college when there was always another assignment to work on and a friend right down the hall.

She had never learned how to do nothing. But hadn't she gotten the hang of it in the medical ward? How could she forget so quickly?

She sat at her desk, turned the chair to face the window, and pushed aside the curtains enough to see out. The rain had stopped. This disappointed her greatly.

She was just contemplating looking through Alexa's things—papers and objects strewn across the other desk—when the door swung open and Alexa spilled through.

"Oh, you're back!"

Sara looked up, feeling guilty for even having thought of snooping. "Hi!"

"Where'd you go this morning?" Alexa asked, dumping the contents of a bag across her bed. "You were up early!"

"Some team-building exercise," Sara said. "With my intro group."

Alexa laughed. "I guess they make us all do that."

"Was it tag for you, too?" Sara asked. "It didn't feel like a bonding moment."

"No, we had dodgeball." Alexa slumped onto her bed, facing Sara.

"They have a thing for schoolyard games, huh?"

Alexa shrugged. "Guess so. So, did you win?"

Sara snorted. "I don't think winning was an option."

"It was very lopsided?" Alexa asked. "Us, too! There were three of us and a dozen of them."

Sara frowned. "Interesting."

"What?"

Sara shook her head. "Nothing. So is this going to keep happening?"

"You mean are they going to keep assigning activities?" Alexa replied. "I don't think so. They'll leave us alone eventually."

"Hasn't happened to you yet, though?"

"I've only been here a week longer than you!"

Sara kept forgetting that. "It seems like you know so much more than me."

"I like knowing things," Alexa said. "I'm just that kind of person."

"Yeah, but how?" Sara heard how plaintive her voice sounded and hated it. "There's no way to learn anything here!"

Alexa looked at her like she had two heads. "There's information everywhere! I've never been anywhere so easy to figure out."

"I have no idea what you mean."

"Okay, it's like high school, you know? Nobody tells you the rules, but they're there, and they're not hard to follow."

Sara had definitely not understood the rules of high school, and she didn't want to live in a community that anyone could happily compare to it. "You're going to have to explain more than that."

Alexa shuffled toward the end of the bed closer to Sara and leaned forward intently. "They never told us what they really want, but we all know, right? They need us, but not *that* much. But they also want to feel good about themselves, so they treat us really well. Get it?"

"Kind of." Not at all.

"We just have to be happy and they'll be happy! And they'll continue to need us, and we'll continue to have this great place to live."

It bothered Sara that Alexa so easily spoke of some unnamed *they* who she thought she had figured out. Sara suspected that no person made all the decisions about this world and was almost certain that nothing was decided based on what made that person feel good. But Alexa told a nice story.

"They think this bland place with games will keep people happy?" she asked, trying to poke holes in Alexa's theory without revealing that she found the whole thing ridiculous. "I'm pretty sure everything is fake. Even the alcohol is fake."

Alexa waved that off. "At the official events, sure. But there are ways to get real alcohol."

Sara blinked. "What?"

"Sure," Alexa said. "One thing people crave is a way to break rules, so they give us that too. Just like high school."

And just like high school, Sara thought, I'm not the cool one.

28

Four years before the Community

SARA AND BEA SAT OUTSIDE A PHILZ, SIPPING SWEET, STRONG COFFEE and luxuriating in the sun. It was one of those autumn days where the sun was still strong but not too hot, when it touches your skin like an old friend. It was midmorning and Bea had just recounted how she'd already had six coffees that morning.

"How are you not jittery?" Sara asked.

Bea shrugged. She did look a little antsy to Sara, but remarkably calm for someone with a near-fatal dose of caffeine in her veins. "It's what it takes to get me awake these days."

"You need to take better care of yourself."

"Like sleeping more?"

"Exactly like sleeping more."

"Easy for you to say, Ms. I-have-an-office-job," Bea replied.

"You're right, I'm sorry," Sara said, relenting. "But how long are you going to go on like this? You're running yourself ragged."

Bea was working fifty-something hours a week as a nanny—however many hours the tech-rich parents would give her—and filling every other waking moment with microwork crammed together from various apps and online services. Every hour, that is, except...

"I made time for you, didn't I?"

Sara glanced at her wrist theatrically. "What do I get, an hour?"

"Something like that," Bea said. "Gotta pay the bills."

"I'm sure you'll get a better job soon, Bea," Sara said. Her mint mojito coffee tasted bitter as she considered her position in comparison to her friend's.

"Yeah, who would have thought an ethnic studies degree wouldn't get me a good job?" she said sarcastically. "Should've seen this coming."

Sara shook her head. "You're one of the smartest people I know, friend."

"Does it matter?" she replied. "Anyway, I'm not really complaining. The kids are fun, and I get by. Let's talk about something else."

"Let's," Sara agreed. Relieved.

"Seeing anyone?" Bea asked.

Sara was going to lie and say no, but she felt herself blush and knew she could never get away with a lie to Bea.

Bea leaned forward, eyes lighting up. "Ooh, who? Tell me!"

Sara looked away, as if suddenly fascinated by the parked cars across the street. "It's really dumb."

"How?" Bea pressed. "You know saying that just makes me more curious."

Sara laughed in spite of herself. "I know."

"Tell!"

"It's…my boss."

"Your *boss?*" Bea asked, her glee replaced by shock. "Sara, how'd that *happen?*"

Sara shrugged. "We got drunk."

"I can see getting drunk and hooking up, but getting drunk and starting to *date?*"

"I've never been one for one-night-stands," Sara said.

Bea leaned back in her chair, gazing up at the blue sky above. "Do people know?"

"No, it's a secret, so don't tell anyone!"

"Who would I tell?" Bea replied. "I only ever talk to toddlers."

"Seriously," Sara said.

Bea rolled her eyes. "Seriously, I won't. But…are you okay?"

Sara scoffed. "I know how it looks, Bea, but I'm not some weak-willed little girl tricked into sleeping with her boss."

"No, you're a strong, independent woman, dumbly sleeping with her boss."

Sara smiled because it was mean but also true. "And having a damn good time doing it."

29

THAT EVENING A NOTIFICATION FLASHED ACROSS THEIR VISION. There would be a cocktail party to celebrate the end of another week, and everyone was encouraged to attend. Dress up!

The invitation actually ended like that: *Dress up!* As if spoken in an excited whisper from a friend.

Now that Alexa had put the high school analogy in her head, Sara couldn't stop thinking about it, which only made her even more uncomfortable.

Alexa showed her how to properly dismiss the notification with a brisk swiping gesture in the air, and a few minutes later the door buzzed with a set of simple black dresses for them to wear. No one was there; they wouldn't send an actual person to make deliveries.

The jobs available here were pretty mundane, but none quite so sporadic and boring as that, Sara thought.

"Oh, this is so cute!" Alexa enthused, draping the dress over her clothes.

Sara had no opinion until she put something on. How could Alexa even tell?

The fabric felt cheap and almost disposable. Probably it was, but at least she could be reasonably sure it hadn't been made in a sweatshop overseas. The company would never do something like that when uncomplaining machines could do things faster and cheaper than people.

Better to displace jobs than create terrible ones, right?

"You know, I used to always wear dresses," Alexa said. "I was thoroughly Team No Pants."

Sara laughed. "I can't even imagine."

"I think I'd have been that way even if I was a guy," Alexa went on. "I'd have been that weird kid in kilts. Did every high school have one of those? Mine certainly did."

"I don't know," Sara said. "When I picture people, they're always wearing jeans."

"Right?" Alexa said. "So boring!"

"I guess."

"Anyway, I'm so excited about this, is the point," Alexa said. She was twirling the soft fabric through the air. Hers felt so flimsy in her hands that Sara worried Alexa would break it before she got a chance to put it on.

"Couldn't you get a dress in town?" Sara asked. "I thought I saw lots of shops."

"I looked," Alexa said. "Nothing."

"Hmm," Sara asked. She hadn't noticed a time on the invitation, but it was still light out. It seemed a bit early to get ready.

But what else was there to do?

"When does this event start?"

Alexa shrugged. "I always like to spend the whole afternoon getting ready."

"You mean since you've been here?" Sara asked. "Are there events like this often?"

"How should I know?" Alexa replied. "I mean since *always*. So fun."

Sara decided to give into Alexa's excitement. "Okay, let's get beautiful."

Alexa scoffed and fluffed her hair. "Bitch, I'm always beautiful."

Sara laughed. "I wish I had your confidence."

"Oh, please, how old are you, twenty-five?" Alexa said. "Women just get prettier through their twenties. Own it."

Sara was not at all sure that was true. "I'm twenty-eight."

"See, even better!" Alexa was laughing, too, now. "I wish we had some good get-hype music."

"Isn't there some way to—"

"There used to be speakers in everyone's room, apparently, but they took them away a couple months ago," Alexa said, pouting.

"Why would they do that?"

"There's enough music out in the town, I guess."

Sara didn't agree, but she saw no point in pushing the issue. "I guess we're back to a time before not just smartphones, but also record players."

Alexa snorted. "We'll have to sing for entertainment like a Jane Austin heroine."

"I don't sing!"

"Sing the first thing you think of!" Alexa urged.

Sara drew a blank, waited what felt like an awkwardly long time, then started, "A, B, C..."

Alexa started laughing, harder than the joke really warranted. "Oh, that's the best!"

But Sara stopped, because she hated the sound of her unaccompanied voice.

"No, no, keep going!" Alexa said. "And turn around! I'm getting dressed."

Sara turned but did not resume the song, feeling ridiculous since privacy was a concept long-since abandoned by everyone in the Community, then dutifully changed into her own dress when Alexa pointedly asked what was taking so long. It fit well—of course it did—hitting just above the knee and plunging low in the back. She expected it not to work with the bra they provided, but somehow it did.

"Normally I'd spend the next two hours putting on makeup and taking it back off again," Alexa said. "But…you know."

Sara was turning in slow circles, trying to decide how she looked since she couldn't check herself out in a mirror.

"Here," Alexa said, handing her a tube of red lipstick.

"Where'd you get this?"

During her day of wandering through town with Drew, Sara hadn't seen any makeup in any of the shops. And she had certainly been looking.

Alexa shrugged, smirked. "I have my ways."

"Are they the same as the ways to get illicit alcohol?" Sara asked. Staring at the lipstick like it might bite her.

Alexa laughed. "Are you an alcoholic or something?"

"No, just asking," Sara said, maybe too quickly. She definitely wasn't an alcoholic by any reasonable standards, but every social activity since college had involved a drink. Even when they were broke and she could barely make her student loan payments, there was cheap grocery store wine. It felt like an essential part of adulthood; living in a dorm where alcohol was inaccessible made her feel like a kid again in a way she hated.

But she couldn't explain all of that to Alexa, or at least didn't want to, so she didn't try.

"Are you wearing it or not?" Alexa asked.

Sara smeared it across her lips, wishing even more for a mirror.

"You're a natural blonde, right?" Alexa asked. "Once your hair grows out, you'll have a serious Taylor Swift circa 2016 vibe, I think."

Sara snorted. "I guess you can't get any hair dye, either?"

Alexa shrugged. "Eh, maybe. But I mean let's be real. Nothing's as worth the risk as some statement lipstick, right?"

Sara just shook her head, then struck a pose in her sock feet as if she walked a runway. "How do I look?"

Alexa grinned. "Perfect! Too bad we only have these athletic shoes, though. Another thing they took away in the last year, apparently, were the shoe stores."

Sara looked at her shoes, muddy and damp from the morning. "That could be a look."

"It'll have to be," Alexa said with a slight scowl. That telltale eye flicker that Sara was coming to recognize as checking the time. "Shall we?"

It felt odd to set out for the night without a purse and with only a single friend in tow, but everything about her new life felt odd. Sara shook off her discomfort and they departed into the falling night arm in arm.

30

THE MORNING'S TORRENTIAL DOWNPOUR HAD FADED INTO A LIGHT rain, so subtle it could only be seen in the streetlights. Sara's hair twinkled with a thousand tiny water droplets.

Groups of people converged on a restaurant that was set up far fancier than she remembered. Tables were draped with white tablecloths, glasses sparkled in artificial candlelight, and throngs of people in cheap black clothes mingled. The lights were dimmed low and the place settings shone.

"Look, I think she got some mascara," Alexa whispered, nodding to a dark-haired woman as she passed.

"Her eyelashes might just be like that," Sara replied.

Alexa inclined her head in thought. "That's why I got red lipstick," she replied. "So no one could possibly say that about me."

"If that's your goal, you should probably have gone for black."

Alexa laughed. "But I also wanted to look good!"

Just then, Drew materialized out of the crowd with two other women Sara recognized from the group that morning, all in the same black dresses as Sara and Alexa.

"You guys look awesome!" said the tall Asian girl who Sara had given a hair tie that morning.

Sara indicated Alexa. "All her doing."

"So lucky," said the other woman, the redhead from their intro group. Sara would have pegged her for a counter-culture type based on her statement haircut and the telltale hole in her nose where a piercing once was. "My roommate is so—and I can't believe I'm about to say this—straight edge."

They all laughed, though Sara wasn't totally sure why.

"See what I mean?" Alexa said, voice low so only Sara heard. "Just like high school."

"You remember May and Lacey, right?" Drew said. The tall girl and the nose ring woman, respectively.

Sara nodded. "And this is my roommate, Alexa."

Everyone exchanged pleasantries, then Drew asked, "Did you get caught in that storm this morning? You have to walk a long way."

Sara shrugged. "It was refreshing."

"Not my idea of refreshing," Lacey said. "I want a fucking spa day."

Laughter again. Sara joined in.

"Did you think this place was a luxury resort or something?" May asked.

"It *is* though," Drew insisted. "Free food, free bed. Basically Disney World."

"Last I checked Disney cost a couple hundred a day," Lacey said.

"My point exactly," Drew went on. "Maybe they have spas, but none of it's free."

"Right?" Alexa said. "I always heard there was no free lunch, but, well…"

Everyone laughed, including Sara, who didn't even have to pretend that time. Though it was a bit of a sardonic laugh, all things considered—she'd lived a very free-lunch life for years working at startups and knew that there were always hidden costs.

Like slipping into dating the boss. This realization made her laugh even harder. She'd sublimated the weirdness there for so many years that it felt exhilarating to admit how weird it was, even to herself.

At the thought of him, she self-consciously glanced around for Zach. But she no longer really expected to see him. She'd come to the conclusion that he, like Bea, was not the kind of person the company would let in. Too much of a planner, too wedded to the idea of steering his own life, Zach would never be happy with all the strangeness within the Community, not like all of her new friends who seemed so grateful. Sara wondered what it said about her that she had been admitted.

Emily, though. If Sara belonged, then so did Emily.

Lacey announced that she was going to go get them drinks.

Sara wondered if she knew they were nonalcoholic but figured it didn't matter. She'd read somewhere that if people thought they were getting drunk they would act as if they were. It was certainly cheaper that way.

"Did you ever go to Disney?" May was asking. "It was kind of a shit show, honestly."

"How so? Crowds, fakeness?" Drew asked.

"Sounds familiar," Sara said, gesturing around at the room.

Drew shook her head, still laughing. "I'm all for fakeness, I guess."

Lacey returned, impossibly quickly, and distributed five identical glasses of amber liquid.

"How'd you carry so much?" Sara asked.

"Waitress for fifteen years, baby!" Lacey said. "Free at last, thank God."

"What is it?" Alexa asked, sniffing.

"No idea," Lacey said, sipping hers. "Tastes like sour honey, so basically, delicious."

Sara rolled her eyes and tipped the glass back and forth. She'd had it thoroughly ingrained in her not to ever drink something she couldn't identify, but knowing the Community, this was a safe time to start. An ice cube clinked in the glass.

"So, you were saying something about fakeness?" Lacey asked.

Laughter, then Drew saying, "Just comparing our lovely new home to Disneyland."

Sara couldn't tell if there was any sarcasm in her voice.

"I just love fake things," Lacey said. When the group laughed, she held up a hand. "You think I'm kidding? I'm not even kidding. Listen."

"Listening," Alexa said.

This prompted even Lacey to laugh. "You got that joke a lot growing up?"

Alexa rolled her eyes. "No, seriously, I want to hear your paean to fakeness."

"Paean?" Drew said.

"Right, *you're* an English teacher," Sara said, laughing at her.

"I know what it means!" Drew protested. "I'm just surprised she does! No offense."

Alexa laughed loudly. Almost obnoxiously. "You don't have to go to college to know things!"

Lacey took control of the conversation again. "Anyway, as I was saying," she said, trying to sound annoyed and authoritative but barely containing her laughter. "I fucking *love* fakeness. Fake fur? Superior. Fake wood? Love that damn rain forest, leave it alone. Fake *people*? Hilarious!"

"You had me there until the end," Drew said.

"To fakeness!" said May, lifting her drink in a toast.

To all that's left, thought Sara, clinking her untouched drink against May's.

She looked over May's shoulder, deeper into the crowd, and the face she saw staring back made her forget to breathe.

Bea, decked out like one of the rejected girls in a glittery dress and full face of makeup, a plastic smile on her painted lips. Their eyes met and Sara's jaw dropped.

31

SARA AWOKE EARLY AND COULD IMMEDIATELY TELL THAT SHE WASN'T hungover in the least: confirmation that the alcohol was as fake as she had guessed.

At least no alarm had pulled her abruptly from sleep this time, so she snuggled back into her blankets and let them comfort her. Nothing like a bed in the morning to make everything feel perfect. When embraced by fabric and cushions, the haze of sleep still hovering around her, the rest of the world didn't matter.

She couldn't remember her dreams at all, which was unusual. Something about awakening without an alarm, she guessed. Her most recent dream taunted her, just outside her reach, its emotions—anticipation, mostly, but also joy—making her ache for the details. Probably it was something ridiculous, but still she wished to know.

If she could properly remember her dreams, she would understand herself better.

Eyes closed, she sent her mind off to wander, searching for what it conjured while she was out. Something about wood, its texture when you ran your hand along the grain. She felt like she should remember the smell of it—cedar? Fresh-cut bark? So many ways it might have smelled. Like a Christmas tree inside by the fire or like the wood in the fire itself. The healthy wash of broken boughs after a storm or the freshness of sawdust in her high school woodshop class.

But did dreams ever have aromas? Suddenly she found she didn't know. This one hadn't, and that made her sad.

The night before was a bit of a blur, melted into a montage even without the help of wine. She knew she'd spent hours laughing with that same group, but none of their conversation felt solid or real. All of it might have been a dream. Eventually Alexa's friends walked past and for a while they were there, too, before Alexa wandered off with them.

Flashbacks to high school again, when the cool kids temporarily deemed her worth an interaction.

But why did she think that? There was nothing about Alexa and her friends that divided them from Sara. Everyone here had been equally selected.

They were, she decided, equally useless and bland. Not like *some* people.

After catching Bea's eye during the toast, Sara had dashed off across the room in pursuit. She left the conversation in the middle without excusing herself, dodging laughing clusters of black-clad people, stepping carefully around untucked chairs and unattended tables. Practically climbing over a deadlock of wooden furniture and well-dressed human legs.

She figured Bea would wait for her, but when Sara reached the place where her friend had stood, she was gone.

Sara had felt like the party spun around her, nondescript music that she had just noticed drifting through the throng of sameness, voices just loud enough to be annoying but not so loud that she would ever be moved to complain. All of it swirled together into something utterly familiar and forgettable and real.

Had she actually seen Bea? She wanted to be sure, but she wasn't at all.

32

Four years before the Community

THE MUSIC THAT HAD BEEN PLAYING THROUGH HER EARBUDS CUT off when Sara answered the phone, replaced by her mother's voice.

"You doing okay, sweetie?"

"Let's just cut straight to it, then?"

She could practically hear her mother rolling her eyes. "You can't blame me for worrying."

Sara looked up from the cutting board and out the window. The smoke was so thick that she couldn't even see across the courtyard outside her apartment. "I guess I can't."

"So?"

She laughed a little and resumed mincing garlic. The whole apartment smelled comfortingly of tomato sauce and onions, simmering in the pan. "I'm fine, Mom. I have an air purifier running in every room."

"Are the filters fresh?"

"I'd hope so," Sara replied. She pulled a pot out of the cabinet and started filling it with water for pasta. "I just bought them this week."

Her mother sighed. "I wish you were here." The air wasn't much better there, but her mom just wanted her close.

Sara smiled and leaned against the counter, gazing across the open-plan apartment to the window. The smoke outside didn't curl prettily like she would have imagined; it just hung there, chokingly, hiding the world. She'd lived with this for her entire life, so it was familiar in a broken way, but somehow it still managed to surprise her how dead it looked every time. "I know, Mom. I wish I were there too. I saw on an air quality map that you guys had breathable air yesterday!"

"You say that like it's funny, Sara," her mom chided her. "It's not funny."

"I know," she said. "I get it. But it is a little funny—I live in the richest county in America and can't even breathe the air! What the hell are we paying for, anyway?"

"Not to mention the air quality laws," her mom said. "Did you see the mayor of San Francisco's trying to ban cars in the city?"

Sara snorted. "Like that'll help."

She stirred the sauce and listened to her mother breathe. Something about talking to her mom always calmed her down, like she was still a child and all it took to make everything okay was her mother's word. The truth was, she had been freaking out before her mom called—this air had made her new apartment a prison cell.

As if she could read her mind, her mom asked, "How are you liking the new place otherwise?"

"Oh, I love it," she gushed. "The carpet in the bedroom is so plush and the water pressure is amazing. I feel like I'm living in the nicest hotel I've ever been to."

"I suppose you haven't tried the pool yet, if you can't go outside."

The pool had been a major point in the apartment's favor. She didn't strictly need such a nice place, and there were plenty of apartments just as close to work that cost several hundred dollars per month less. But the pool looked amazing and made her think back fondly to her childhood on the swim team. She told herself, when she signed the lease, that if she had a pool right outside her door she would actually exercise regularly.

"No, but the smoke will clear up soon enough," she said. She hoped, anyway.

"I can't wait to visit," her mom said.

"Give me some time to set it up properly first!" Sara protested, dumping pasta into the pot.

The apartment was still mostly empty; she'd only lived with her parents or roommates before and didn't have much of her own furniture. She'd considered buying it all online but was trying to use fewer resources. Buying things in a store was better for that, she figured, with last mile problems and such.

"Well, just let me know when and we'll drive down," her mom said. "And, honey, you know you can come up anytime, too. Are they making you go into the office when it's this bad?"

The conversation hadn't stayed away from the smoke for long, Sara thought wryly. It made its presence unavoidable. No one could really talk about—or even think about—anything else. What might the world look like if important things were so omnipresent?

"Nah, I'm working from home. Good thing my internet is fast here."

"So you could come home!"

Sara pulled a noodle from the boiling water and tasted it. While she chewed, she said, "I guess."

"You don't want to?" Her mom sounded more surprised than insulted, which was a relief.

"It just seems like an overreaction."

"This is a natural disaster, Sara!" her mom protested. "If it was a hurricane, wouldn't you run?"

Sara laughed. "It's not nearly as bad as a hurricane."

Her mom sighed, knowing she wasn't going to win this one. "Anyway, honey, I have to go—the dog's losing his mind about something."

"Okay. Love you."

"Come here if you want to!"

"I said I love you!"

Her mom laughed, finally. "Love you too."

When she hung up the phone, the music did not resume. Her wireless earbuds suddenly felt ridiculous, hanging uselessly from her ears. The silence came rushing in like smoke.

She turned away from the window and took a deep breath of the stale indoors air. It would smell like tomato sauce until the smoke cleared and she could open a window. And who knew how long that would be?

With a sigh, she served herself a bowl of spaghetti and sauce, forking some chicken out of a can into the warm food. Pathetic, boring, eating alone kind of dinner. She hadn't even bought cheese.

She thought about pouring herself a glass of wine—red was good with tomato sauce, right?—but decided that would be silly. Even the nice bottle of wine she'd gotten for graduation and not drunk in the two years since couldn't dress up such a lame dinner. Better to save it for an occasion that deserved it.

She carried her meal around the counter and into the living room, which had only a bookshelf, a rug, and a coffee table, and sat cross-legged on the floor facing the window. The evening light filtering through the toxic smoke was oddly beautiful—a rich purplish color that she might have liked if she hadn't known what it was.

The weather alert on her phone that morning said the fires reached some kind of manufacturing facility and that the air was even worse than it seemed, which prompted Zach to tell people to stay home. But she imagined the chemicals in the air weren't any worse than after flames devoured a neighborhood, gulping down paint and bathroom cleaner and synthetic fabric.

If a fire consumed her apartment, how many toxins would it release into the air? More than she wanted to think about. The rug she sat on was plastic and so was the fake wood of the floor. Now that she thought about it, so was the veneer of the coffee table where she sat.

She was suddenly repulsed by the things around her, so much fakeness, artificial coatings and carefully engineered designs that she was supposed to love. Who decided petroleum should reach into everything she touched?

But she was lucky, even if everything *was* flammable. She should stop thinking about depressing things that she couldn't do anything about.

She took a deep breath again, relishing that the air didn't burn at her lungs or taste terrible in her mouth. Some people had lost their homes this summer, like every summer for the last twenty years. The seasonal lottery that no one ever thought they'd lose.

If only it would rain. She willed the smoke to morph into clouds, wished she could make such a thing happen. The fires, like each one before, would only end when the rains came and washed the world clean. Wind might blow the smoke away, but only rain could actually cleanse it from the air. Otherwise, it would always become someone else's problem.

If she'd believed praying would do any good, she would have prayed. Instead, she just ate her spaghetti and hoped a storm would roll in soon.

33

"BRUNCH?" ALEXA ASKED.

Sara blinked a few times, clearing her bleary morning eyes, and sat up. She'd fallen asleep again, apparently. "What?"

Alexa was already dressed—in the black dress from the night before—and had her hair in a high ponytail as if going to the gym. "I'm thinking omelets. You in?"

Sara almost said no, but then considered how stupid that would be and nodded instead. If she didn't go with Alexa, she'd just have to go by herself later. "Give me a sec."

The clock in her peripheral vision said it was past ten in the morning, which she probably would have guessed by the brilliance of the sun coming in the window. How had she slept through that?

Unlike Alexa, she didn't love the dress. She pulled on one of her identical sets of black athleisure clothes and slipped on her shoes, which were finally dry. "Do you have somewhere in mind?"

Alexa didn't, but it wouldn't be much of a challenge: in the morning the whole town converted into a brunch place, it seemed. Storefronts that she felt sure belonged to shops or yoga studios later in the day served breakfast food before noon.

"Who staffs all these places?" Sara asked as they strolled down the street. The paving stones were almost dry under the bright morning sky.

"Residents," Alexa said. "You get bored eventually and find a job."

Sara wrinkled her nose. "And that helps?"

"It's something to do," Alexa said, laughter in her voice. "Don't be such a snob."

"I'm not—" Sara started to protest, then realized Alexa was teasing. "It's just that these are the kinds of jobs I thought we wanted to escape."

Alexa shrugged. "They have real employees do the grunt work, I've heard," she said. "But that's invisible. Behind the scenes. Just a rumor. And anyway, I worked in a restaurant in high school. It was a lot of fun, actually."

Sara thought back to her own teenage service industry days and had to admit that she agreed. "I didn't like burning my hands in the pizza oven, though."

"Guess you should work in an ice cream parlor, then," Alexa said. "Far away from ovens."

Sara laughed. "Not the worst plan."

They picked a place based purely on the ratio of pancakes to omelets on the diners' plates and were seated almost immediately. Sara gave barely a thought to what she ordered and promptly forgot it.

"It's just strange," she mused. "I thought these jobs would all be replaced by now."

"You think too much," Alexa replied, taking a sip of orange juice.

"Seriously."

Alexa shrugged. "It's simple, really. People like people."

"You think you've got it all figured out, huh?" Sara asked.

Alexa laughed, but she didn't seem to be joking when she replied. "I do have it all figured out. Just relax and you'll see."

Sara decided to let her go on believing that. Pleasant delusions, she supposed, were worth sustaining if they didn't hurt anyone else.

Their meals arrived, a pair of perfectly cooked omelets, and they ate mostly in silence. It wasn't uncomfortable in the least, which Sara was grateful for, and wished she could achieve reliably. So much of socializing felt like a puzzle she could almost solve and she was relieved that, for the moment, she was succeeding at a rate well above her historical average.

Sara asked more about what Alexa had learned in her week there, trying to tease out information she herself would probably take far more time to uncover. The strangest revelation was that, until very recently, everyone had had their own room. Sara had assumed that the roommates were assigned to keep people from being too lonely and to make more efficient use of space, but Alexa assured her it was a new development. "Talk to the people who have been here a while—it's all they talk about!"

Alexa reported that already the frequency of her enrichment activities was declining, so she could sleep in more. But one of the guys from her intro group had just disappeared! No one knew where he had gone or whether he had left because he wanted to. Maybe the company had kicked him out! But why?

Sara took it all in contemplatively, trying to assimilate the new information with what she already understood. So people *did* leave, after all. For some reason, she had assumed no one did.

It felt wrong to just get up and walk away after eating, but she knew it wasn't. The illusion of a transgression was kind of nice, actually. Freeing.

As they walked back toward their apartment, moving slowly against the flow of people on their way toward the bank of restaurants, Sara found herself scanning faces for Bea. If it was Bea she saw the night before, she could be anywhere now.

Faces became dissociated from humanity as she looked at so many of them, their constituent parts fungible and strange. Eyes emoting and mouths speaking and noses wrinkling and cheeks dimpling. A cacophony of humanity that somehow her mind parsed effortlessly into identities. It was remarkable that it was so easy.

Alexa was talking, but Sara wasn't listening.

She marveled at the uniqueness of each face that passed her and how simultaneously the same they appeared. How could billions of people all be made up of the same few pieces? How did they always fit together so cohesively? There had to be a person somewhere who looked incorrectly put together, but she'd never seen them.

They approached the metal message cylinder, looming above the crowd, and then passed it by. Sara let herself go a few feet away before turning around; it wasn't necessary to wait to check her messages until she could come alone.

"What are you doing?" Alexa asked as Sara stopped.

Sara walked right up to it and the familiar contacts list materialized before her. The message thread with her parents was in bold.

"Haven't you sent any messages?" Sara asked.

She barely heard Alexa's laugh and dismissive reply: "Why, shouldn't I live in the moment?"

Sara hungrily read her parents' responses.

So good to hear from you, honey! Keep us posted. Emily texted when she was about to enter. Have you seen her yet? We are still in the shelter, doing as well as can be expected. The pets are great. Love you so much!

Hi. Send pics if you can. Love you.

She could practically hear each of their voices in their words, her mother's ebullient information dump and her father's matter-of-fact-ness. It made her smile to feel them thinking of her, but the warmth couldn't last long.

Emily had entered, then. It was only a matter of time.

She decided she would reply later, when Alexa wasn't around. It had been silly stopping like this.

She could send something to Bea, too. Did those on the edge of this strange society use this kind of message? If it had reached her parents so far away, it would reach Bea, too, wherever she was.

And she would finally check on Zach, she decided. It was the right thing to do, even if the conversation it started would inevitably end with them breaking up. The universe—or the company, anyway—had already decided that for them. She wasn't complaining.

34

WEEKENDS AND WEEKDAYS DIDN'T MEAN MUCH IN HER NEW LIFE,
but she was used to that: unemployment had taught her to expect a lot of
sameness from every day. Perhaps she should be grateful that the disappoint-
ments in her life prepared her for this.

Alexa was called off to some community-building experience early the next
morning, making some flippant remark about forced friendship and college
sororities that Sara didn't quite understand in her half-asleep state. After lying
in bed for a while, she set out to face a beautiful, sunny Monday with a smile.

She decided to be intentional about noticing her surroundings. Living in
the moment, as Alexa had put it. Something that she'd heard every day of her
childhood, she thought, needling her and her peers for too much time spent
staring at a screen and not enough appreciating how lucky they were.

Lucky for what, she'd never known, but that hadn't seemed to be the point.

She was never much good at it, but now was as good a time as any to
become the kind of person her elementary school teachers had wanted her to
be. With her phone gone already she figured the hard part was over.

So, she noticed.

A sun too bright to look at—how reassuring that at least that was still true.

Bricks in several shades of gray pressed together, barely a seam between them.

A shop Sara passed that most definitely sold dresses, much as Alexa said
she knew of no such place.

Slight movement as the waves set the floating town back down onto the
sand and retreated out to sea.

Moss clinging to the side of a tree.

Bark more silver than brown.

Leaves loosely tethered to their branches, threatening to drift away if
picked up by a breeze.

Tamed nature: local succulents in a row beside young trees, attended to by
human-acclimated squirrels.

A bird singing somewhere she couldn't see.

The overhang on the building roofs, a consistent size across all of the
different architectural styles. Something about it must be optimal. But what?

That word, *optimal*. It used to be something she thought about so much,
back in school and at the startup.

Constantly trying to optimize something—maximize user engagement, minimize customer wait time, find the ideal values for some complex function so a computer could translate between two languages or recognize faces or categorize images. Tiny granular steps in the right direction.

She had, at one point, wrapped up the whole of her life in such a philosophy, believed wholeheartedly that there was a way to optimize every day, an ideal way to arrange appointments and tasks onto her calendar so not a moment was wasted. There was a cost function that could be applied to every decision and if only she could find it, she could solve it and live perfectly.

But optimal didn't mean the same thing as perfect, did it? Perfect implied so much more; it encapsulated some completeness that optimal dared not touch.

Everyone in Silicon Valley—that microcosm of exploding capitalism—seemed to buy into the same idea. Money was so much more than currency. They let it guide them. They defined and tracked a plethora of tiny metrics, each a minuscule proxy for the only thing that really mattered, whatever it was. Millions of people made a thousand decisions each a day, inevitably revealing which ideas and idea-havers were the best.

She couldn't lose the thought, an itch deep in her skull, that something was off with the system. They had optimized so much and ended up here and this could *not* have been the goal. This place was not the perfection it seemed; the economics of it all did not add up, and she didn't understand why it was allowed to exist.

If they hadn't solved the meta-problem of the ideal life that they thought they were solving, what had it all been for?

Was the race over and the conclusion now foregone? Was it too late to rewrite the program into something else, complicate the cost function enough to find a different, better version of optimal?

She sighed and gazed out at the waves, a little surprised to realize she'd wandered right up to the edge of the town, where the division between floating city and untamed waves was most explicit and harsh. A brick wall was the only thing between her and the water below, always moving, always trying to weather away what humanity had built.

Something large splashed in the ocean. A whale? She hoped so, thought it unlikely but decided that was what she wanted to believe.

It was too far away for her to be able to identify it by sight, but she could almost hear the crash of it colliding with the surface and imagine the cold of the water droplets on her face. Its impact left ripples across the rough surface, a great smooth oval of disturbed ocean spreading and morphing, a mirror against the sky.

She watched the memory of it long after it had disappeared.

35

SHE ATE A SANDWICH FOR LUNCH, CHEESE AND TOMATOES ON freshly baked bread, sitting on a bench under a young tree with the sun directly overhead, then felt like an idiot for selecting a meal that was over so quickly.

Efficiency was not something she needed to strive for any longer. Why did she keep forgetting that?

The bread had been as good as she could ever remember, though, and for lack of anything better to do, she decided to find the bakery it came from. Everything was made here somewhere, she figured. In keeping with the image of the place—sustainable, pseudo-small-town living—it had to be.

She set off down the street, walking along the side of it cast in shadow. The sun was not really hot enough on this winter afternoon to drive her into the shade, but sometimes making a choice felt good, even if it was an arbitrary one.

Past a florist (a florist? How antiquated!), past a shoe store, past a couple more cafes. Shoes: another thing Alexa had been certain they could not buy.

How much of this place *was* self-sustaining? She had somehow gotten it into her head that everything consumed here was made here, but that didn't seem possible. The electricity, probably. Perhaps the food. But the shoes could not have been made in this place; who would know how? Where would they get the materials? Another of the company's illusions. There was no sign of anything being imported or exported, but it had to happen. They were not truly sheltered from the crumbling world. If supply chains collapsed again, they would be just as likely to suffer as anyone else.

At least disease could be kept out, most likely.

Maybe there was no bakery to find. Probably she was creating ridiculous missions for herself. Just something to pass the time. Missions felt good—people liked having goals. She would keep herself happy longer if she continued to do this.

She was intentionally putting off returning her parents' messages and reaching out to Bea and Zach because it gave her something to look forward to; messaging all of them was a sliver of her old purposeful life. It would be a reward at the end of the day, if she managed to stay out that long.

She walked a whole block without noticing anything, then shook her head, telling herself to be present, *intentional*.

This was just a phase she had to break free of, a hump she had to get over, and her mind would reset, acclimatize to this life. It really wasn't so bad. The true problem here was that she kept thinking that it was.

She closed her eyes and stepped into the sunlight, feeling it on her face. See that? That's real.

A deep breath, two, calming herself. Imagining the ten thousand ways things could be much worse, because, really, she lived a charmed life and always had. She chose to not picture worse outcomes too vividly, lest the guilt of complaining drag her down even farther.

The deep breath brought the scent of fresh baking into her lungs.

Her eyes opened, her head swiveling like a predator. A bread-seeking drone.

She smiled at the image and crossed the street to the bakery. Each little shop had its own appearance and this one was charming: the front had lightly carved concrete done up like marble columns, reminiscent of some ancient cathedral, hilariously offering baked goods instead of prayers. Was it some joke she didn't get? Probably, but she didn't care.

Or maybe someone just thought it looked nice beside the wood panels of a stationery shop and the faux-rusted metal fronting of a yoga studio. Contrasts, or something like that.

When she reached out to touch the ornate wall, her fingers found smooth cement. She grimaced.

The door was propped open, letting the aroma spill forth onto the sidewalk. She thought she would have gone inside even if she hadn't been in search of the bread from lunch.

The man behind the counter was in a good mood, like everyone. Was there something in the water? Something she was not getting?

Maybe she needed to drink more water.

She smiled, not sure how to handle such cheer.

"How can I help you?"

He was portly and pleasant, pretty much exactly how she imagined the kind of man who made cookies and cupcakes all day long. Like something out of a storybook.

Do they select us to fill roles? she wondered. Like casting an enormously complex play.

She glanced around, taking in stacks of baked goods. It did not seem like the sort of bakery she'd been looking for. "You don't supply the bread to any of the cafes around here, by any chance?"

The man made an apologetic smile and shook his head. "No, I'm sorry, no bread. But we do have some lovely offerings today!"

He gestured at the spread of sweets. She'd never been much of a cookie person, but cupcakes were a weakness. Multicolored and thickly frosted, arranged like jewels for perfect viewing.

Perfect was in fact the word here, she decided. Not optimal.

"You have enough customers to go through all of these every day?" she asked, realizing only after asking that it was possibly a rude question.

"Sometimes! But nothing goes to waste, you know. Don't worry."

It was kind of an ominous answer, but she didn't press. "Great," she said, because she had to say something.

He looked very eager to have a customer, and she realized she couldn't leave in good conscience yet. Maybe it was her imagination, but in her eyes, he looked lonely.

"You know," she said slowly, thinking up the lie as she went along. "It's almost my birthday. I think I should order a cake. Do you do that?"

Her birthday was months away. But wasn't the whole point of this society—any society—keeping everyone else afloat? Giving each other something to do? What were other people for but to occupy your time?

A lie that gave him a purpose was a good one, she decided.

Though she did wonder if someone in a corporate office somewhere was watching and judging her for lying, guessing at her rationale and coming up with no good explanations. A mark against her in some ledger that she didn't want to think about. Deciding when she would be kicked out for lack of cheer or inability to assimilate or who knew what else.

The same things that had nudged people out of society for centuries, really. Behaving the wrong way had always been a crime in one manner or another. She had just never lived in a culture where her way of thinking was anything but celebrated, and it was strange to realize pessimistic striving could be as problematic here as lack of ambition or starry-eyed naivete had been in her previous life.

"Your birthday?" he said. "Perfect! We can do that! What do you want on the cake?"

She had no idea. She'd never ordered a cake before, least of all for herself. Did people even do that?

"Well, what do you like to do?" she asked finally.

He grinned and then stepped out from around the counter. She took an awkward step back in surprise, but nothing about him was threatening, strange as his approach might be. "Let me show you!" He proceeded right past her and out onto the street. She frowned but followed.

"This, here," he said, running a hand down the fancy carved facade of the shop. "I love this."

She tilted her head to one side and nodded, not understanding in the least. "I see."

"I'm an architect, you know," he said. "The cakes, the frosting, it's just the current expression of my creativity. This building, though…"

"You designed this building?" she asked. Trying to keep up.

He shrugged. "Or something like that."

"Right." The glee in his eyes was more than she was comfortable with, and her meditations on insanity and the edges of society felt more relevant than ever. "You were an architect before coming here?" she tried again.

He nodded. "And I still am, like I said."

"Of course," she said. Feeling like she was talking to a crazy person, or at least someone who didn't understand metaphors. "So, the cake?"

"Would you like it like this?" he asked, gesturing toward the wall and its ornate carvings.

"Like the wall?" she asked dumbly. "Sure. Love it."

"It'll be ready tomorrow!" he said.

She took that as a dismissal and nodded, smiling, retreating into the crowd that had grown as the evening approached. He waved to her like they were great friends.

What a strange interaction, she thought. Had he been crazy when he arrived, or did he become like that since coming here? There was no way to know, really.

Or maybe he really had designed the building and she was being too harsh. Maybe he was entirely sane, just a bit odd. Maybe she was a terrible person.

That was probably it, she concluded with a private smile. Best to acknowledge and come to terms with that now, early in the game.

And then, as if her own grip on reality were slipping, she laughed and had to hold herself back from skipping down the street. Because, even if sanity and appearances scarcely mattered, she did still have a tiny amount of dignity.

36

"SO, BEA," SARA'S MOM SAID AS SHE REACHED FOR THE SALAD BOWL, "tell me what you think of Sara's new boyfriend."

Sara felt herself flush, more from horror than embarrassment.

Bea's eyes cut across the table to meet Sara's, silently asking a question. Sara just grimaced and shrugged.

"Honestly?" Bea asked, setting down her glass of wine. "I am not convinced."

"Bea!" Sara protested.

"Convinced?" Sara's mom asked.

"She means she doesn't like him, Mom," Sara jumped in. "She thinks I'm making a mistake, that he's not good enough for me."

"Well, are you making a mistake? He can't *possibly* be good enough for you."

Sara rolled her eyes. "No one could be, eh? But seriously, could you two be a little supportive?"

"I'm not supportive either," Emily piped up.

The four of them were eating dinner at her parents' house while her dad was getting beers with friends. A girls' night, Sara's mom called it, but really her dad would have been welcome, too. Nights like this one had started when Bea came home with Sara one weekend early in college and so thoroughly charmed her parents that they insisted she bring her along all the time. Bea and her mom talked on the phone sometimes.

"Just tell me that you're not being taken advantage of," her mother said.

"Zach is actually really great," Sara said. "I know it's weird, but you must see the appeal, right? He has his shit together so much more than anyone else I know!"

"Yeah, yeah, he runs a company, we know," Bea said. "You're attracted to success, ambition, blah, blah, blah. But Sara—that's just *not* sexy."

Sara glanced at her mom, uncomfortable, but her mom was laughing.

"She's right, honey!"

Emily kicked Sara's leg under the table. "Sara has always liked nerds."

"I *am* a nerd," Sara said. "We have a lot in common."

"Except you actually graduated," Bea said. "Unlike him."

"Like a degree makes you so special," Sara said.

"I'm just saying."

"Do you want me to list everything I like about him?" Sara asked.

Emily laughed. "Could you, please?"

"Well," Sara said, pretending to deliberate. "He's tall."

Bea shook her head vehemently. "We've talked about this, Sara. *Tall* is not a reason to like someone."

Emily wrinkled her nose. "You know, I think it might be."

"You'll grow out of that, honey," their mom said. That made everyone laugh—Sara's father was exactly the average height for an American man.

"Seriously, though," Sara said. "None of you have even met him. You'll understand when you do."

And they did, as it turned out. The next time they had a girls' night, it wasn't just the girls—Sara's dad and Zach were both invited, and the seven of them sat around her parents' big antique dining table eating pizza and drinking the bottle of wine Zach had insisted on bringing.

"It's not local," her dad had chided, pretending to be upset. "Don't you care about the local economy?"

Zach had taken this in stride. "I care about the dock workers who unload crates, too," he replied. "It's more of an economic stimulus to buy things that have been shipped a long way because so many people were involved."

Bea murmured to Sara that she found this doubtful, but she had to admit it was a good recovery.

"So, Zach, tell us about yourself," Sara's mom said once they were all settled with their food.

He'd looked at Sara, smirked, and said, "I've heard the main appeal is that I'm tall."

Making Sara blush was a sure-fire way to get everyone laughing, so this was a promising start to the evening.

Zach hadn't expressed any nerves about meeting her family, though Sara would have been intolerably anxious to meet his parents. He figured out the dynamic effortlessly and even had Bea honestly impressed by the end of the night.

"To be clear," Bea whispered to Sara as they all parted hours later, "I still think you're being dumb, sleeping with your boss."

"But?"

"He *is* tall."

Girls' nights continued, but so did family dinners, complete with the men. Zach loved her parents as much as Bea did, which Emily and Sara found both hilarious and kind of wonderful. Their parents were never the neighborhood favorites when the girls were young, but had managed the transition to having adult children more deftly than most. Even if she still kept her relationship with Zach a secret from her coworkers, it felt great to share him with the people who really mattered.

37

SARA FOUND HER WAY BACK TO THE PILLAR AND COULDN'T BRING herself to message Zach. But she was desperate to message Bea.

She struggled to find the words, though she had so much to say. She felt her mind tripping over itself. Bea would never take something she said the wrong way, would always understand the subtext and jokes. Writing to her had always been easy, so why was it suddenly so hard?

Heyyy

With the full three *y*s, of course.

I SWEAR I saw you the other day here, dressed like one of the, idk, marginal women? Honestly not sure what to call them. But I hope you're here and you get this! Would love to see you, obv. Miss you a thousand.

Before she could send it, something bright flared in the sky.

She flinched, glanced upward, some instinctive fear coursing through her. Was it falling, or flying?

Her chest tightened and her breath caught and she watched the rocket or weapon or whatever it was racing overhead, impossibly fast but also strangely slow. Great rippling clouds rolled off it, colors that lifelong experience with airplanes had not prepared her to see.

Someone nearby was laughing at her.

She forced her eyes away from the thing in the sky and met the eyes of her mocker, a woman decked out in faintly ridiculous jogging clothes. Paused on her run to watch the rocket overhead, amused at Sara's surprise.

"You looked terrified!" the woman managed to get out between guffaws. "Didn't you hear about the spaceport?"

Sara's face grew hot. She looked away from the woman, ignoring her and the rocket overhead, and skimmed the message once more. It had felt so important a moment before, but now all she could feel was the heat on the back of her neck, the embarrassment. She'd heard of the spaceport, of course, but not that it was operational. And not that it would be visible from here.

Sara returned her attention to the screen, skimming back over her note to

Bea. It would never be perfect, but it didn't need to be. She hit send.

The screen pulsed once, glowing brighter blue and then returning to its usual benign white. Beneath her message, an italicized message in red appeared:

Message cannot be delivered: contacts within the Community are not supported at this time.

Sara blinked and took a startled step back, then peered closer at the message again. Bea had been accepted? Who had Sara seen, then, the other night among the marginal people? And why had she been unable to find Bea anywhere amid the crowded streets?

She told herself not to be surprised by that: there were so many people in the Community, it was not too strange that she hadn't run into one of them yet. But she *had* been looking.

Impulsively, she typed Emily's name next, needing to know.

Whether it went through or not wouldn't necessarily tell her anything, she thought. Perhaps the messages could go through to someone still in quarantine, though obviously their intended recipient would not read them.

Already bargaining, as if she knew before she even tried what the result would be.

Hi! Hope you're doing okay! Let me know if you get this!

The message did not bounce back.

38

SHE DIDN'T GO BACK FOR HER CAKE THE NEXT MORNING.

It rained until noon; cozy in her warm, dry room, she didn't want to venture out into the wet. She could barely bring herself to get out of bed, and it occurred to her that she was behaving as if she were depressed. But she couldn't be: life was too good, compared to what it had once been. There were so many luxuries and so few worries. Any discomfort had to be overridden by her relief.

One major downside of this life was dependence on leaving the apartment. She supposed she could have acquired snacks and kept them in her room, but the Community was structured around leaving for every meal. She suspected it was by design, a way to get people out of their homes and interacting with each other. It probably did them well, but it didn't come naturally to her.

It was the kind of morning that would have been absolutely perfect with a book in her lap and a mug of tea in her hands, but she didn't have either of those things.

There had to be a library around here somewhere. As she understood it, the main purveyor of e-books was as verboten as the other tech giants that competed with the company, but surely physical books were allowed. She just had to find them.

Adjusting to life with the products of a single corporation was more difficult than she had expected. It hadn't been a consideration when she chose this place. Because why would it be? She was not so dependent on any one company as to truly miss its services, she had thought.

But she didn't realize how much her life was a blend of just a few companies, typing on the keyboard of one and the phone of another with the software of the third and relying on the final one for everything else, from entertainment to the procurement of objects in the physical world. She used a hundred apps and tools and products, but they belonged to just a few billionaires.

And now, to her surprise, even the company's own products had faded into the ether. Because the familiar was not what she was here to test. They had real users for that, not these strange, almost captive employees.

She forced herself to stop lamenting how bored she was, how isolated.

This place was a choice. She *chose* this. She should appreciate what she had.

Eventually her boredom and hunger drew her from her bed and into the strange little world. She went out in her pajamas without a jacket, just shrugging into a bra and pulling on shoes. Something she never would have done before, but like so much else, her appearance no longer mattered. *She* no longer mattered.

There were probably people here who cared about their appearances more than ever, she thought. Lots more time for dating, and everyone so healthy and young.

Maybe that drive to look good was why everyone here seemed so fit. Or maybe they ejected you if you gained too much weight—you were no longer part of their utopian vision. It was a dark thought, such a sad and broken way of looking at the world that it almost made her laugh. The ridiculousness of Silicon Valley, percolating into everything. Wellness culture intoxicating our brains.

The rain was beginning to let up and she walked through it languidly, letting it land on her unhooded head and drip down her bare arms. She was cold, but not uncomfortably so.

She crossed the courtyard and entered the first cafe she reached, ordering a latte and breakfast sandwich, sitting by the window while she ate to watch the raindrops on the glass. People's voices murmured through the air around her, but she didn't eavesdrop, something that took actual effort to avoid. So strange that other people's thoughts intruded so easily.

After eating, she returned to the promenade and walked along it slowly, letting the gentle rocking of the waves and the sound of their insistent washing against the shore blend with the last of the rain to make the whole world water.

She could almost believe that if she closed her eyes, she would find herself beneath the surface, sunlight bending through the deep, sea life flying through the sky above her. She thought back to the kelp forests and the deep blue of the tanks at the aquarium so many years before, how small she had felt, how calm.

Instead, she leaned against the low wall on her elbows, watching the white caps out in the bay and the storm clouds gathering again in the distance. The deck beneath her feet rocked gently on the high tide. The sun had defeated the clouds directly above town, but it would not last. It never lasted, did it?

Birds dipped and dove, splashing into the surface like downed fighter pilots and then emerging again, triumphant. She thought their antics should make her smile, but they didn't, and she wasn't sure why.

She became aware of another body standing beside her but did not turn her head. The person was larger than she was, standing close enough that she couldn't quite see them with her eyes fixed ahead of her. Familiarly close. Could she guess who it was?

The stupid games she played to fill the hours.

The slightest turn of her head gave it all away, ruining her fun. Huh, not who she had expected, but that, too, made sense.

"So what kind of a name is Everest?" she asked.

He made a sound like he was more amused than insulted, which had been exactly what she was going for. "My parents wanted me to aim high."

She smiled. Tapped a hand against the wall. "And did you?"

A shrug. "I didn't not."

"I know the feeling," she said.

Silence then, for a while. Or not silence: a bird crying overheard, the waves brushing against the sand as they receded, wind in the grass and through the leaves. What hubris to call these things silence.

"Who were you, before?" she asked eventually.

It was a strange question, one she had mulled over for a while. What she wanted to ask—so what do you do?—no longer made sense here. Like for the poor baker architect. How was he supposed to answer such a question?

She could hear the smile in his voice when he replied. "Wouldn't you rather know who I am here?"

She kept her body angled out toward the water but hazarded a glance in his direction. "I'm getting pretty used to not getting what I want. But I think that's what the company would want, yes."

He was looking back at her, too, and smiling now. Such perfect white teeth. "But that's a boring question, isn't it?"

"Which is why I didn't ask it."

No reply.

"It's okay, you don't have to tell me," she said. Retreating by habit.

"Well, let me ask something," he said. "You want to know what I used to do, right?"

When she nodded, he went on.

"What does that matter? Why did that ever matter?"

She snorted. Started to reply but then found all of her almost-answers woefully inadequate. "It's a heuristic," she finally settled on. "Always imperfect."

"And shouldn't we strive for perfection, Sara?"

Something in his tone was grating to her. As if he knew so much more than she did. It reminded her of Zach in the worst way. "Is that what we're doing here?"

He seemed to shrink slightly. Let his line of questioning go.

She wished she knew what the two of them were doing, exactly.

"What do you think happens here?" he asked after a long pause, in which the freshness of the waves had rushed in to fill her ears, so complete she didn't know why they bothered talking.

Something about that question felt different from the others. More sincere. Less like he already knew what she should say.

But she also didn't know what she should say. "Testing things, right?" she offered, lamely.

"That's the company line," he replied.

She decided to be fully honest, though perhaps that was stupid. "I think we're hiding, actually."

"From what?" he asked.

Not like he disagreed, though.

"From everything."

"Letting the company shield us from the refugees and the storms and the melting of everything from ice caps to political norms?" he said.

She shrugged. Not ready to go quite that far out loud, though that was exactly what she had been thinking. "Just hiding."

"Hmm."

She blushed, feeling suddenly ridiculous.

"How long have you been here?" he asked.

She was startled by the abrupt pivot, but grateful too. Such an easy question to answer.

"A week," she replied. "Approximately."

He smiled and looked down. Like he was laughing at her and didn't want to be. "You'll get used to it."

"People get used to all kinds of things," she said.

"And you're just wondering, should they?"

"It's like you read my mind."

Once again, she found herself deep into a conversation with him that was more substantive than any she'd had with anyone else. And how much total time had they spent talking, ten minutes?

"What about your old life was so great?" he asked.

"Well, nothing, really," she said. "That's why I'm here."

"But?"

"But I understood how that world worked," she said. "You know, steeped in the logic of Silicon Valley. Not…whatever this communist pseudo-paradise shit is."

Now he laughed outright. "Communist? This isn't the 1960s."

"What do you call it, then?" she challenged. "Everything is free."

"This is what communism wishes it could be," he replied. "Do you see any bread lines?"

She understood, of course. Only the pure, uncaring greed of information-age markets, unfettered in the world, left to eat everything, could yield a company so rich it could employ thousands of people to do nothing at all.

"Doesn't matter what you call it," she said. "It's still strange."

"That, I'll give you," he said. "Like—what ever happened to the Protestant work ethic?"

She shrugged. "I'm not religious."

That laughter again, at her expense. "Are you sure about that?"

39

Three years before the Community

"WHAT'VE YOU GOT TODAY?" SARA ASKED, SITTING DOWN AT THE lunch table across from Hakim, the head business guy for One, and Zach, who were already eating.

Zach peeled back the wrapper on his sandwich. "Some vegan shit, I think."

Sara laughed lightly and checked the label on her salad. "The Tree Hugger," she read.

Hakim nodded. "I think they're putting us on a diet."

"Who is?" one of the software engineers, a guy from SoCal named Zhang, asked.

"The caterer," Zach said around a bite of sandwich.

Zhang shrugged. "I've got fried chicken."

The other three groaned.

"Did you hear about the new tax proposal?" Hakim asked.

"Taxes? Really? That's what we're gonna talk about?" Zach asked.

Sara shot him an exasperated look. Their relationship was still a secret from the rest of the company, but everyone was good enough of friends that their familiarity was easy to explain away. "Yeah," she said to Hakim. "Raising the top marginal rate to ninety, was it? And a carbon tax."

"And a wealth tax," Zhang added.

"But that's been a thing for a decade at least," Sara said. "Abolish billionaires and all that."

"I hope billionaires aren't going anywhere," Zach said. "I aim to be one soon."

"Well, I think it's not a bad idea," Sara said. "But it'll never happen, of course."

"I don't understand why not," Zhang said. "It's so obvious."

"What?" Zach asked.

"It will solve all of our problems," Zhang continued. "I don't know why no one's thought of it."

At the same time Sara said, "I wouldn't go that far..." Hakim said, "Tons of people have thought of it!"

"Yeah, man," Zach said. "You think you're the only genius in the world?"

Zhang raised his eyebrows and held his hands out in a dramatic shrug. "Maybe!"

"Narcissist," Sara said.

He just shrugged again. "Or there's a reason it hasn't happened."

"Yeah, no one can agree on the details!"

"Or there's a group who doesn't want it to happen, like—"

"I'm gonna stop you before you say something anti-Semitic," Hakim cut in.

"I was going to say lobbyists," Zhang said, glaring. "But I'm glad to hear how poorly you think of me."

Sara met Zach's eyes across the table and mouthed "de-escalate."

Instead, he just went on chewing his sandwich silently.

"You're treading dangerous ground, my friend," Hakim said.

"I wasn't!" Zhang said. "It really is so simple, though, I just don't see…"

"You know some people think we're rich," said Lina, another engineer, as she joined them.

"Laughable," Zhang said.

"See, you're a total hypocrite," Hakim said.

"Well, what's the lowest salary around this table? $200k?" Lina said. She glanced around at their faces and no one contradicted her. "Higher, then. You know that's three times the annual household income in America?"

Zhang scoffed. "You saying you want to pay more taxes?"

Hakim shook his head. "You were just saying that it's so simple! How can you—"

"Am I working with a bunch of socialists?" Zach bellowed.

Sara resisted the urge to put her face in her hands.

She certainly wasn't a socialist, but she wouldn't be surprised if Lina was—everything about her screamed "I went to Berkeley," in the most stereotypical ways. But Sara knew she grew up with rich parents in Upstate New York, so looks weren't everything.

Sara certainly didn't feel rich, interminably paying down her student loans. It had been four years and she felt like she hadn't made a dent. And she knew she'd probably never own a house, but who did, these days? Only the billionaires Zach aspired to join, not the regular, broke-but-supposedly-rich class that Lina insisted they all belonged to.

She knew that if there were a line drawn between the global haves and have-nots, she would be on the privileged side of it. But a line could also be drawn between those scraping out a life in a difficult world and those floating above the fray, and she would not be on the lucky side of that one. She felt more solidarity with the cashier at the grocery store than the venture capitalists throwing money at One, or even her home-owning neighbors who consistently voted against the construction of more apartments.

Once, she heard that in America there were no poor people, only temporarily embarrassed millionaires. Maybe that used to be true, but she felt like now there were no millionaires, only the poor who briefly attained a bit of stability.

She pushed her chair away from the table and went back to work, bringing her sad half-eaten salad with her.

40

THAT AFTERNOON SHE RELUCTANTLY RETURNED FOR HER CAKE.

In the real world she never would have ordered something and then failed to pick it up. What kind of person did that? It was basically as bad as eating at a restaurant and then leaving without paying.

The sun had now broken free decisively from the clouds and the sky was a brilliant eggshell blue. The kind of weather that, to anyone not California born-and-raised, precluded a bad mood, but Sara was immune to such effects. She was in a good mood for her own reasons, no thanks to the sky.

Something about her conversation with Everest had left her feeling electrified. It had been utterly unsatisfying, but in the best possible way.

A different person worked the bakery that day.

Sara had stood outside the door studying the facade for at least a minute, trying to see in it what that man saw, trying to understand. It was a relief not to have to.

Instead, a young woman stood behind the counter, carefully frosting cookies and humming to herself. Her hair pulled back in a low ponytail and her hands in plastic gloves, she would have fit in at a hospital as much as a bakery.

She was pleasantly unchatty. The kind of service Sara preferred.

After a few exchanged pleasantries, the girl revealed the cake, an extravagant concoction in white and cream with thick swirls of frosting curving up the sides. Sara didn't see how it resembled the building and the girl didn't say anything about that, so she didn't have to lie.

Without any writing scrawled across the top it looked oddly empty, naked, but that was just as well. She didn't want to be reminded of her fake birthday while eating it.

She felt ridiculous walking home with her cake in hand, the neat, white box held against her chest proclaiming her lie. Surely someone was watching her and judging, but as far as she could tell none of the passersby noticed her, which meant the judgment she deserved had to come from afar.

Maybe people turned to religion because they craved this sense of distant, silent judgment, she thought. She adjusted to being forever spied on far more quickly than she had expected to.

The sweet smell of frosting wafted out of the box. She wouldn't normally eat a cake on her own, but she knew she'd have some of this one as soon as she reached her apartment. Sitting outside and eating it alone in public was far too pathetic, even for her current state.

She hadn't planned to, but when she found herself passing the message column, she stopped.

She set the cake in its box on the ground, among the green leaves and loamy soil, tucked away so seagulls wouldn't get into it while her attention was diverted.

She turned to the column and watched as the screen illuminated before her. She desperately wanted to see a new one from Emily, apologizing for having been rejected, assuring Sara she was okay now, hoping Sara was all right on the inside alone. Emily would take being rejected as a mark of failure.

Though Sara didn't want to have to make her little sister feel better, that had always been her role; Emily needed far more reassurance than any reasonable adult should. But was she herself any better? Wasn't all this moping just her wishing the universe would prove to her that she made the right call?

But there was no message from Emily, no obligation to encourage her to not feel guilty or bad for not being accepted.

Something curdled in Sara's stomach. She pushed the fear away.

Replying to their parents didn't need to be hard, but she felt herself making it into a challenge. What she really wanted was a phone call, for them to tell her that she would be fine, because no matter how many times she thought it to herself it would never be as effective as hearing it from them just once. She realized she craved exactly the reassurances she begrudged Emily for needing.

She didn't even know what kind of comfort would have made her feel better, though. Coming to the Community hadn't been a difficult decision, not in the end; they had been out of options. This had been the right choice, and also the only one. What reassurance was needed after that?

Everything was temporary, anyway. This was just buyer's remorse. This fear that she was throwing her life away, giving up too easily, was all an exaggeration. She couldn't ask her parents to tell her what to do because they had no idea.

Instead, she regaled them with stories of her time there thus far. A mention of Alexa's joke of a name, a description of the floating city at high tide, the ridiculousness of the tag game, the beauty of the sky and the sea. How nice it was to slow down without stress, how different it felt from unemployment—to have open days stretched out before her when their presence did not make her a failure.

Was that last part a lie? She couldn't decide. Life in the Community did feel different, distinctly so, but she didn't know that it was actually better. Her emotions were far too complex to summarize in a missive dashed out on a screen.

Putting her thoughts down in writing, though, made them feel more truthful. She doubted it all while she thought through what to say, but reading back over the message, seeing the words she had chosen and congratulating herself on telling it right, she felt the truth in them.

This was better than sitting in her apartment forever fine-tuning her resume, going to never-ending interviews for positions she was ever more overqualified for. This was better than watching Zach waste hours on the couch, lost in virtual reality. This was better than wondering what would happen when her savings ran out.

This was *better*.

She clicked send before she could second guess anymore and opened a new message, this one to Zach. Surprised a bit that her parents hadn't mentioned him, but then they had not said much.

Zach had been in her life long enough for her parents to know him well. They'd been skeptical at first to hear she was dating her boss, but came around, at least when she was present. Probably they still questioned what she was thinking, especially since she spent so much time complaining about him to her mother. But, as she told them and everyone else, nobody was perfect, and mothers were ideal to complain to.

If he had been rejected from the Community, he would have contacted her parents looking for her, and maybe also just because he was bored.

He liked her parents; he liked everyone. They were dependable, middle-aged people who were kind and friendly, which had always fascinated Zach.

His own parents were rambunctious, never staying in one city or with one person very long. He grew up in Hawaii, but on three different islands and half the time on a boat. The concept of parents who owned a home and remained married blew his mind.

So the fact that her parents hadn't mentioned anything about him concerned her. It was her duty as a girlfriend to reach out to him, but more than that, she wanted to know what had happened. She was increasingly sure she hadn't loved him in a long time, but that didn't mean she didn't care about him.

Still, it was a hard message to write.

Hey there, just checking in

It sounded like she was out of town for the weekend and dropping a line to make sure he'd done the dishes.

I'm sure you know by now that I've been accepted. One week in, 259 to go!

Was that overly presumptuous? Did he know enough about this place to understand what she meant? If he had been rejected, possibly not.

Miss you

Was a lie.

Hope you're well!

Was true but vapid, almost a waste of characters on the screen.

It's been almost a month since I last saw you.

Just a fact. No point in sending that.

I'm one week into this new life and haven't seen you, so I figure you're not here. Let me know if I should be worried!

She smirked, thinking the message too flippant and relaxed, then decided it was perfect. The message did not bounce back: confirmation that Zach had been rejected. She thought she should feel something about that, the way she had when Emily's message went through, but she didn't. She walked home, forgetting her cake in the mud.

41

THE NEXT DAY WAS SIMILARLY BRIGHT AND AIRY. THE LAST OF THE
water in the cracks between the paving stones and the mud around the planters evaporated under the sun. It smelled and felt like spring, though it was far
too early. Though when had that ever stopped spring in the past?

Sara and Alexa went to breakfast together in the midmorning, then parted
ways. Alexa said she was going to a yoga class, insisting it was calming and
also a good way to pass an hour. Sara didn't think she'd reached that point yet.

She decided that today would be the day she set up her half of the room.
When she arrived, Alexa had only been there a week and had already selected
a bedspread and some tasteful decor. Sara's part of the little apartment was
still as bare as the college dorm of a broke stoner.

Strolling the streets in the sunlight, she caught herself humming. Sara
wondered what song it was, since she hadn't really listened to music since
coming here, just heard snippets in the background, and couldn't remember
the lyrics that accompanied the tune in her head. In her old life, she listened
to music constantly.

There had to be a way to play music here. Another thing to look for
while shopping.

It had been a long time since she set up a living space. In college her dorm
was simple, the same pink bedspread from her childhood bedroom trans-
planted a hundred miles to the south, a ribbon with printed photos pinned
and strung across the wall, Christmas lights hung around the window. She
often turned on just those lights, setting the mood for romantic encounters
she rarely had.

Her first apartment, like all first apartments, was sparse. IKEA furniture
and a rug she rescued from the side of the road. Bea had found that hilarious
and her mother had been horrified, afraid of bedbugs, but it was large and
soft and geometrically blue. Just grown up enough that she wanted it. She
bought cheap blankets that were on sale at CVS and stole her plates from the
dining hall before senior year ended and lit the whole place with more strings
of Christmas lights.

If she really thought about it, she had never set out to decorate a space
intentionally. It had always just happened over time, by way of living.

Impulse-buy succulents in the jewel toned pots they came in, arranged behind the kitchen sink. Free calendars that arrived in the mail, thanking her parents for a donation to some cause. Candles given as an office gift.

But this time she would choose exactly what she wanted. She would come up with a vision for her space and execute it.

Assuming she *could* come up with a vision for her space. Which she wasn't at all sure about.

She wandered in and out of shops for an hour, telling herself she was just getting a sense of the options, what range of choices she had. Since the furniture had been chosen for her, and she was restricted by Alexa's choices on the other half of the room, she felt comfortable treating this as a bit of a challenge. Trying to *optimize*, whatever that meant now. Such things came naturally to her.

As she went about her day, she kept the question of music in the back of her mind. She noticed the light instrumental sounds that played in one shop, and the washed-out old pop music in another, and concluded they were not intentionally keeping music away from the residents. She could find it if she wanted, and without much effort.

But she encountered no speakers, no earbuds, no devices on which to choose her soundtrack. The music she experienced was chosen for her, deemed appropriate for each scenario by someone else—or some algorithm. The more she thought about it, the emptier her life felt.

What was the point of this? Humans had always had music. It was as much a part of human nature as cooking or storytelling. What did they hope to learn by depriving people of music, or at least their choice in it?

Maybe she was coming at it all wrong. Maybe they were trying to coerce their residents into resorting to an older form of musical appreciation. Alexa had suggested they sing like Jane Austen characters. Maybe that was the entire point.

Sara shivered at the thought and dedicated herself back to the immediate task: adorning her room. Even if it would all be artificial, mere projections before her eyes, it had to be better than the plain white towels and bedding she had.

She was considering a wall stacked full of sheets in every color, tucked incongruously behind a pane of glass, when she saw a familiar form passing outside the shop. Everest, walking with his face toward the sky and a wide grin, like nothing on Earth mattered.

Seeing him rattled her, and she hated that it did. But she returned to the bedding, studying all the options—trying to imagine sleeping in any of them, and failing. She'd always just bought the cheapest sheets and felt a bit unmoored without prices to guide her.

She didn't end up selecting any of them. It felt like the wrong place to start. Maybe lighting, or a statement piece of wall art. She could choose her sheets to support something more important.

Of course, it all was a bit ridiculous. If she slowed down long enough to let her thoughts creep back in, she could feel herself descend into a kind of existential panic. If she remembered why she was here and what had happened in her life, and if she stopped to consider that the big decisions she contemplated now amounted to choosing a texture pack for the video game that was real life, she thought she might just curl up in a ball on the floor and give up right then and there.

She couldn't let herself slow down long enough to think about it, which was hard when the pace of life was so slow.

How had people survived for the hundreds of generations when there was no hope that anything would ever change?

42

EVEREST LEANED AGAINST THE WALL OUTSIDE THE NEXT SHOP, ARMS folded across his chest, watching her approach.

She smiled. She could hardly ask *Were you waiting for me?* Though she did wonder.

"Doing some shopping?" he asked, a note of amusement in his voice.

She felt even more scrutinized than usual.

"My room still looks the way it did when I arrived," she said. As if she owed him an explanation.

She continued walking, pretending she didn't care whether this conversation happened or not. To her relief, he walked along with her. "All of ours do, if you really look."

She nodded. Took a guess at what he meant. "Without the contacts, you mean?"

He laughed. "I didn't even mean that, but yes."

It was subtle, how much of this place didn't match how it looked when you reached out and touched it. But she had noticed almost immediately. It was impossible not to, when moving through a physical space. The illusion held from a distance, but people know how wood should feel beneath their fingers, how sound should carry through a shop full of fabric, how paper on a wall should move when they walk by. Even without touching the sheets projected on the shelves she knew they were not really there.

"What did you mean, then?" she asked.

"When was the last time you couldn't change your living space if you wanted to?" he asked. "College? High school?"

She shrugged. "I hated my most recent apartment, but it was the only one I could afford."

He smiled. "Fine, then. Maybe this isn't so different."

The conversation slowed, stopped. They walked on in silence. She hadn't picked out anything for her room but felt now that there was nothing better than to continue on in the sunlight here. At least she knew that was real.

She wondered if he had in fact been waiting for her. If they had run into each other randomly. If such a thing as a coincidence even existed in a place like this.

"You know that I've been here a week and hated my old apartment," she said. "But I know nothing about you."

"Everyone here has the same story," he replied.

"Yeah, but what's yours?" she asked.

"I could lie to you," he said, as if musing about it, as if just stating his thoughts. "You'd never know."

She nodded. "I wouldn't."

"But I could also tell you the truth, and nothing I said would matter."

"Remember," she said. "*Nothing* matters."

A pause. The hum of other people's conversations around them. She assumed they were inane, but what did she know, really?

"Nothing matters," he agreed. The pause had been him deciding whether it was true or not, whether he wanted to go on the record about agreeing. As if such things *mattered*.

It was almost enough to make her laugh, but she didn't. She wanted to know what else he would say.

"I've been here for a year, almost," he said.

"Or you could be lying," she said, smiling. A joke.

He smiled too. "I'm not, though."

"Anything you've learned in a year here?" she asked. "Anything I should know?"

"I'm sure I've learned something," he said.

"I heard…" she started to say, meaning to mention what Alexa had told her about contraband. She thought better of it.

But he didn't let it drop. When she was silent for a long moment, he asked, "What?"

She shrugged. "My roommate got lipstick somehow."

"You're wondering if I know how to get lipstick here?"

"Obviously not lipstick, but…"

He laughed. She wasn't sure what was funny.

"Perhaps I do know, Sara. But why should I tell you?"

Sara bristled at that. He wasn't teasing; he was actively avoiding being honest. She hated it but didn't know how to reply. She had no right to his honesty, did she?

And he had a point, even if he hadn't quite come out and said it. If the contraband items were some enrichment challenge the architects of this place had included to keep people thinking and striving—to give the residents some way to break rules and struggle for something—it didn't make sense for someone to just tell her what to do. Maybe as a longer-standing resident Everest understood the need to keep yourself busy better than Sara did.

Perhaps she was just making excuses for him, but it felt like a caring gesture, much as it bothered her. Don't give up the secrets of this place too quickly. She needed some mystery to sustain her.

As if there weren't enough questions.

43

Three years before the Community

THE MOVING TRUCK ARRIVED OUTSIDE OF ZACH'S HOUSE FIFTEEN minutes early and sat idling in the street, apparently confused by the proliferation of furniture and boxes arrayed in the driveway.

"Next time we shell out for humans," Zach said, laughing at the car's caution.

Sara was just glad it hadn't run into the couch. It was a much nicer one than she had.

"At least robots are prompt," she said.

Zach climbed into the vehicle and tried to switch it out of autonomous mode to maneuver it closer, cursing in frustration when it made him sign a waiver first—and then again when the eye tracker wouldn't let him skip to the signature field at the bottom.

"They really think this thing is a better driver than me?"

Sara, standing at the ready to direct him in, noted the irony. "You're about to attempt something the car wouldn't try."

He backed into the driveway and they loaded up the back of the vehicle, its lift and guided dolly streamlining the process and the computer suggesting strategic locations for each box, artfully tessellating things into place. She'd never moved with the help of human movers, but she'd struggled through it alone enough times to know this was an improvement.

They climbed in the front and were presented with a different set of waivers across the dashboard, then the car pulled away, leaving Zach's dilapidated two-million-dollar rental bungalow behind.

The van was even more useless pulling into her—now *their*—apartment complex, stymied by the lifting gate which it seemed to fear might come back down prematurely. Rather than coax it into the parking garage, they left it in the driveway with the flashers on and ferried Zach's stuff inside.

Sara mostly watched as Zach and the robots worked, following right behind him. His first trip he made the mistake of going up the stairs, leaving the guided dolly unable to follow and beeping angrily.

As a child, watching sci-fi movies where robots played central roles, she never imagined they'd be quite so pitiable as this.

But hadn't her mother's most frequent words to the Roomba been "I'm sorry" when it had to clean up after the pets or got stuck in a corner?

When everything was unloaded, Zach signed off on the move's completion and the van drove itself off, waiting an uncomfortably long time to merge cautiously into traffic.

It was strange not to think of this apartment as hers alone anymore, but she was glad to be halving the rent. In the two years she'd lived there the rent had gone up five percent each year, which sounded like less than the hundreds of dollars a month it actually was.

Zach's things didn't look like much stacked neatly in boxes, but as the afternoon wore on, she began to worry that it wouldn't all fit in the cupboards and closets. Ridiculous how bowls and Band-Aids and sweaters expanded when freed from their cardboard prisons.

"Still sure you don't want my help?" she called from the kitchen, where she was making herself tea.

Zach had started by delivering each box to the appropriate room and was now attacking them systematically. Besides moving the couch, he insisted he could do it all alone.

Instead of answering her question, he shouted, "Hair dye!?"

She rushed into the bathroom, sure she'd misheard him, reacting to the anguish in his voice.

He sat on the tile in the middle of the room, a half-unpacked box of razors and cleaning supplies beside him, a box of brown hair dye clutched in his hands like it might injure him.

She laughed, relieved that he was okay.

"You dye your hair?" he asked. Looking betrayed.

"Yeah," she replied, not sure why he would act like it was a big deal. "I have for years."

"I don't know what you actually look like!"

"Is that what this is about?" she asked, laughing again. "I look like this, silly. The same."

"What are you really?" he asked.

"What a way to phrase it," she replied.

Suddenly she didn't want to tell him, just because she could see how much it bothered him.

"I would think I'd know," he said, staring down at the box of dye, deep in thought. "Or do you dye your pubes, too?"

She sank down to his level and lifted the box delicately from his hands. "It's fine, Zach. Really. I'll tell you."

But she would drag it out a little longer, goading him. Having some fun at his expense.

"So?" he asked, eyes wide. She didn't think he'd ever looked so curious about anything about her.

"I dye it brown so people will take me more seriously," she said. "I never want to be the dumb blonde."

"You're a *blonde*?" he asked, jaw dropping. As if it was some big revelation.

She wondered if he was hamming it up, too, but from the look in his eyes she thought he wasn't kidding.

"I'm dating a blonde and didn't even know it?" he went on.

He reached out and grabbed her by the shoulders, like she was something precious. The way he looked at her made her uncomfortable and she wouldn't have been able to articulate why.

"I'm dating a brilliant, hot, *blonde* and no one else knows, either?"

Ah, that was why.

She leaned forward, kissed him, then got up before he could get any ideas, and went back to her still-hot tea.

44

THE NEXT MORNING, ALEXA WAS SUMMONED TO DO ANOTHER BOND-
ing activity. As she went, she joked that Sara could come along, but who
would want to leave so ungodly early to play schoolyard games with disin-
terested adults?

Squalls of rain came and went throughout the morning and for once Sara
didn't want to dive into it; she wanted to enjoy modern conveniences that
allowed her to pretend the weather was something other than what it was.
She sat by the window in the apartment, sipping water from the reusable
mug and dreaming that it was coffee for as long as she could maintain the
fiction. As soon as the sun broke free of the clouds, in a manner that did not
inspire confidence, she ventured out into the day in search of the real thing.
She wondered vaguely if the coffee was any more real than the wine, then
wondered why she hadn't thought of that before.

Without Alexa to guide her toward any restaurant in particular, she
headed to the nearest cafe right across the courtyard again, on the corner
facing out to the water. Compared to places more thoroughly surrounded
by lodgings and other activities, foot traffic was low, which of course didn't
matter in the least.

Still, there was a slight line and she begrudgingly joined it, suddenly
impatient for coffee now that it was so near. She was fixated on its scent
in the air, thanking someone somewhere for not banning caffeine as they
had banned alcohol, because she surely would have noticed, when someone
tapped on her shoulder.

She turned around ready to complain about the pre-coffee disruption,
like some cliche, but before she could say anything she recognized the girl
standing there. Her eyes went wide with surprise and relief. "Priya!"

Priya shocked Sara by wrapping her arms around her in a tight hug and
saying, "I'm so *incredibly* glad to see you!"

Since they'd only known each other for a few days before entering the
Community, Sara thought this was a bit much, but let it happen.

The woman behind the counter cleared her throat as the line moved forward, getting Sara's attention to take her order. Sara extracted herself from
Priya's embrace and said, "Just a shot of espresso, please."

She felt like she should offer to buy Priya a drink, since the other girl was clearly so much more aggrieved than she was, but neither of them were actually buying anything.

As the barista pulled the espresso shot, Priya said, "Sorry to ambush you like that, I've just been starved for human attention since I got here."

"Don't worry about it," Sara said, accepting her drink and nodding to Priya to place her own order—a latte, which would take a minute to put together. They drifted down the counter to wait.

Sara was glad to see Priya; in the early days in quarantine, she had longed for her new friends along with the old. But she found herself studying Priya's face, trying to guess why the company had let her in when they rejected Emily, and uncharitably thinking that they had made the wrong choice.

"When did you get here?" Priya asked.

Sara had to stop and think. "I think ten days ago, now."

"So, you're old hat at all this now, huh?" Priya said. "I arrived just a couple days ago."

If Priya had only been there a few days, how had Sara managed to encounter her so quickly? Surely if she could run into Priya, she could run into Bea.

It had occurred to her that her actions were guided by the Community, steering her toward some people and away from others. She couldn't guess why they would want to do this, but surely it was within their power. They could change what she saw! Back in the old world, where companies only controlled what you saw *online*, they could still affect your mood and choices. Their influence could reach even further here.

Sara downed her espresso and shivered a little at the bitterness, then placed the cup back on the counter. "Drinking espresso standing up like this feels very European," she commented.

"How'd you get into that, anyway?" Priya said, eyes darting about like she wasn't quite comfortable here. Perhaps, Sara thought, still feeling like a thief for not having paid.

"Espresso?" she asked. "College, I guess. Wanted to seem like a badass."

Priya laughed and picked up her latte. "I like that they still have people here making the drinks."

"And doing *everything*," Sara said.

Priya nodded and started walking toward the exit with Sara trailing behind. "And everything else," she affirmed. "But it is a little weird, don't you think?"

Sara shrugged, suddenly finding herself in the opposite role to where she'd been since she arrived. "They want it to feel normal, I guess."

"*They*," Priya said, sipping her drink. "Who is *they* anyway?"

"The company, you know, corporate people in suits somewhere," Sara said. "I guess."

"More likely an algorithm decides everything, right?" Priya said. "No way a committee's deciding what to do with our lives."

"I don't think anyone's deciding what to do with our lives," Sara said.

Priya laughed. "Certainly not us!"

They sat on the seawall and watched the waves. The tide was out enough that the town had been set down onto the sand and was stationary, which had come to feel strange to Sara after so much time afloat. Like something was missing, but something so subtle and mild that she would never have been able to identify it if someone had asked.

"You know what's funny?" Priya said. "Usually, one of us would have to rush off somewhere, but there's nowhere to go."

"It does feel weird not to have obligations," Sara agreed. "I'm not sure how to socialize without a set end."

"How are you supposed to leave without being rude?"

"If you're trying to say that you want to leave, you can just go," Sara said.

Priya laughed. "No, that's not it at all! I like talking to you. It's just… if there's something you'd rather be doing you don't have to stick with me."

Sara turned toward her a little to see what her expression was, but Priya's face was down, staring into her coffee, and Sara couldn't really see. "You said you've been starved for human attention?"

Priya laughed again, awkwardly this time. "Yeah, there were only four other people in my intro group, which I guess is small? And I haven't run into any of them, and everyone has their own friends here, so…"

"What about your roommate?" Sara asked.

Priya shrugged. "I don't have a roommate."

Sara nodded, considering this. She had joined Alexa's apartment, so obviously Alexa had faced her first week alone, too. Somehow, she didn't think Alexa had struggled like Priya seemed to be.

"My roommate arrived a week before me," Sara said, "so you'll probably get one soon."

"I hope so. I'm honestly more lonely here in town, surrounded by people I don't know, than I was in that hospital all alone."

"That was a wild experience, right?" Sara said, not knowing what else to say about it. "I've never been so bored."

"And yet it was also so…zen?" Priya said. "I don't know. Like I was in a cocoon or something."

Sara wasn't sure she would put it that way, but she understood. "Since you *couldn't* know anything, it was okay to not know anything."

Not unlike this place, she thought. Though the lack of knowledge felt worse and worse all the time.

"But still, I was very ready to be out of there."

"You were there a whole week longer than me!" Sara said. "Any idea why?"

"How should I know?" Priya replied. "It was just a constant string of doctor appointments. Maybe they had to wait on some test or something, see if I was good to enter."

"Huh."

"Have you seen anyone else? From our group?"

Sara shook her head, not sure why she didn't bring up Bea. "I'd about given up hope, to be honest."

"So, are they just out there in the real world, then?" Priya asked, more musing to herself than asking Sara. "Seems so far away."

Sara nodded. It certainly did.

45

SHE ABANDONED HER PLAN TO DECORATE HER ROOM AND INSTEAD decided to get a job. It didn't make sense to decorate, she decided; maybe this would be her home for five years, but that was still temporary. She wanted it to feel that way. She did not want to make a home with augmented-reality goggles. If her cramped dorm somehow began to feel like home, Sara wanted it to happen organically, over time and from good memories, not because she tried to force it through a feat of artificial interior design.

Some part of her malaise, she thought, was due to a lack of purpose; empty days were intimidating and made her lose the point of living.

She doubted any of the jobs here would give her the sort of validation she craved, but at least they would help her run from her thoughts. Give her somewhere to be, assign a task, put people in front of her who depended on something she did. Even if it was a fiction, it would be a useful one.

A job, she had realized in her year without one, was far more than a means to money. Here a job was distilled down to its essence, what it truly was: in a world broken free of subsistence and handed over to the search for meaning, a job was a purpose. It could become your meaning, give you an identity. Without that, what were you?

When she first arrived, she had marveled at all the jobs staffed by people in the Community that could be—and were—done by robots out in the real world, but she didn't wonder about it anymore. People did things here not because any specific task had to be done by a person, but because people had to do something to fill their days. Leave too many people without any kind of task and they would lose their minds.

The jobs that existed in the Community might leave you drained and despondent in the outside world, but here they could be fulfilling. How many people cooked as a hobby, for fun? Make it a job to give it structure, then remove the stress of trying to pay your bills on a meager wage, and it could be communal and joyful and creative. Making things felt good.

Some people in the old world probably took joy in being a yoga instructor or working in a movie theatre, but here they could enjoy it even more. These were hobbies turned careers, where teaching something or sharing some beloved activity could be removed from the fear of judgment for not being the kind of professional the world insisted everyone should long to be.

She remembered little children dreaming of being a pizza delivery driver because that would mean they got to spend a lot of time around pizza. No one dreamt of being a delivery driver once they were adults. But had the appeal really gone away?

She had spent a lot of the past year wishing to go back to childhood, when such questions did not haunt her. As a child she never wondered what her purpose was, didn't strive to fill her precious hours with meaningful work that fulfilled her or contributed to the future or solved problems. She didn't need to exercise her mind or her limbs to feel like she had spent her time well. It had been so much simpler.

And why was that so impossible, anyway? Regression to a childlike state. Weren't they most of the way there already?

Like in childhood, she lived here at the behest of strange people more powerful than her, who she did not understand and who did not consult her for decisions. People she had to trust. Her basic needs were met, but the expectations of life were unclear.

At some point while growing up, these dynamics had shifted. She couldn't remember when. Now the transition back to a paternalistic life was distinctly uncomfortable. Even incomprehensible, if she let herself fully put it into words. It felt profoundly wrong.

And so she fought it, and they let her fight it, by getting a job. It wasn't like it would pay her, she guessed, and she found that she didn't care. She just needed something unnameable to make her feel like an adult again, and a job might give her that.

The streets became increasingly artificial the more Sara looked at them.

She kept catching herself flickering her eyes away and back, trying to trip up the software—to see what was really there instead of what the company wanted her to see. Exhausting and futile, but irresistible, too.

She could take out the contacts.

Her hands were at her eyes, but she stopped herself. What problem would it solve, blocking out this virtual world that was meant to be real?

She had spent several days wandering these streets, but until that afternoon she didn't really consider the options. Each storefront had its own appearance, but they blended together in her memory, her mind barely registering whether they sold stir fries or sandwiches or sundries.

Now the patterns in the shops slowly settled into her mind, beginning to make a kind of sense. She saw the logic of it, the rhythms in how the streets were laid out: always dominated by food, but intermixed with different sorts of places depending on the block.

None of the little trinkets and consumer goods that filled cities in her childhood, no little signs to hang on a wall or knickknacks to place on a shelf. Not even the shelf to put it on. Why did we ever need so many objects to fill our space? Why did we have so much space to fill?

Instead, the shops were far more practical: food, ready to eat or in pieces to be prepared (so some people had kitchens? How?), and the tools to prepare it with. The yoga studio Alexa disappeared to so often, and gyms, and art studios. The whole town set up around humans consuming and then expending energy. Like hamsters in a wheel.

It struck her that the only indulgences from the world outside were the interminable rows of cafes and restaurants. Besides that, it was all bare and sparse, minimalistic as a design vision but also as a philosophy.

Displays of virtual objects to personalize rooms with. Basics for modern survival—new shoes, hairbrushes, nail clippers. The most basic mall in the world. Everything so *simple*.

But what did people do all day? There had to be more to life than eating and exercising and painting. Such leisure would make anyone crazy.

She thought again how strange it was that everyone exercised so much. Perhaps the company really was encouraging them: subliminally guiding people to a gym when they had eaten too much, highlighting the active members running by while fading the less active into the background.

Could they do all that with the contacts? Augmented reality was not the sort of software engineering she ever learned about, but she guessed they could.

She hoped it was something as benign as that, the kind of social engineering these mega tech companies had engaged in since their inception, and not something more extreme. If you became too depressed to exercise, if you just didn't want to, would they eject you? She wondered what one had to do to be evicted from this life, spat back out into their fragile old one.

Finally, she reached the last block. She couldn't remember if she had walked down this street before but guessed that she probably had. The entire town looked more or less the same, all built at the same recent date, none of it weathered, all of it crisp and new despite whatever attempts its architects had made to give it character.

The first place she noticed was, against all odds, a movie theater. It had a low roof and simple glass front, not at all in keeping with her mental image of a theater. Too small. And a bit of a culture shock, given the palace of boredom she'd constructed for herself as her future in this place, but it was a strange, vertiginous relief to see something so familiar and mundane.

Across the street and two storefronts down was something even more disorienting: a VR entertainment center. She pressed her face against the glass, peering into the gloom, and saw the booths arrayed into the darkness, people in them moving strangely, off in faraway worlds.

A place like that would thrive in a place like this, of course. She did what she could to resist the escapist temptation to imagine herself in another, better, reality. One that emulated just a little more of the world she'd left.

She would give in eventually, she thought. And then it would be over.

In the meantime, she *needed* to find a job to keep her mind in this almost-real world, such as it was. In that single afternoon her nerves had frayed more than in all the time so far. But nothing yet appealed to her.

She remembered her years in the restaurant industry as tolerable solely for their brevity, for their status as a stepping-stone to something better. They would not be that now, and she didn't think she could stand it.

But could she stand not to try it?

She reached the last store on the block, and indeed the last in this entire branch of the town. The grid and gray dissolved here into the curves of nature, hills rising inland and sand reaching out onto the pavement, trees stretching toward the sky that bent down to meet them.

The kind of place they were assured would die with the rise of the internet: a bookstore.

Staring at this facade—wood, rough and unpainted, with a yellow door propped open to the seaside air—she felt her anxiety evaporate for the moment. Even if she did not work here, knowing that it existed in a place like this—in the disintegrating vestiges of civilization—reassured her.

Sara told herself that giving her conscious mind over to the imaginings of an author from a simpler time was more forgivable than being swallowed into a virtual world. Knew that she was lying to herself about this but didn't care. It was older and that meant it was better, right? It was at least less complete, leaving her mind free rather than seeking to control every sense. That was something.

No matter how unconvincing her arguments were, she chose to believe them, and knew this place would become a refuge, one way or another.

She walked in, expecting there to be a bell on the door, and there was. What a relief to have her expectations met for once.

The woman behind the counter was sitting perched on a stool, reading a book: the first person she had seen in the entire town who, in Sara's mind, was not bored. She suspected that was just her own bias coloring the world around her.

"Are you hiring?" Sara asked, without even a hello.

The woman looked up, blinking a few times. Emerging from a kind of VR Sara felt less guilty about drowning in, ridiculous as that was. She smiled, shrugged, and said, "Isn't everyone?"

And then Sara had a job.

46

Two and a half years before the Community

"HAPPY ANNIVERSARY!" ZACH SAID, LIFTING HIS GLASS OF EXPENSIVE champagne toward her.

Sara clinked her glass against his. "Congratulations on closing the series B!"

"Can you believe it's been two whole years?" he asked, sipping the champagne.

"Of our relationship or One?" she asked, grinning.

He waved a hand. "It's been two and a half years of One. Now...to at least two and a half more!"

They toasted again and she laughed. "Not trying to sell before then?"

"I love my job, Sara," he replied, very earnest. "And," he added pointedly, "I love you."

"Glad I made the list."

"Right behind innovation and genius and success!"

She wasn't even insulted, both because she was pretty sure he was kidding and also because she had known what she was getting into dating a startup CEO. "Is that three things or one?"

He grinned. "One!"

The waitress arrived then and asked how they were enjoying the champagne, and if they were ready to order. Zach met Sara's eyes over the bottle. "Are we ready?"

Sara shrugged. "I assumed this was a prix fixe, multicourse deal."

"Yes, but we have several options," the waitress said quickly. "Are either of you vegetarians? Any allergies?"

Sara made a face. "I'm trying to eat less meat, you know, it's better for the planet."

"I hope that doesn't mean *all* meat," Zach said, raising his eyebrows suggestively.

Sara blushed and the waitress pretended not to notice.

"So that's one vegetarian order, and one lamb? Fish?"

"Lamb," Zach said, closing the menu decisively. "And we don't need any other drinks."

Sara hadn't looked at the drink menu yet, but she was used to Zach making little decisions for her, and really the champagne was fine. As long as he let her contribute to the more momentous decisions, she was happy to let him control stupid little things like what she drank with dinner if it made him feel better.

The waitress walked off to put in their orders and Zach's hand found Sara's thigh under the table.

"I love this dress," he said, his voice low. "Is it new?"

She smirked and took a sip of her drink. "I know what's coming next."

"Oh, yeah?"

"You'll love it even more on the bedroom floor."

He grinned. "You know me so well!"

She tipped her flute back and forth, watching the glittering liquid slosh. "Drink up," she said, nodding to his full glass and her own almost empty one. "You're falling behind."

He downed the rest of his champagne and refilled first his glass, then hers, humming some song she didn't recognize as he did so.

"I think you're supposed to savor champagne, not guzzle it," she said.

"You're the one telling me to drink faster."

"What is this, anyway?" she asked, taking another sip. Her head felt pleasantly buzzy.

He shrugged. "I dunno, I just asked for the most expensive one they had."

"Look at you, Mr. Conspicuous Consumption."

He raised his glass in the air like an athlete celebrating a victory. "What's the point of the $20 million I just raised if not this?"

She laughed. "I don't know, maybe building your company?"

"I have the best company imaginable," he said, and she wondered whether he was talking about her or the startup.

"So, what's next, then?"

It was highly unusual for them to have an entire evening set aside just to talk and spend time together, and she found it harder to fill the air between them with words than she had expected. After two years it was easy just being with him, but that didn't make the actual conversation part equally easy. Talking about work felt like a bit of a cop out, but it was a topic he usually wanted to expound upon.

"Well, you know," he said, swirling his glass with one hand and fiddling with the silverware with the other. "We're going to expand out of food and office supplies into…other things."

"Like?"

"Anything! I'm thinking putting it out to the customer—what do you wish you had just one of? Get them thinking."

The conversation was spiraling the drain a bit, so Sara was relieved when the first course arrived, an arrangement of colorful vegetables and some delicate white cream sauce on tiny plates. Beautiful and expensive, just like Zach liked.

The course only lasted about two bites, though, and she found herself back in the position of forcing the conversation. "How'd you find this place, anyway?"

"A VC recommended it," he said. "Apparently lots of deals get made here."

"Imagine how much money has exchanged hands here, then," she replied, searching for the right thing to say. "The *future*."

"Speaking of, have you heard about these Cities of the Future that keep popping up?"

"Peripherally," she said. "I think I saw some headlines."

"You should really keep more on top of the industry, if you ever want to make anything in your own right," he chided her.

"Who says I do?"

He laughed a little. "You're cute, but not *that* cute."

She rolled her eyes, ignoring the jibe. Sometimes Zach could be so immature. "You were saying."

"Very trendy right now," he said. "All the big tech companies are trying to get in on it, and VCs are searching for the startup version. Micro capitalist corporate city-states, basically."

"Sounds horrific."

"Or like a dream, right?" he said. "Depends who runs it and what they're aiming for."

"Right, so I imagine there's no homelessness, no carbon footprint, universal healthcare, and people pay to live the gentrified dream?"

"Sometimes."

She frowned, but he just raised his eyebrows in response, waiting for her to guess the twist.

"Um…if it's so idyllic, and they put their workers there, they'll be happier and more productive. Logical endgame of what Google started thirty years ago."

"Or what if it's not their workers?"

"What, like a haven for worker drones that companies pay for? Like company towns?"

"Or a thousand other business models. Maybe the whole place is full of ads and the people are supposed to buy things. Maybe big companies and universities can pay to run experiments on the residents. Maybe it's for beta testing. Who knows?"

"Like I said, horrifying."

"Or the future."

"Would you live in one of these places?"

"Of course not," he said. "But I'd be down to run one."

She shook her head. "My point exactly."

He laughed, maybe at the concept, maybe at her.

Their next course arrived.

47

SARA SPENT MORE THAN AN HOUR IN THE BOOKSTORE, CONSIDERING her options. They seemed to have every genre she could imagine, but very few titles she was familiar with. She wasn't sure whether that was a surprise or not, but she didn't feel disappointed by it. A bookstore full of books she had never heard of was a bookstore full of books she had never read.

She trailed her fingers along the worn spines, noting that most books seemed to be used and almost all were paperback. So fragile. She felt a bit awed that all of it was free. In a closed community the difference between a library and a used bookstore began to break down.

Cradling a small book in her hands, something with a dramatic dragon curving on its cover and the familiar smell of aging paper wafting from within, Sara felt the need to see this place for what it really was. This book felt exactly right, smelled exactly right. The contacts could not ruin those other senses.

But the book could be something other than it seemed. Every book there could be blank, varied pages populated with unique words for each reader based on what the company thought they would want to read. As long as she kept the contacts in, she would never know.

With a sharp intake of breath, she set the book back on the shelf and raised her finger to her face again, peeling the contact from her left eye.

Suddenly, her eye felt exposed and vulnerable. She hadn't realized how accustomed to the contacts she had become.

She blinked furiously, waiting for her vision to clear, then at last gathered the nerve to look at the shelf before her.

It was exactly the same, whether she used her free eye or the one that still wore a contact.

Hurriedly, and feeling very foolish, she placed the contact back in her left eye. What had she been expecting? Why would it have mattered, anyway? Whether the story was on a book's physical page or projected there, it would be just as transportive.

No sooner did her vision clear again than a message flashed across her vision in blaring red letters:

DO NOT REMOVE YOUR CONTACTS

There was no explanation, but she didn't need one. She couldn't dismiss the message, not for the painfully long minute it blinked before her eyes, baking a headache into her forehead. At last, the reprimanding message ceased and she shook her head to clear it, returning her attention resolutely to the bookshelf.

She couldn't find the book with the dragon on the cover. A chill went down her spine, some fear that what she thought she remembered and knew was not reality, but she pushed the fear aside as forcefully as she could.

No matter. There were so many other options.

Eventually the employee, a thirty-something Black woman with short-cropped hair and smiling eyes, announced that the shop was closing, and Sara retreated into the evening. It was early enough still that the sun had yet to go down, but the light was beginning to fade, the shadows stretched long and the hue turned golden. She could have gone home, could have gone back toward town to eat, but instead she turned away from the buildings, facing the hills.

Without really thinking about what she was doing, she stepped off the pavement and onto the sand, then began to hike through the plants, trying to avoid stepping on them out of a desire not to cause any more harm to what was left of nature. The streets receded behind her.

She moved surreptitiously, though she didn't think there was any real reason to. Leaving at any time was allowed, and she wasn't really leaving. Just stepping away for the moment.

Still, it felt dangerous, exposing herself to whatever might lurk in these hills as night fell. Not that she really thought there was anything risky in the descending darkness.

She climbed steadily upward, scrambling at times for purchase in the loose sand, not sure where she was going but also not wanting to stop.

It was a different hill than the one she had ascended during the game of tag, but it loomed above the town and the ocean just the same. Large and momentous; ignored and abandoned. No one else here and no one else looking.

Mere anonymity was enough to feel freeing and strange.

She reached the summit while the light still glowed, vibrant even though the sun had touched the horizon and was now disappearing rapidly. The water and sky were no longer blue, the land no longer dull brown and ashy green, but everything a perfect, glowing amber. Light shone through the waves and burst into brilliant stars. Blades of grass became a work of glittering art.

She perched on a rock with her shoes off and feet pressed into the sand—thick like clay—and leaned back, resting her hands on the ground, staring up and out at the world.

Sitting there, letting her eyes unfocus slightly in the fading day, she thought how strange it was that they had separated themselves from this. The buildings with their sharp edges and hard walls, the streets with their precision and the people with their eyes on each other's faces and nothing else, all just below this untamed reality.

Everyone in the town was close to this view, but they did not see it. She didn't, either, most days—and in that moment, she hated herself for it.

How many thousands of sunsets had she missed?

Watching the sun drop, she felt more full and alive than she had in months. The fresh air and the silence, the color gradually changing, made her feel a part of something, though she couldn't explain exactly what. The sky around her changed so slowly that she felt it should have lost her attention, but she couldn't look away.

A bird or a bat flitted across the sky above her, a tiny black speck silhouetted in the last of the sun's light. Racing off, home or to eat, with urgency that she no longer had to feel. She felt solidarity with the tiny creature, eking out a meaningless life against a beautiful backdrop it never regarded.

There was a tickle on her ankle and she looked down to see an ant crawling across her skin. Leaving a trail for its fellows, one they would not be able to follow when she moved. A tragedy in its tiny life.

So many small dramas of the animals out for the evening just like she was, wandering through the twilight. Did they know how much their world had changed? Did they sense in some instinctive way that things were not as they should have been?

In her old life, she would have taken a picture. She wondered if it would have come out, and knew, even if it had, that it would not have captured the perfection of the moment. So much of it was in the slight scent of the ocean and the soil, the freshness of the succulents and the seagrass. The gentle motion of the life around her could not exist in a still image. Her expression in the photo would never have conveyed how she felt.

But still, she longed to take a souvenir of that sunset home with her. Something to look back on when she sat in her sterile gray room. Something to show to Alexa—or to Bea, if she ever found her. Something to prove it had all been real.

The sun disappeared and the breeze picked up and the temperature dropped, and Sara returned to the town, feeling empty all over again.

48

THE NEXT DAY, SARA WAS SCHEDULED TO WORK IN THE BOOKSTORE in the afternoon, but she still needed to fill her morning. Anticipating having an actual plan for the later hours drove her away from her previous aimless wandering; she couldn't sit still or people watch. She craved a routine.

After their breakfast, opposite each other at a cafe with barely a word exchanged, Alexa announced she would be going to yoga again. For what seemed to Sara like the thousandth time.

And for the first time, Sara decided to go along.

She had tried yoga once in her old life and found it simultaneously intimidating and mind-numbing, but not in a meditative way—in an excruciating way. But that was her old self, she thought. She now had an attention span she could not have once imagined. Surely now she could stomach it.

"I'm so glad you're coming!" Alexa gushed as they walked down the street.

The sun continued to shine down on them. Sara already regretted her choice to go into a dark studio, but she couldn't back out now.

The room was filled with smiling and vaguely identical young women, dressed in the same athleisure style that had started in gyms like this twenty years earlier and slowly infected the entire world. Tight ponytails and fit bodies. Maybe this was what people did all day to keep from losing their minds, Sara thought. Exercise was supposed to release endorphins, after all.

But did yoga even count as exercise?

The class was exactly as she remembered from the single other time she'd done yoga, proceeding with gradual calming cheer and encouragement. Everyone else moved confidently and fluidly; Sara felt ridiculous. She knew yoga could be intense and exhausting, but this felt more like therapy for a stressed-out life she no longer lived.

The atmosphere had been thoroughly stripped of any references to Eastern philosophy, which struck her as both disappointing and unsurprising, but also somehow right. Anything even a little bit devotional—for any religion—would have been out of place in the Community.

Everyone had been standardized, she thought. The faithful weeded out selectively, or maybe just the demographic that tried to enter. Or perhaps, she thought, it was what society had become, performative enough that even those who, before joining, would have spent Sundays in church or lit candles on Hanukkah or fasted for Ramadan would now dutifully engage with the new religion of whatever this place was.

What were the values here, anyway? Patience? Obedience? Calm? Certainly not the frenetic intensity of Silicon Valley's unquenchable growth or the consumer culture that had trampled the world. She should be glad for that—those had been precisely what she aimed to escape. Still, the underlying culture of a society had to be replaced with something, didn't it? A common ground of accepted givens that everyone implicitly agreed upon.

Maybe the literal shifting of the ground beneath her feet was not why she felt so unmoored. Maybe it was because she didn't know what undergirded her new home, didn't understand the principles shaping life here.

Had she been told? No, she was quite sure they hadn't said. Was she somehow defective as a human, unable to discover such things on her own?

The yoga class stretched onward through the morning, with breaks for water and snacks and murmured conversations but never a clear indication to leave. Though she followed along as best she could, Sara's body felt flimsy and unused by the end of it. At the second break, she said goodbye to Alexa and went back out onto the street, determined to get the workout she had naively expected.

Luckily, the streets were organized such that there were several other gyms within a short walk. She'd never been inside—she wasn't much of a gym person—but she expected them to be full of bedraggled people moving reluctantly through workouts they dreaded.

To her surprise, the generic fitness center she chose was full of people, most apparently in good moods. The dance studio and spin class on either side of the gym were probably just as full. Many people were sitting or standing on the periphery and chatting with those near them, but plenty used the sleek silver machines or racks of free weights, evidently comfortable and expert at such things in a way she had never been.

And suddenly many things made sense. What did people do all day? How did they spend so much time eating and remain thin and healthy? What did the Community revolve around, if not any of the hubs of identity she was used to?

She still felt out of place, but resolved to join in, trying to melt into this community she had chosen and been chosen to join.

Have I really become this person, who follows the crowd? she wondered. Her parents raised her to be an independent thinker, to make her own choices.

But, she reasoned, doing as others did could be a good thing, and was in this case. She wasn't following them into vice or the wilderness. And more to the point, she needed to blend in for once, to make friends, to adapt to a new way of living more suited for a splintering civilization. In that moment, it seemed obvious how to do it.

She climbed onto a treadmill, lights glowing blue across its readout and the track beginning to hum as she moved, and began to run, hating every minute of it.

49

SHE ARRIVED AT THE BOOKSTORE IN THE MIDAFTERNOON, CARRYING a coffee and a pastry, and traded places with a thirty-something man who didn't stick around to chat. The woman the day before had explained a little of how things worked, but in essence it was very simple: since nothing cost anything and the inventory was almost entirely fixed, she really just needed to be there because customers expected it. An algorithm decided who would work when and sent them all notifications; occasionally new shipments of books arrived, but no one placed orders for them.

"There's nothing you'll do that a robot couldn't," she had said nonchalantly. "But bookstores are supposed to be friendly and cozy, so people are better."

Almost as soon as she had told Sara she could have a job, a message had appeared before her eyes—visible to them both, apparently—listing a four-hour block the following afternoon. And so there Sara was, alone in the bookstore, with no further instruction and nothing to do besides remain there.

Which was still enormously better than the alternative. Just having this tiny amount of structure returned a sense of normalcy to her life that she had craved.

She guessed correctly that there would be very few customers, but since there was no need to pay rent or earn wages, it didn't matter. In her entire four hours she saw only a few people walk past. No one came inside. If not for her newly acquired tolerance for boredom she might have resented it, but instead she spent the time exploring the place.

At first, she perched behind the counter on the wooden stool, assuming the position of an idealized bookstore worker. Staring eagerly at the door, then thumbing through the papers scattered about—flyers and bookmarks, handwritten notes—and the drawers in the desk. Most of them were empty, where in a real bookstore she thought there would probably be folders filled with records and receipts, money for making change, orders placed for people who wanted something in particular. Maybe a phone book, since this store felt like a time capsule going back not ten but perhaps fifty years, to a time when things like that were common.

She gradually strayed from her post, first sticking to the front of the store where she could have ducked back to the counter in a few steps, then delving deeper between the shelves. Inhaling the scent of mildewed pages and old ink. Letting it take her back to childhood and rainy days spent reading her mother's old paperbacks.

The place was exactly the warren of shelves she pictured in her mind when she thought of a used bookstore, stacks interlocking together with colorful book spines lined up neatly along them. The ceiling was lower than the other shops she'd entered here, the lighting dim. Like someone had decided to build this store exactly as they had seen in movies.

And probably they had, she decided. Because why not? This whole town felt like an alien's idea of how to make people comfortable, and for a certain kind of person a nostalgia-laden used bookstore would be an essential piece of that. The kind of person like her, apparently.

The thought of some anonymous corporate committee brainstorming what was missing from the cutesy cafes and sleek gyms made her laugh, alone amid the books. Laughing by herself made her laugh even harder. Maybe, like the man at the bakery who still believed himself an architect, she was beginning to succumb to this place.

50

SARA HAD NOT GROWN UP HIKING. HER PARENTS WERE TOO LAZY FOR it, too suburban to take their children on real camping trips that involved a longer walk than the twenty feet from the car to the tent. Backpacking had been introduced to her in college, when it seemed like that was all any Bay Area twenty-something wanted to do on the weekends, and she'd gone along with it skeptically.

How much prettier could the woods look after a day of hauling heavy gear on your back? How could it possibly be worth it?

She'd protested so much, in fact, that when she went and fell in love with it, she was embarrassed to admit just how wrong she had been. Getting out in nature, uncontactable and quiet amid the enormity of the mountains and trees, made her feel small and inconsequential in the best possible way. She relished the soreness in her legs and back and neck at the end of a long day on a trail, found herself addicted to that pain. Never had she slept so well than in a sleeping bag on the cold, hard ground.

But life moved quickly, making such trips a rarity. After college that was especially true.

So she was determined to enjoy a stolen weekend in the High Sierra with Zach and Christina and X, who had started dating not long after they met at Eric's party, though the weather was hotter than she'd hoped and Zach was a whiny backpacker.

They drove five hours on Friday night and set off with the sun on Saturday morning, climbing upward through the trees. Her heart pounded in her chest in a way that made her feel very alive.

Zach began complaining of sore feet shortly after they stopped for lunch, which made it harder for Sara to ignore her own complaints, but the aroma of pine trees in the air soothed her. She'd read something about the chemistry of the oils they released into the air, but she couldn't remember the details just then. It didn't matter.

In the afternoon, the pine air was replaced with a strange deadness which

Sara didn't understand until they rounded a ridge and saw the great expanse of blackness before them: what had once been trees were now ashes, washed away in a deluge of spring rains after they burned at the end of a hot summer. The sight was epic, but not in the way a glimpse of Yosemite Valley might be. It was awesome in the antiquated sense of the word.

"Wow," Christina said, coming to a halt beside her.

Zach, panting up the hill behind them, took a few minutes to catch up. To Sara's relief he didn't make any snarky comment about the destruction, just looked out at it in silence.

"Guess we better keep on," X said.

They continued, following a ridge that kept the bowl of late forest to their right for the next several hours. Sara always read the acreage counts of the annual fires, but the enormity had not hit her until that moment.

She didn't really feel anything in response to the desolation, though she wanted to. What it left her with was a strange emptiness. She liked it when the wild made her feel tiny, but not like this. Not like she was useless.

She yearned for something she couldn't name. She frequently felt like she was wasting her life, and this fire's remains drove that home. In the past she'd always been able to push it away, but now the impulse to even try felt ridiculous.

Who was she to ignore anything?

She wanted to live, really *live*, whatever that meant. She wanted to climb every mountain and shout into the wind. She wanted to punch someone in the face, but who? She wanted to win an election, wanted to comfort a crying child—wanted to make the future better on a grand or tiny scale. Better, or at least different. She *wanted.*

At one point, after they entered living greenery again, when the day started fading into evening, she asked, "Do you think any of this will still be here for our kids to see?"

Christina scoffed. "Do you really think anyone like us is going to have kids?"

X laughed bitterly. "And the answer to your question, Sara, is no."

51

OVER THE NEXT WEEK SHE ENFORCED A RHYTHM FOR HERSELF, GET-
ting up with Alexa and eating together, then walking to the yoga studio where
they parted ways. After that dreadful hour on the treadmill Sara resolved to
run outside, though it was somewhat less of a break from her usual habits of
walking in a curious daze around town. Like during her walks, she let her
mind wander, contemplating the people she passed and the decisions they
had all made that brought them together in this strange place.

Half the days she worked the afternoons in the bookstore, pleasant hours
where she had a purpose. It was strange to have work so thoroughly de-
coupled from survival, and even stranger to realize that she barely noticed
the difference.

She got to know the rows of books and where each belonged. Partway
through her third shift she picked a book, almost at random, and began to
read, relaxed in a way she hadn't been with a book since childhood when the
pressures of time hadn't been so intense. She realized how much of her more
recent lack of reading had come from a sense of there being far too many
books to ever read and far too many other things to do, a stress that crept in
no matter how interesting the argument or compelling the story.

Now, without that, every book had merit. She had five years before her in
which she could read every one of these books, if she wanted.

She wondered at each word, realized that someone once had sat at a
keyboard and considered it carefully, choosing to forgo or include punc-
tuation and deciding when to start a new chapter. Someone, separated by
time and space, had labored over the pages she now read. Transmitting ideas
to her imperfectly but in the best way that person knew how: these words
were a window into the author's distant mind, as much as they were a story
to be consumed.

Of the myriad options for losing oneself in someone else's imagination,
Sara decided that books felt more pure because of the simplicity of writing,
the directness. A single other person had created this. They were constrained
so much more than a three-dimensional virtual artist or cinematic team of
storytellers, restricted to tiny black squiggles that at some point in history
people had collectively imbued with meaning. How incredibly *human*.

On the days she did not work, she tried to meet up with people besides

Alexa. Usually that meant Priya part of the time, and Drew and the other introductory group girls the rest, though she kept an eye out for Bea or Everest, both people she found far more interesting than the others. Almost every day, she saw someone out of the corner of her eye who she was sure was Bea— women the right build, moving a certain way that felt so familiar. But it was never Bea, and Sara began to despair that it never would be.

She found herself wondering if the message column was honest. She exchanged more messages with her parents and even sent more messages to Bea, all of which bounced back. Perhaps none of it was real.

She *wanted* none of it to be real. After a few days of avoiding it, she told her parents that she thought Emily had been rejected from the Community but wasn't replying to her messages. Her parents hadn't heard from Emily either.

She could read between the lines in her mother's messages that she was frantic with worry; both parents tried to say that Emily was surely fine, but Sara didn't believe that they meant it. Yes, the world was chaotic. But Emily was clever and resilient! Yes, Emily wouldn't know where to find them—they had relocated to different temporary housing; their childhood home had, in fact, burned down the day after Sara's apartment.

Right—that was another thing that made Sara flighty and afraid and unnerved. *Unmoored*, that was the word. There was nowhere left to run.

Zach replied, after an agonizing week. He had just been ejected from their quarantine, he said. Two full weeks longer in there than Sara. When she asked him where he would go now, he did not reply.

She desperately hoped the messages were not real. She couldn't stand the image of the world they painted.

The group outings with her Community friends were fine, even fun sometimes, but in Sara's mind were filed away as time fillers, just something to do. She noticed her memory of them fading almost immediately, every one of their conversations painfully similar and every meal unremarkable.

It struck her just how much of her previous life had been that way, too. Conversations not working to achieve anything (but what was so wrong with that?) and friendships constructed out of shared appetizers and tipsy evenings of no substance. Could she say anything specific about any of the people she had once counted as friends? Who were they, besides avatars in her personal history?

By her sixth shift in the bookstore her new routine had begun to feel easy, even natural. Her morning runs had begun to settle into a familiar route through and around the town; her walk to work was memorized. She woke up in the morning and knew how she would spend her day. A limitation of her horizons that instead felt like a twisted sort of freedom.

That afternoon she had three hours alone with the books and did not anticipate any customers; there had been an average of less than one per shift in her time so far, and even when someone did come in, they rarely wanted to talk. She saw how this life could devolve into drudgery even with the new obligation of a job, but it hadn't happened yet.

She was deep in the store, scanning the backs of worn paperbacks in a meandering search for something to spend the next few hours reading when the bell hung on the door tinkled. She considered getting up to greet whoever had just walked in but decided it was unnecessary.

The sound of someone moving through the shop, footsteps and breath, strange after so much silence. But not unwelcome.

She replaced the book she had been looking at and moved on to the next.

The person approached, their athletic-shod feet in her peripheral vision, and still she did not look up.

As they sat down beside her and reached for the book in her hands, she finally caught a glimpse of their face.

"Of course," she said, trying to sound mad but too pleased to pull it off.

Everest skimmed the back of the book and slid it back onto the shelf. It was in the wrong place, and crooked, but she made no move to replace it. A sign that she had not yet worked there long enough to be changed by the experience.

"Thought I might find you here," he said.

"Why's that?" she asked, curious and also teasing.

A shrug. "You're here a lot."

She hadn't seen him since their last conversation, but evidently, he had seen her. "Have you been following me?" she asked.

He sounded amused when he answered, "No."

"It's alright if you have," she went on, realizing only as she said it that it was true. And how strange was that? Such a thing should not be welcomed.

"I'm just observant," he said. "I usually know where most people are, I think."

She narrowed her eyes, trying to figure out if he was joking, and if so, what the punchline actually was. "Is that so?"

He shrugged again. "And this place makes sense for you."

"Am I that predictable?" she asked. Trying to decide now if she wanted to flirt with him or drive him away to leave her with the distant authors.

"More than most of us here, you're still grappling with modernity," he said, speaking slowly. Like either he was figuring out the words or explaining something to a child. "Where better to engage with old ideas?"

"You say that like it's a bad thing," she said.

"We all get to decide for ourselves what's good and bad," he said. "But I try not to look too deeply."

She scowled. "And here I thought I liked you."

She surprised herself a bit with that, but it was true. And didn't help her decide between flirting and pushing him away.

But he smiled, slowly. Not offended, then. "You asked what I'd learned in a year here."

A pause.

"That was just about the beginning of this place, right?"

"Close to it," he said. Perhaps too quickly, she thought.

"What made you sign up for something like this? Being a guinea pig here?"

"People came for all the reasons they always have," he said. "You know, a pioneering spirit. Seeing the future before anybody else. Escaping something or somewhere or someone."

"I didn't ask about *people*."

He laughed. Knowing she had caught him. "I don't know. I just wanted a change."

He was lying and they both knew it, but she wasn't going to press.

They sat beside each other, her tucked in the corner with her knees bent toward her chest, him reclining casually, like a sunbather on a beach. Angled so they didn't have to meet eyes but could look at each other if they wanted to. On consideration, Sara thought that was his favorite way of arranging things.

"You wouldn't tell me what you did before," she said. He looked toward her, and she could tell he didn't want her to ask any more questions about that and feared that she would. Instead, she said, "What do you do now?"

"A little of everything," he said. "Like everyone."

"How boring."

He laughed. "Aren't you the same?"

"I'm trying not to be!" she said. "Life should have meaning. Or else…"

He let her thought hang in the air for a moment, then asked, "Or else it doesn't matter?"

"That's circular reasoning," she pointed out. "But yeah."

"Well, it doesn't," he said. "You should come to terms with that. No one has ever mattered, and you are not an exception."

Just when she thought she was getting somewhere with him.

"I matter to myself," she said. "To my mother, my friends, to…"

To you, maybe? she thought but did not say.

"I mean in the larger sense," he said. "Let yourself feel small."

"Sounds like a sad way to live," she said.

"It's very freeing, actually," he replied. "Don't you want to be free?"

She knew what he was getting at, but chose to needle him a bit instead of going down the road he wanted. "Am I not free?"

"You're here," he said. The first irrefutable indication that he had doubts just like she did. "You tell me."

"We all chose this," she pointed out. Perhaps arguing for her own benefit, as she did so often.

"But from among what options?" he lamented. "It's hard to say no to a life of ease among your fellow selected."

She burst out laughing, making a connection on that word, *select*, that she had not made before.

"What?"

She waved a hand, telling him to let it go.

In high school, her history class had studied world religions. Everyone had been thoroughly steeped in vaguely Christian theology, of course, but until that class she had not thought about it much, certainly not in any kind of rational way. Heaven was supposed to be what you wanted and hell what you did not, but in her decidedly agnostic Christmas-celebrating family, that was as far as it went.

Then, in tenth grade, they discussed the many sins that might deem you inadmissible for eternal reward and the ways different flavors of Christianity enumerated selection for salvation, and it had hit her suddenly. There were sects of Christianity that believed some people were among the select from birth, chosen by God for heavenly reward no matter what they did. No one could be certain whether they had been chosen or not, so they all had to live as if they had a chance. All the while, a vast many were doomed. How dark, how limiting, how sad.

And heaven looked down on or outright banned all the things that made life exciting—the anticipation and heat of romance, the debauchery of alcohol, the drama of conflict and triumph of being right when other people were wrong. Heaven wasn't desirable. Heaven was *boring*.

Hell might have been a punishment—in some cases for things people did knowingly, in some cases for things no fault of their own—but at least it maintained all that gave life vibrancy and all the humans that made it worth living. Just like the world melting down outside this simple town of pleasant drudgery.

There are so few rules left to break, though, she thought. All the useful vices that in high school loomed so impressive and thrilling now felt dull and done. What was the point anymore?

"How much longer do you work?" he asked.

She smirked. "Is that your version of *wanna get out of here*?"

He spread his hands as if to show they didn't hold a weapon, some vestige of a world where what we had to fear from each other was material violence instead of everything else.

"Where would we go, if we left?" she asked.

He opened his mouth as if to say something, then paused, frowned, and asked, "Have I misread something?"

So, she thought, the maybe-flirting had in fact come across that way. Which was fine.

"You think they're more or less likely to be watching this bookshelf or your bedroom?"

His face was somewhere between surprise and laughter, hers a kind of forced stoicism and steely determination. Because when had she ever hooked up with someone just because she wanted to?

She leaned across the distance between them and wasn't sure that it actually was what she wanted—but waiting for Zach to reply again so she could break up with him was not what she wanted, she knew that much. Following unspoken rules that probably no longer applied certainly wasn't, either.

Who cared if she was technically at work, and that he was practically a stranger, and that he annoyed her as much as he fascinated her? At least he made her feel *something*.

52

THEY STAYED IN THE STORE UNTIL WELL AFTER THE SUN HAD SET, not bothering to lock the door in all that time but knowing that no one would come in. The slightest thrill of nudity in this almost public place made the encounter more interesting than it otherwise would have been. But still she insisted on parting ways on the street corner in the light rain without even a kiss on the cheek, as if there were any appearances to maintain.

She walked home alone, buzzing with the unfamiliar joy of a new secret. Of course, she would have told Bea if she had known where she was, and nothing was stopping her from gushing to Alexa or Drew or anyone else. But in a life where nothing important happened and where probably someone knew everything, it felt crucial to have something to keep to herself. Even if it was an illusion.

Not dressed for the rain and not caring, she strode along smoothly. Pretending nothing had changed, since of course it hadn't.

Still, it felt momentous: giving up on Zach and with him the rest of the world, pivoting to this new place and the people in it.

It had been fun, sneaking around like a teenager, letting herself enjoy the touch of a new person, the feeling of excitingly unfamiliar skin against hers and unknown breathing in the dim light.

She ducked into the first restaurant that emanated good smells and ate a steaming bowl of noodle soup alone at a table near the window, gusted by the wind each time someone opened the door. She relished the brush of cold against her face in between bites, a reminder that the world went on blustering outside.

When she finally reached her apartment, Alexa wasn't there. A glance at the clock in her peripheral vision confirmed that it was early enough that this was not unusual, but still it felt like a blessing, a reward. As if such things existed.

She lay in her bed and set her mind adrift back to that afternoon, to allowing herself to indulge in frivolities she usually dismissed as stupid and silly. She let her head grow light and her smile wide, daydreaming like a child and confirming to herself that, though she had been unsure in this decision as with so many others lately, this choice had been, if not correct, at least what she wanted.

Perhaps those could be the same thing.

53

THE NEXT MORNING, SARA LEFT FOR HER USUAL RUN BEFORE ALEXA woke up, leaving her to eat breakfast alone. She considered for a second how she would feel to be abandoned like that and decided that she wouldn't care, so could safely assume that Alexa wouldn't either.

It was the earliest she'd been out since the first couple days in the community and the sun shone weak but bright, the kind of thin winter light that used to frustrate her as a child. Why wouldn't the sun just make up its mind? But that morning it was rejuvenating; she felt like she was floating through her run, each step fluid and easier than the last.

In her old life, she never would have exercised without a good workout playlist, or if she was forced to, she would have actively despised it. Some part of her mind did notice how her lungs burned and her nose ran in the cold air, but where she once would have called it miserable, today she called it happy instead, and she couldn't say why.

If only she understood that, perhaps she could employ the same trick with her entire life.

Most of her route wrapped around the perimeter of the village, stringing past the coast to the sound of crying seagulls and crashing waves, then dipping inland along the edge of the dunes, one foot landing on sand and the other on pavement. There was one place, though, about three quarters of the way around the town, where brambles descended upon the rear of the buildings and she had to turn into the streets to continue, dodging people and cafe tables arranged to catch the sun.

It was there that she was wrenched from her meditative rhythm.

"Bea!" she cried, certain the woman facing away from her a block away was her friend, though her vibrant blue hair had faded to an ugly near-gray and her black dress was boring, something the old Beatrice would never wear.

Bea turned around and broke out in a laugh as she saw Sara, and Sara laughed too, though she didn't know what was so funny.

"Are you on a run?" Bea shouted, jogging toward her, looking incredulous.

"Can you believe it?" Sara replied, understanding now.

They reached each other and collided into a brief hug. Sara didn't think she'd ever been so happy to see anyone.

"I'm so glad you're here," she said.

Bea laughed again. Sardonically? "I'm not sure about that, but I'm so glad to see you."

"I've looked for you in here every day."

"You too, honestly," Bea said, always having to put some joking distance between them. Sara wondered if she had, in fact, seen Bea at that party. "Since when do you *run?*"

Sara laughed again. "I recognize myself as little as you do."

Sara had a million things she wanted to say to Bea, but in that moment, nothing was important enough to surface above the milieu. She was happy just to see her friend, to know that there was someone here who knew her. They fell into step beside each other, bubbling with minor remarks about the morning and little questions about their lives.

"What are the apartments here like?" Bea asked eventually. Confirming that her life was as separate from the Community's usual path as it had seemed.

"Dorms, basically," Sara replied. "I've got this roommate who is actually named after Alexa."

"No! That's hilarious."

"Where do you live?"

A shrug. "A co-op, basically. On the edge of town."

"What a dream."

Bea laughed. "It's much cleaner than the ones in college, but just as much fun. I guess even co-op people grow up."

"Imagine that," Sara said. "And, um, is it true...?"

"Is what true?"

"Like, why you're allowed to be here?" Sara asked. It was a delicate question, she felt.

Bea didn't seem to agree. "I feel like I've got the best of it all, honestly," she said. "My life is fucking awesome, Sara."

"Really? You don't mind being..." Sara trailed off, waving her hand in the air vaguely.

Bea scoffed. "Dating in exchange for a place in some tech bro's world is all I ever did in Silicon Valley, and it's just as freeing here. Really. I get to come in here and eat the fancy food, but I get to go home to the kind of wild people I've always preferred."

"If you say so."

Bea stepped in front of her and whirled around, walking backwards so she could look at Sara's face. "You think I'm lying to you?"

Sara smiled. "I think you're gonna trip if you don't turn around."

"You're really drinking the Kool-Aid, huh?" Bea said, looking concerned, but stopping her backwards walk. "They want you to think being chosen is so great, but it's not."

Sara shrugged. "I wouldn't say I think that. I just…"

Bea stopped and put a hand on Sara's shoulder. "You're worried about me?"

"Of course I am! You're my best friend!"

Bea's expression softened. "I've been worried about you, too."

"I'm fine," Sara assured her.

Bea's smirk suggested she wasn't convinced.

"So what do you do all day?" Sara asked, changing the subject before Bea could press the issue. "Where are you headed right now?"

It was early enough that very few people were out.

"Here, actually," Bea said, gesturing toward a large squarish building that Sara had walked by at least a dozen times but never given much notice. "I'm going to a discussion group."

"A discussion group?" Sara asked.

"You know—complaining, discussing the philosophy of this place. Protesting, at least among ourselves," Bea said.

"That can't possibly be sanctioned," Sara said slowly, suddenly worried that Bea didn't understand the fundamentals of their lives.

Bea rolled her eyes and launched into an explanation of empowerment and ideas and how important it was to give people an outlet to consider different views even if there could be no change and, "Perhaps especially in places like this, so rudderless and where we all truly have no voice."

Sara stood there blinking, listening to Bea's tirade and feeling the words wash over her, thinking how useless it all sounded.

"But what's the point of agitating for change if there can be no change?" she finally asked. Trying to put her wonder and skepticism into words that made sense.

"It only seems like nothing can change until it does," Bea said.

"But we're not in the…"

"Real world anymore?" Bea supplied. "I know. But you can't pretend there's nothing that could be improved."

"There's nothing that we *can* improve. They change things—take away music, transition physical to virtual—and there's nothing we can do!"

Bea smirked. "Sounds like you should join us!"

Sara grimaced and found herself, oddly, glancing around. She had never spotted a camera on any of her runs, but she knew they were always watching. "It sounds like a good way to be singled out."

"Singled out?"

"If you were the company," Sara said slowly, "and you wanted to identify which people might cause problems within the Community, what would you do?"

"You sound paranoid, love," Bea said, patting her on the arm.

"You don't understand," Sara protested. "You're—what are you, anyway? If not a full member, what *are* you?"

"What am I?" Bea mocked, laughing. Sara felt herself lightening up at just the sound of Bea's laughter. "I'm the same as I've always been, just mooching off the profits of Silicon Valley. And no one kicked me out of Silicon Valley before!"

Sara laughed for real at that. "I do sound paranoid, huh."

"You do. You really do. But I've gotta get going."

"Got much to discuss." Sara raised an eyebrow.

Bea snorted. "As fruitless as you think it might be."

Bea started to go, but Sara reached out and caught her arm before she could duck through the door, pulling her into a hug. Bea struggled for just a moment, because she never could go along with any form of intimacy without registering her disapproval, but then she hugged Sara back, burying her face in Sara's hair. "I'll see you soon, okay?"

Sara sniffled, surprising herself with her impending tears. "Soon."

54

Fourteen months before the Community

IT WAS A FRIDAY NIGHT AFTER WORK AND THEIR TINY APARTMENT was crowded, just the way she liked it.

When she and Zach first downgraded from the luxury apartment in the new complex to the dingy place with 1990s fixtures and a wall-mounted AC, she'd assumed they would stop having people over. The place may have been half the price—something they very much needed, as Zach stopped taking a salary and cut everyone else's in a desperate bid to keep the company afloat—but it was also kind of embarrassing. Her parents' generation had been buying houses at this point in their lives, not subleasing shitty apartments!

But instead, they started having people over more often, because how else do you make a depressing place feel like home besides filling it with people you love?

The walls were a sickly yellow that was once white, the bathroom counter had grout that was impossible to keep clean, and the hardwood floor in the hall squeaked constantly, but the presence of friends made it cozy.

And since it had a careless landlord, candles were allowed. She filled every horizontal surface with them, keeping them lit and the space warm as often as possible—tamed fire, kept captive in a glass on the counter.

Hakim and Lina from work, dating now, were chopping vegetables in the kitchen. Since there wasn't room for anyone else in there, Bea and Sara and Zach sat in the living room, clicking through songs on an old playlist of Sara's from middle school, alternately mocking and praising her childhood taste.

"Oh, I remember this song!" Bea said. "Remember when Ariana Grande was coming out with a new album every six months?"

Sara snapped her fingers, getting the speaker's attention, and swished her hand through the air to skip the song. "And I've heard every one of them way too many times."

"I always thought all her music sounded the same," Zach said.

"Sacrilege," Sara replied.

Bea picked something vaguely electronic that Sara barely remembered.

She leaned forward to get some food from the spread on the coffee table, smearing cheese across a cracker.

"So, how're things with you, Beatrice?" Zach asked. They'd known each other for years and yet he never shortened her name to Bea.

"I live a glamorous existence, you know," she said, striking a pose like a model.

"Oh yeah?" Zach asked.

"Sara didn't tell you?" Bea asked. Sara cringed. "Turns out there's an appetite for washed up twenty-seven-year-olds among the millionaire set."

Zach frowned. "Got a new boyfriend?"

"She's signed up to be a sugar baby," Sara said.

Zach's jaw dropped.

Lina shouted from the kitchen, "I want to hear everything!"

"Some rich dude pays you to date him?"

"It's not much," Bea said, eyes twinkling, "but it's honest work."

"It's one step away from prostitution!" Zach protested.

Bea shrugged. "Oldest profession there is."

Lina entered the room, carrying a salad bowl. She nodded back toward the kitchen. "He'll finish up. I don't want to miss you breaking Zach with this news."

Bea laughed. "It's really no big deal, guys. Mostly I just go out in public with him, showing that he can get a girl at all."

"Just the one guy?" Lina asked.

"I dated around a bit at first, but mostly they want consistency. They're less comfortable with it than I am."

"No one should be surprised by that," Sara said.

Bea and Sara turned toward each other and laughed.

Hakim entered then, carrying some pasta and a baked filet of fish. "I thought you were a big feminist," he said. "Aren't you always going to marches and stuff?"

Bea gestured at him, standing there wearing an apron and holding their dinner. "That's feminism," she said. "And besides, part of what our grandmothers fought for was the right to fuck whoever they want."

"For money," Zach said.

Bea smiled. "For any reason at all."

"But there's a right reason…" Zach trailed off, clearly deciding he didn't want to actually engage.

"And a wrong one?" Bea finished for him. "Who's to say which reasons are right?"

"You wouldn't be interested in any of these guys if they weren't paying you for it!"

"Maybe I would," Bea said. "I guess we'll never know."

"But it was their money that got you out with them in the first place," he insisted.

Sara started loading up a plate. With her attention on the pasta bowl, she said, "Well, we only started dating because you were my boss."

She glanced over her shoulder at Zach, who looked decidedly uncomfortable. Lina and Hakim were laughing.

It was true, whether or not he wanted to admit it. All romantic relationships were in some sense also business relationships; people spent so much money on each other. But a relationship with your boss harkened back to the days of marriage as a woman's way to sell her life into the care of a man. What Sara had done may not have been motivated by money—she hadn't intended to sleep her way to the top by any means—but it amounted to an exchange of security for affection, and wasn't that almost the same?

"Anyway, it's positively feminist to keep a roof over my head," Bea said. "And, really, what's feminism when the world is melting down?"

Lina rolled her eyes. "Speaking of—you hear the latest about the Yellow Fever outbreak in Georgia?"

"I assume you don't mean Eastern Europe?" Zach asked.

"Or the million refugees in Bangladesh, riots in Paris again, a deadly heatwave in Australia, blah, blah, blah," Hakim said.

Bea raised her eyebrows. "I'd expect such nonchalance about death and destruction from Zach, not the two of you."

Hakim shrugged. "I'm just glad I live in a suburban wonderland. No outbreaks or riots here, everyone's too NIMBY and stressed."

Sara found herself laughing, though there really was nothing funny about the state of the world. At some point, she'd become inured to it. Wasn't it inevitable? Hadn't it always been this way? Or if not, hadn't they begun a march off the cliff long ago, a march that could only end one way?

There was nothing to do but laugh.

55

EVEREST STOPPED INTO THE BOOKSTORE THAT EVENING SHORTLY BE-
fore Sara's shift ended. She knew that he knew she would be there, but he
behaved as if running into her was a coincidence, leaning casually against the
counter and asking, "Got any book recommendations?"

She was sitting behind the counter about a third of the way through a
thriller set during the Cold War. She slid the book toward him.

"Could be fun to lose yourself in the threat of nuclear annihilation."

He raised his eyebrows. "Sounds cheerful."

"Positively lovely to dread the end of the world, rather than expect it."

He picked up the book and looked at the cover. A rather ridiculous drawing of a man in a suit looking furtively over his shoulder. "You think this man
would want to think the future he was fighting for would be so dreary?"

"The guy on the cover is the Soviet spy," she replied. "He fought for
a different future."

"Ah, so then he'd be vindicated to see how we turned out."

She laughed lightly. "What're you doing here?"

"Well, in a post-cellphone world I have to actually see you if I want
to see you."

Her stomach warmed at the fact that he wanted to see her, and she
couldn't keep the smile off her face. "What's up with that, anyway? You must
know more about this no-phone rule than I do."

He shrugged. "Unimportant, I think."

"What, phones, or why we don't have them?"

He walked over to the nearest shelf and scanned the books there as he
said, "It's like this: they have the online patterns of every other person. What
do they not have? The offline behavior. That's what we're for."

"Seems suspect," she said, coming out from behind the counter to see what
he was looking at: the psychology shelf. How appropriate. "We change our
behavior without phones. What can we tell them about the outside world?"

"We change our behavior anyway," he said. He pulled what looked like
a college textbook from the shelf, heavy and shiny and unread. He began
flipping through it and stopped on the first chapter heading, pointing to a
sidebar on the scientific method. "It's a controlled experiment."

"Very smooth," she said, laughing. "Did you know that would be there?"

He laughed, too. "It would have been awkward if I just kept turning the pages until I found it, so I guess I got lucky."

She glanced at the time and then said, "My shift is over in a few minutes. But you knew that."

He grinned. "I figure we'll have to see each other outside this store occasionally."

"What makes you think I want to be seen in public with you?" she asked.

"You're new here, not me," he replied. "I'm the one with a reputation to uphold. I think I should worry about that."

She laughed. "Ouch."

"So, dinner?"

"Like a date?" she asked.

"Hard to say, when we'll both be going to a restaurant anyway and neither of us will pay," he said. "But sure. Like a date."

She shrugged. "I've always thought a dine and dash would make a good first date. Too bad that's sanctioned here."

"I can't tell if you're joking."

"And I'll just leave you wondering," she said. "But they let me in here, so what do you think?"

"Well, you did ask me about the black market in our first conversation," he said.

She began closing up the shop for the night, which was a very minimal process of making sure the windows were shut and then flipping the Open sign on the door to Closed. "I'm still wondering about that, by the way."

"Of course you are," he said. "But you know no one calls it that."

"Sure, just like no one calls the marginal women *prostitutes*."

Everest looked shocked at that and Sara felt herself flush, not sure why that had been the line it was scandalous to cross.

"They're not all women," he said.

This caught her a bit off guard. "Do you hang out with a lot of male hookers?"

He rolled his eyes. "Trying so hard to be edgy, huh?"

She harrumphed.

"But seriously," he said. "It's just like society at large. There have always been and always will be people on the edge, only a part of the main culture. It's not going away, but it's so much better than it could be."

She raised a skeptical eyebrow.

Seeing that she didn't buy his argument yet, he went on. "The analogy would be...undocumented immigrants. Or even slaves, where slavery still exists. People without a place."

"You're saying the marginal people are the company's slaves?" Sara thought about Bea, so happy on the fringes. "Slaves are compelled to work, and hidden away. I wouldn't say either of those things about the marginal people."

"So it wasn't a perfect analogy!"

"Nobody's forcing them to be here," she said. "I'm sure undocumented immigrants would love to change their situation. Slaves *certainly* would."

"You're right, okay?" he conceded, holding up his hands. Sara was glad to see that she could win an argument. Until that moment, she hadn't been sure she still had it in her. "But aren't we all kind of the same, here? What are you doing, that's different than that? Everyone is *compelled to work*, to use your term."

"That's not the same, and you know it."

"I'm not discounting atrocities, Sara." He sounded almost mad, though his voice retained its levity. "My point is that it's all the same, really, when you look at it from far enough away: no society can fit everyone, and every society has twisted ways of slotting us all together."

"Is this society you imagine just the Community, or the whole world?"

He paused. Sighed. "All I'm saying is that putting some people in gray athleisure and simple apartments and others in short skirts and rundown houses makes things easier. For them."

For *them*. She knew who that meant.

"It's all so imperfect," she said, knowing that was a ridiculous understatement.

"I'm surprised you hadn't come to this conclusion yourself," he said. "You jump straight to the worst explanation for everything. But it's not about survival, or necessity—just order. They're just organizing the world, the same way they always have."

"The grand illusion of choice," Sara concluded, surprising herself as the words left her mouth. Heavy with truth.

"Exactly."

"I might have gotten there eventually," she replied. It was a disgusting thought, a tragic way to see the world, but she didn't think he was wrong. No one had ever accused her of being an optimist. She felt a bit sour, but also hungry—and uninterested in eating alone. "Food?"

They stepped out into the evening: a light breeze flitting between the buildings in the last of the sun, the sky a telling shade of rich pink that made her cringe. Nothing caused by wildfire smoke and pollution should get to look so incomparably lovely.

"Beautiful sky tonight," Everest said.

"Yeah," she replied. Why ruin two peoples' moods?

They walked on in silence, not comfortable. Very much a first date kind of silence, she thought, though she was basing that off of media she'd consumed rather than her own experience.

They approached the message tower and she considered walking past it, remembering Alexa's reaction to seeing her use it, but concluded in an instant that she was too curious about what Everest might say. She held up a hand as they neared it and said, "Just a sec."

He didn't make any immediate snarky comments, which was a mark in his favor.

The familiar message screen materialized before her and she clicked on the notification from her mother. A general life update, longer than Sara ever would have sent, rambling a bit through news of their neighbors, who were strangers to Sara, comments on growing unrest in the area and *We had the most lovely dinner with Zach the other night, he says he misses you!*

"Who's Zach?" Everest asked, peering over her shoulder.

"No one," Sara said, before realizing that if he'd read her message, it wasn't visible only through her contacts, as she'd thought. "You can see these?" she asked. Another illusion—her last remaining semblance of privacy—shattered.

He blanched, took a step back and said, "Um, I guess so."

She tried to shrug it off. "I just figured since it's in the contacts that meant—"

"It must be malfunctioning," he said. "Strange."

"Yeah…"

"Things are always so buggy," he said. "You know."

"Oh, believe me, I know," she said, mind still turning. "I used to work for a startup."

"She divulges something about herself!"

She laughed and they began to walk away. She wondered if there was a proper way to close her messages or if they remained there, public for everyone to see. Like everything else. "Now if only *you* would."

"What kind of startup was it?" he asked instead of answering. "Nothing too frivolous, I hope."

She shrugged. "They're all a bit frivolous, aren't they? Not solving problems like world hunger."

"There are plenty of apps about getting food," he said. "I'm sure they'd tell you they had something to do with feeding the hungry."

She thought back to their gimmicky breakthrough project, delivering a single french fry to new users of their service. It was admittedly tongue in cheek, but she found it hilarious at the time. Now she found it emblematic of an excess she had once been blind to.

"I'm so glad I never worked anywhere like that," Everest said.

"Yeah," said Sara, unsure how to feel. "Me too."

But wasn't their new job, whatever it actually was, no better?

56

THEY WANDERED THE TOWN, THE CONVERSATION LIGHTENING UNTIL they were both laughing, until her smile felt genuine and semi-permanent in a way it hadn't in years. The jokes were mostly dark and self-deprecating, old stories of her own ineptness or his state of entirely having given up. Anything else would have been insincere.

At some point, impulsively, Sara took Everest's hand. She couldn't remember ever holding Zach's hand in public, a habit born out of a year of hiding their relationship from their coworkers that continued into their regular lives even once the secret broke. Holding hands felt almost unbearably intimate.

The sky faded to light pink and lovely, as if nature agreed with her assessment of how things were going. Maybe it didn't come from smoke after all; maybe it was natural and thus deserving of her awe. Nauseatingly romantic, either way.

If they spoke, it was not anything remarkable enough that she could remember it later. Commenting on the pleasantness of the breeze, the beauty of the sky, the perfection of the light at that time of evening. If only it could be late evening all day long, Sara thought, everything would be better in the world. Nothing bad could happen at this time of day.

They stopped for ice cream and called it dinner.

"Want to go back to my place?" Everest asked, but he didn't really need to.

His place, inexplicably, was an apartment all to himself, set above some shops in the heart of town. Besides the fact that it had a single bed instead of the mirrored twins her room had, it resembled hers in every way.

She thought to ask why he had no roommate, but was distracted when he kissed her. There was something vaguely suspicious in his privacy, something that made her pause, but it wasn't enough to make her push him away. Her mind refused to divert any attention from the feeling of his mouth on hers and his muscles under her hands and his hands on her back.

57

SHE WAS STILL AND SILENT IN A WORLD SO BLUE IT PUSHED OUT ANY other thought. The memory of things not this vibrant hung just out of reach; the awareness of all she could not recall hovered there, impossible to grasp. The strain of trying was exhausting, so she stopped.

Nothing changed perceptibly, but the particular shade became gradually darker, as if she sunk deeper below the ocean or the light above was drawn slowly, delicately from the world. It made her feel cold, but not uncomfortable. Her fingers seemed impossibly far away.

A jellyfish appeared before her, or maybe it had always been there. A beautiful pale orange, tendrils stretching off into obscurity, pulsing like a heartbeat, buffeted by a light breeze and swaying. She lost herself in its motion, eyes going unfocused as she watched it floating through the air before her.

Except it wasn't air, she realized all at once—of course it wasn't—and as soon as she knew this, the water invaded. Pressure squeezed her every pore and held her arms heavy and flooded lungs that begged for breath. The cold was suddenly intense and inescapable instead of distant, but oh, it didn't matter because every thought was drawn inward to her desperation for air.

The jellyfish hung before her, forgotten, translucent.

Her lungs aching, burning, her skin on fire, the water pushing in so strong she might collapse upon herself at any moment, her struggles ineffectual and the surface invisible and the jellyfish just *floating* there in front of her. So gentle and small and pristine.

Going nowhere while her heart beat erratically, spiraling toward breakdown, driving wildly faster. Her hair tangled around her pounding head and her arms thrashed against the incredible smoothness of the frigid water. Tears pricked in her eyes.

The jellyfish pulsed past, calm amid the panic.

All at once, she knew what she had to do. But could she do it?

She stared at the jellyfish through salt-stung eyes, pushing any fear or pain away, watching its simplicity and perfection, so bright against the blue darkness. She fought the urge to struggle. Fought the urge to flee.

Her heartbeat gradually slowed, matching the jellyfish's every contraction, pushing blood through her veins like the jellyfish pushed through the water—reliable, steady, mimicking the jellyfish, so gentle and safe.

And then, heart in her ears and tears in her eyes, she drew a breath, so deep and profound that she could feel the air reaching her even through the weight of all that water and—

She opened her eyes to the reality of Everest's bed, warm and dry and utterly unlike where she had just been. Her heart still pounding, her lungs labored for air. But everything was fine now, she told herself, it had all been fine, and she quieted her breath so as not to wake him and rolled to one side to await morning.

58

Eighteen months before the Community

"YOU'VE HEARD OF THE NEW INTENTIONAL COMMUNITIES?" BEA ASKED.

Zach and Sara were sitting on Bea's couch drinking tea, and Bea had emerged from the kitchen with a plate piled high with pancakes.

"You need any help with that?" Sara offered.

Bea shook her head. "Well, have you?"

"Yes, we have," Zach said. "Sara thinks they're ridiculous and I think they're fascinating."

Bea set the pancakes on the coffee table and sank into the couch beside Sara. "But do either of you think they're the future?"

"Are you going to bring any syrup, or…" Sara asked.

"These are finger pancakes."

"What?" Zach looked perplexed.

"I don't have any clean dishes." The price of water had spiked recently, and Sara guessed that was Bea's excuse for not running the dishwasher.

Sara laughed and shook her head. "You're just assuming our hands are clean."

"Your hands are always clean," Bea said. "Zach, though, I don't know."

He looked down at his own hands as if he didn't know either, then got up to go wash them in the kitchen. Bea chuckled and reached for a pancake, rolling it up and starting to eat it like a hot dog. "Anyway, answer the question."

"The future?" Sara asked, sipping her tea. "I don't know about that. They seem to be part of the present."

Bea snorted. "Don't be cute. You know what I mean."

"I hope it doesn't come to that, I guess," Sara said. "I don't love the idea of a company controlling even more of my life."

"Maybe they can manage it better than you can."

Sara looked at her sharply. "You think I need the help?"

"I know *I* could do better, anyway."

Sara frowned. "Where's the confident Bea I know and love?"

Bea opened her mouth to reply, but before she could, Zach re-entered the room, waving his wet hands. "I'm super skeptical of this finger pancake concept," he announced, even as he reached for one. "How am I supposed to do this?"

Bea grinned. "You can figure this out."

Zach considered the pancake and started eating it like a piece of bread. He chewed dramatically and squinted. "Bit dry."

Sara held up his cup of tea.

"Sara was just saying that she's not a fan of the intentional communities," Bea said to Zach. "What do you think?"

"Some are better than others," he said. "Like any startup ecosystem, some are doomed to fail. But the concept is compelling. I can see why investors are all over it."

"You're analyzing the business case."

"Of course," he said. "How else should I assess it? Based on the user experience? I'm not their target audience."

"Oh, and who is?" Bea asked.

"Depends which one you're talking about."

"How about one of the religious ones," Sara said. "They make it easy by telling you outright who they won't accept."

"It's an ingenious innovation on church planting," Zach said. "Certainly not for me, but man, megachurches rake in the dough."

"It's basically a cult," Bea said.

"And cults are famously so successful," Zach said. "Until they...aren't."

Bea laughed at that.

"The only ones that sound at all interesting to me are the eco-city places," Sara said. "I really like how green they are."

"In every sense of the word," Bea said.

Sara had to acknowledge she was right about that. They may have been carbon negative and full of plants, but they also charged exorbitantly to be part of their experiment in future living.

"Are you betting on an individual startup or an offshoot from a megacorporation?" Bea asked.

"The startups are way more interesting," Sara said. "More creative— far more radical relative to the real world, which is what we need, I think. But probably too risky. I'd never live there. What happens if your home goes belly up?"

"Exactly," Bea agreed. "I've been having this conversation with everyone lately, and no one gets that. The big companies can offer stability, but it's all a bit creepy."

"They're mostly A/B testing, right?" Sara asked. "You live there for free, but you can use only their products. They have you try things out that they might turn around and sell to richer people?"

"Something like that," Bea said. "I've heard it's really basic and a lot of tedium."

"But hey, no rent!" Sara said.

"The ones that attempt to be a real business are most interesting to me," Zach said.

"Of course they would be," Bea said.

"If you can successfully connect good living to a profit motive, life will actually improve for a lot of people," Zach said. "Set it up and let the free market run away with it. We know our current system isn't working, and we also know that things like providing housing for all is cheaper than providing all the services unhoused people need. You just have to align the incentives."

"Such a social justice warrior," Bea teased.

Zach shook his head. "It's just good business. Take better care of people, they'll be better consumers."

"And there it is!" Sara said.

Zach laughed. "No one spends money when they're afraid of the future."

"Or when they don't have any!"

"That, too." He chomped on another pancake. "You know, these aren't half-bad."

59

SHE NEVER EXPECTED TO GROW ACCUSTOMED TO THIS NEW LIFE, BUT it became ordinary just like all of her previous lives. She adjusted to college and meager employment and going to an office every day and raucous startup life and then unemployment. Each radically different schedule felt inevitable after a few weeks; this was no different. The disorientation of the first days faded quickly into an unsettling sameness, each day just rolling by.

The routine became ever more normal and she became less self-conscious about the constant watching with each passing hour. Even the gentle motion of the town at high tide felt common, expected; it would have been strange to live without the floor ever rocking or bobbing on the waves. She began to understand how Everest could be so dismissive of everything. This place taught complacency.

Her morning run grew faster. Her dyed hair, already showing significant roots when she arrived, grew out noticeably. The line demarcating when she had stopped caring—months before she entered the Community—dropped lower and lower until her hair began to look blonde again, lighter than it had been since freshman year.

One day, a month after arrival, she realized she hadn't thought in terms of algorithms or optimization in days.

She was a bit disturbed by how little she reacted to everything that unnerved her. The shoe store and shop selling dresses were but the first of many places that appeared just after she spoke aloud about needing them. The more she looked, the more she found inconsistencies between the appearance of the town and its physical reality. She continued to search for music that she could choose, rather than just happen upon, but never succeeded.

The frequency with which she checked the message tower declined; she didn't want to know what she would learn when she did. Her parents remained in a shelter. No news came from Emily.

Sara made up elaborate stories about what could have happened to her, telling herself that Emily had found a caravan of roving hippies to live with, or that she had found her way into a high-paying job in San Francisco, or that she had entered a different community much like this one. But she knew that if any of those stories were true, Emily would have found a way to let her know.

Her fear melted into grief, as if the worst had happened, even though of course she couldn't know.

Somehow, despite it all, she woke up calm and went through her day calm. Her emotions, like her mind, dulled through lack of use.

At least she was in the best shape of her life, she thought. She was exercising now more than she had even when forced through the daily rigor of gym class as a child.

About once a week, she was pulled from her bed to compete in some silly game with strangers, each time more routine and absurd than the last. She made no effort at conversation, just participated in a modified version of capture-the-flag in the woods and volleyball on the low-tide's exposed beach. Community building? It felt more like an experiment than anything else they did.

She almost forgot about the pretext of testing anything.

The parties, so frequent in the early days, ceased entirely. She occasionally saw other people summoned to evenings at the museum just like the one she had experienced—some kind of heady entree to their flashy new life, where they could pretend it would be fun and beautiful. She did not envy them.

Her life became smooth and easy, if utterly devoid of any real excitement or joy. Even sleeping with Everest became boring after a few times, the adventure of a new person fading quickly as she got to know him. Everest was compelling, but he could not be enough to make her whole life compelling, and she had the strange feeling that he should have. That he thought he did. She wondered if she believed anything he said. She wondered if *he* did.

She talked to Alexa about stupid things, never bringing up the relationship for reasons she couldn't name. She replied to her parents ever more days after they wrote to her. She chatted with Bea over coffee or lunch but made excuses not to see the co-op, perhaps afraid of what seeing it might shake loose in her.

Sometimes thoughts would resurface of what Everest insisted was not a black market; she would look at him or Alexa differently for a moment, wonder what they knew that she did not. Consider that as much as she thought of herself as a freethinker, she was the only one not breaking any rules. Try to guess what she would buy if she could and realize there was nothing she needed and that she had long ago forgotten what it really felt like to want something.

She didn't grow more content with her place there, not really. No matter that she became used to it, comfortable. Comfort and contentment were not the same. Her life felt like it belonged to someone else, someone quieter. More of a follower than she wanted to be.

Sitting across from Everest in a cafe, not talking much because in a life without external news or internal progress there wasn't much to say, she reflected on her stagnation, trying to convince herself that wasn't what this was. Trying to read his mind through his brown eyes and slight smile.

The life she imagined as a child had been revealed as a delusion, a falsehood that was necessary for a developing brain but useless now. No more possible than time travel back to an age when this was still the future.

Would she be happier now if the generation who'd raised her had not spent so much time lying that everything would be okay? Would she be happier if she had never believed them?

Some part of her was certain she wouldn't be where she was if the fabrications had been more obvious. She had believed them whole-heartedly and chased a future that never could have existed. Having reality laid bare felt like the ultimate betrayal. But if she had never believed at all, she would probably be somewhere worse.

She didn't want to leave, though, much as her subconscious railed against the confines of the Community. Because where would she go, anyway? This might be constraining and boring and a waste of her life, but at least she *had* a life.

What she wanted, she told Everest, was someone to blame.

He found this funny, had laughed and laughed, and she wished for Bea in that moment—but not enough to seek her out. Not enough to admit that being selected for this place meant nothing at all.

They had been told as kids that they could be anything but realized now that *anything* was a much smaller infinity than they'd imagined—one with invisible limits that were nevertheless unbreakable. That's what growing up was supposed to be, of course. But the possibilities that should have been there to explore had been torn away by rising seas and wars over water, by hurricanes and wildfires and a stratified economy that left everyone out.

She wouldn't be happier if she had never believed.

She would be happier if she didn't now feel so complicit in her own failure. She had been far too focused on her own little life to live up to the grand expectations of her younger self. There had been too many protests unattended, too much panic ignored for far too long. It wouldn't have been enough, but at least she could sit here a failure and know that she had tried.

She thought back on all that suburbia that stretched on forever, stoplights and strip malls and silver-painted fire hydrants for miles and miles and years and years. Forever, until it wasn't anymore.

That long list of landmark accords in cities that everyone hailed for their progress—Kyoto and Paris and Copenhagen—but which in the end no one listened to until it was too late.

Parking lots full of Teslas that flowed like rivers, which they thought would save them but didn't, in the end.

And such inadequate caring among the previous generations, such certainty that this could be someone else's problem in perpetuity—that it really wasn't as bad as it seemed; that life went on and always would. Fear and concern came too late.

Did they know this was coming when they told her that if she worked hard and went to college, the world would lay at her feet?

Did they know that the world at her feet would be in ruins?

She felt fear in those long days of pathetic leisure, but mostly resignation. Resentment toward those who got to create the mess but never live with it. Hatred but also pity toward the governments who sat by—so *sure* someone else would act. And, of course, toward the corporations who showed an interest in humanity now because they needed bodies, not because they actually cared.

If you're not the customer, you're the product.

Too bad, she thought, that no one had managed to commoditize things in a way that could leave them with stability and safety and prosperity. Even with the benefit of hindsight, she couldn't imagine what that might have been.

One day, she checked messages and felt her heart sink through the ground at her mother's words.

They had packed up the car again, her mother wrote. They were fleeing, heading inland, away from an outbreak of some spreading tropical disease that spilled out into the city and spurred a surge of violence. They couldn't ignore it anymore.

She imagined her parents and their pets crammed together in an old station wagon, driving into the unknown.

It all fell apart so quickly.

How bad must it have been for her parents to move again, weakening the hope that Emily might find them?

She felt panic crush in around her ears and an urgent need to run to them. The knowledge hit her—overwhelming, desperate—that such a thing was impossible and useless, anyway. It almost brought her to her knees.

She couldn't save them, not by running to them and not by thinking of them. She thought of them anyway, picturing their fear, wondering where they found their meals and where they slept.

Like Everest advised—and like she felt herself doing instinctively—she adopted the mantra that nothing mattered. There was no other way out of a depression fueled by fear and despondency except to see that such gloom, like everything else, was a waste.

There was supposed to be a second part to such a message, though. *Nothing matters* does not tell you how to live your life. It tells you not to live your life at all, and that couldn't be right. There had to be more. But what?

60

SARA LAY IN HER BED IN THE DARK AND ALEXA LAY IN HER OWN BED across the room, deep in the kind of late-night talk that flowed more easily than during the day.

Alexa was lamenting the limits of her childhood—"and that's why I think my dad didn't actually want us to succeed, because it would make him feel worse about himself for going fucking nowhere"—and Sara was pretending to listen.

The parallels to college propelled her back in time, to a similar night with Bea, lying on symmetrical beds and analyzing their lives the way only young adults could. Trying to emerge into the real world but not having any idea what that meant. Convincing each other and themselves that they understood why they were the people they were and how to become the people they wished to be.

"You know how they say you grow up to marry a man like your father?"

It sounded like she wanted a reply, so Sara said, "Yeah, I've heard that."

"Do you think it's true?"

Sara thought of her own father, perfect in her eyes, so silly and calm and kind. Nothing like any of the idiot boys she'd dated, who seemed so young and useless to her even when they were supposedly independent, grown men.

"I don't think I'll find a man like my dad," she said, realizing how sappy and ridiculous that sounded only after she said it.

"Awww, are you a daddy's girl?" Alexa asked, barely containing laughter.

Sara bristled. "I just mean that everyone I've ever dated is a mess."

Alexa sat with that for a moment, then said, "Fine, don't tell me."

Sara laughed. "I'm not hiding anything!"

"Sure you're not, Miss My-Life-Is-Perfect," Alexa snapped. "You're here just like I am, and don't tell me you don't think that means you failed."

"Do *you* think you failed by coming here?" Sara asked softly.

She could practically hear Alexa roll her eyes. "We're talking about you, Sara. I see you every day. You hate it here."

"I don't *hate* it."

"Tell me what you feel, then, if not hate."

"I feel trapped," she said.

"Humanity—for basically ever—lived much more limited lives than we do," Alexa pointed out. "Don't make yourself out to be more special than you are."

Sara sighed dramatically, trying to let Alexa know she wanted her to shut up without having to say it.

"So tell me about some of these guys you dated," Alexa said.

She hadn't planned to tell Alexa about Everest, rather liking how she felt having a man to sneak away to, all of their moments just between the two of them and whoever might watch them on the cameras she knew were hidden somewhere. But suddenly she felt the need to divulge everything spilling up inside her, like the urge to jump off a cliff whenever a wide expanse opened up before her. It felt slightly suicidal but also like a terribly good idea.

"Well, actually, I'm seeing someone now," she said.

"You sound like it's the '50s."

"I don't think people talked that way even then, but fine," Sara said, drawing out the next words extravagantly, "if you want to hear it this way, I'm *fucking* someone."

Alexa burst out laughing. "So much better. And also, I can't believe it! How are you still this cranky?"

Sara laughed. "Guess you just lucked out with roommates."

"Oh my God, you can't leave me hanging like this, you have to tell me more!"

Sara kept laughing. Her mind floated back to the last time she had a conversation like this, with Bea about Zach, and both how different and how similar it had been. Talking back then with a friend she knew far better about a guy she cared about far less, and saying all the same things.

61

Fourteen months before the Community

"WHAT TIME IS YOUR FLIGHT?" SARA ASKED, LEANING AGAINST THE kitchen counter in the apartment that had until that morning been Christina and X's.

"Christina's is at two o'clock and mine's at three thirty," X shouted from the bedroom.

"Shouldn't we get going, then?"

It was almost noon.

"It'll be fine," Christina said, emerging from the bedroom with two backpacks and two enormous suitcases, all in a bright shade of pink.

"I don't drive like Eric," Sara reminded them.

"It'll be *fine*."

"X, come on!" Sara shouted.

"Go load up the car and turn in the keys," X replied, voice muffled. It sounded like they were struggling to close their bag. "Be right there."

Christina smiled conspiratorially at Sara. "This is life with X, always."

"I'd lose my mind," Sara said, opening the door and shouldering one of Christina's backpacks.

"I did, long ago," Christina told her.

They headed off down the hall, Sara shaking the keys to Christina's car in her hand nervously. "You sure about the car?" she asked in the elevator.

Christina laughed. "What am I gonna do with it? Canada outlawed clunkers like that years ago."

"Like a civilized country."

"Maybe the last one left," Christina agreed.

They emerged into the heat of the afternoon, Christina letting out an "oof" in reaction to the temperature. "I will not miss this."

"Vancouver gets heat waves too."

"Not ones that last for months," she replied. She stopped by the car and dropped her things. "Load up and I'll go check out."

Talking as if the apartment she'd lived in for three years was a hotel room.

Sara unlocked the car and stuffed Christina's bags into the trunk, then walked around it slowly, taking in its peeling, rusty paint and completely un-aerodynamic profile. Hideous, but it was the first car that had ever been hers, which made her love it somehow. Christina had sold it to her for a dollar.

Christina returned from the office, twin braids bouncing as she jogged across the parking lot. "No X yet?"

Sara shook her head. "All set?"

Christina nodded. "I'll VR in tomorrow for the walk-through."

Sara cupped her hands around her mouth and shouted, "X! We're gonna be late!"

She had no idea if X could hear her, but it felt good to yell.

Christina chatted idly about her plans—the book she'd downloaded for the flight, the meal she'd preordered, the new suburban Vancouver apartment she'd already leased…

Sara wasn't really listening. She hated being late, and even if it wasn't her flight they were about to miss, it still made her nervous.

Finally, the elevator doors slid open and deposited X into the sunlight. Half their hair was shaved to an inch long and the other half dyed bright red and cut shoulder length; their outfit somehow hearkened back to the '80s and the '50s at the same time, all blocky shoulders and bright colors and feminine skirts; their three duffel bags weighed down their tiny frame.

"I'm here!" they said, shuffling into the back seat with their bags so quickly it almost felt like the other two were the ones making them all late.

Sara got into the driver's seat with a heavy sigh and Christina sat down beside her.

"I can't believe you still have a manual," Sara said, shifting the car into gear.

"*You* still have a manual," Christina replied.

They'd spent the previous weekend making sure Sara knew how to drive it. She hadn't driven in years, let alone a minivan with a manual transmission. The car was at least twenty years old.

They sat in silence for the first few minutes as Sara focused on driving, carefully shifting through stoplights and then accelerating onto the freeway. It was only the second time she'd taken the car up that fast, and it felt like it might rattle apart, but at least she'd avoided a stall. She let out a breath and relaxed.

"Hey, thanks for driving us," X said from the backseat.

"Least I can do," Sara replied. She signaled, moved carefully over into the left lane, and flicked on the cruise control. "So, X, Christina told me all about her plans. Besides melting in the humidity and relishing in a libertarian paradise on the island, what're you thinking?"

"Gee, tell me how you really feel," X said good-naturedly.

Sara laughed a little. They'd been over her skepticism of X's techno-utopian ambitions enough times. "Go on."

"I'm gonna lay on a beach drinking mai tais and let cryptocurrency support a lazy-ass lifestyle while y'all toil in the sawmills of history."

Occasionally X's Texan roots revealed themselves.

"Until a hurricane wipes your hut off the map," Sara replied.

"My *mansion*," X corrected.

"Still."

"I'll take a hurricane over the Big One any day!"

Sara rolled her eyes. X had always said they planned to make a fortune in California and escape before an earthquake leveled the place, and it looked like they were getting their wish. They hadn't exactly made a fortune, but they'd been a blockchain true believer since elementary school and were in it for the long haul.

"Besides, Puerto Rico's been dying for twenty years. They know how to survive the apocalypse better than the rest of us."

"Not to put too fine a point on it," Christina said.

"Isn't that why you're going home?" X said. "Escaping America while you still can?"

They were mostly joking, Sara knew, but the sliver of truth in it sent a chill down her spine.

Christina shrugged. "BC was always the endgame."

Sara looked at her friend out of the corner of her eye, trying to read her expression. Christina gazed out the windshield at the looming empty hangars and barren runways of NASA Ames Research Center, face impassive. She'd gone to school for aerospace engineering but never had a relevant job. Would she find one in Canada?

Sara wished she could be as free spirited as her friends, cheerfully ending their relationship of three years to move far away from one another, leaving their lives behind without any apparent qualms. Just the thought of it stressed her out.

It didn't help, she supposed, that she never really left home. Her whole life she'd lived within thirty miles of the Pacific and the redwoods, with short, wet winters and long, dry summers, the threat of an earthquake always hanging over her head. She couldn't really imagine a life outside the rolling hills of Northern California or with her parents more than an hour's drive away.

62

SARA SAT ON THE SEA WALL A DOZEN FEET ABOVE THE BEACH AT LOW tide, watching a storm thrashing against the ocean in the distance. There was something magical about being able to see all the way to the horizon, watching the weather approach long before it arrived. Growing up nestled between the hills near the Bay, she never experienced such expansiveness.

Lightning flickered down from the clouds, colliding with the surface, looking so gentle from this distance. Like a hand reaching delicately down from above.

She wasn't the only one out, but she was the only one so carefully watching the water. Mesmerized by it, awed by the glowing point in the distance where the sun seeped through the storm clouds and lit the waves a vibrant gold.

Above her the sky was white and overcast, the veil of clouds steady and smooth and far from threatening. The blackness of the storm rolled toward her as she sat there—barely perceptible, but it was happening. Soon she would have to go inside.

The wind had already begun to pick up, teasing her pulled-back hair and rifling her jacket, deviating rapidly from the calm of the early morning. She had barely thought to bring her jacket, it had been so pleasant when she left her apartment. But she had stared down the horizon for hours and in that time things had changed.

She blinked and then saw a ship beneath the storm, devoid of lights, adrift. Almost impossible to make out, gray against the dark sky and silver waves, though it couldn't be so very far away.

She glanced around, looking for someone to confirm what she saw, unnerved. Something seemed not right about the ship, so impassive and dull that she marveled it could stay afloat. Plenty of times she had seen the lights of a hulking behemoth chugging up the coast, headed to the Port of San Francisco, lugging goods that she couldn't believe a market still existed for, crossing from the cheap factories of Asia to the rich purses of the American elite. But such ships did not look like this one, so vulnerable and so still.

A passing pair of young women paused, noticing her anxious look. Considering her, wondering what had agitated her.

"That ship?" she asked.

They both looked. One shrugged and the other laughed. "I think it's one of the techno-utopian projects," she said.

"Like here?" Sara asked.

"I heard people saw them last night," the woman went on. "Rumor is they're adrift and starving."

"Where'd *that* come from?" her friend asked.

"My roommate just arrived a few days ago," the first woman explained. "She said the feds won't let them dock."

"*What?*" Sara asked.

"They gave up their rights when they went out there," the woman said, apparently unconcerned. "Sea-steading, or whatever. They went out into international waters for freedom."

"Freedom," Sara murmured, turning back toward the ocean. Wondering if it was true.

The ship moved slowly beneath the roiling clouds, which gathered higher now. Preparing for another lightning strike.

Like her, the people on that ship had made a choice. An irreversible one, apparently, if the woman was to be believed.

But who knew what was really happening out there? Everything could be entirely fine. She had no way of knowing, just this hearsay, this recounting of news that was itself suspect.

She couldn't possibly know what might be happening on that ship, just like they had no knowledge of what was happening in her town here on the shore. Them and everyone else. So little information bled in or out, they might as well be drifting too, far out to sea.

There could be a parallel woman sitting on that ship in the storm, gazing toward a land that didn't want her anymore, utterly unaware of Sara on the seawall staring back. The people there were every bit as solid and vivid and real as she was, but she couldn't begin to conjure their faces. She knew nothing about them.

If that ship sank once it passed around the point out of sight, she would never know. And, much as she didn't want to believe it about herself, she wasn't sure she would even really care; no one else ever did. Caring was a false emotion that she had to eradicate from herself if she wanted to survive.

Still, she hoped they would be okay.

What a pointless wish, she thought. What good did her hope do for them?

If they were out of fuel and food, she imagined her hope would only infuriate people who needed far more than that from her. How useless were distant peoples' good thoughts? How silly and wasteful it was to spend time wishing others well.

The two women she had spoken with continued on their way, chatting and laughing and not looking toward the sea. Oblivious? Or wise to not concern themselves with what they couldn't change?

The ship continued, its progress as difficult to notice as that of the clouds and the waves. A part of the ocean, though it sat upon it. What might the people out there be thinking? How horrible did they feel, how afraid?

Would the government really abandon people like that? She didn't want to believe it; it contradicted every myth about America she had grown up with. But she knew it was true. It had happened so many times before.

She noted the minutes ticking by in her peripheral vision and wondered briefly if even this was real, this measure of time. The company could show her an incorrect time and she would never know. She decided that wasn't something worth worrying about.

While the clouds drew closer and the sky above darkened and the rain began to fall, Sara watched the ship until it passed around the south end of the bay and disappeared.

63

THAT NIGHT SARA MET UP WITH HER FRIENDS FOR DINNER, INTRO-
ducing Priya to Drew and Lacey and May and Alexa.

She was somewhat gratified to realize that here, in her new life, she had
a more solid group of girlfriends than she had ever had in her old one. Ever
since college her only steady female friend had been Bea. But then, she figured, that wasn't terribly surprising given the demographics in her start-
up-centric social circle.

They sat around a table draped in a white cloth on the sidewalk outside
one of the few places in town that felt like a nice restaurant instead of a simple cafe, drinking wine that almost tasted real and wrapped in furs that she
was glad were not. A gas-burning fire flickered comfortingly beside them,
the flames wrapping up around artificial wood in a half-hearted attempt
at authenticity.

If not for the mild California winter air and stark new buildings, they
might have been in an alpine ski town.

Sara let herself be transfixed by the fire, staring into it while she sipped
her wine and listened to the murmur of the pleasant conversation around
her, voices blurring and laughter lifting. She had been nervous about intro-
ducing Priya to the others, as if either side of the introduction might judge
her for it, but they all seemed to get along perfectly. Just like everyone here,
she thought.

"I really wish I'd met you all before," Drew was saying, drawing Sara into
the conversation. "All my friends back then were other teachers."

"You don't know that we're not teachers," Priya pointed out. "Or have you
guys all talked about that already?"

Lacey and May exchanged glances. Remarkably, they had not.

"No offense, but you do not look like a teacher," Alexa said. "And you're
way too young."

"Teachers can be *babies*," Drew said. "Every year I'd get the new hires
confused with students."

Sara laughed. "I felt the same way at work. And honestly when I started
working too, I did not feel old enough."

"What do you mean?" Alexa asked.

"Right, you wouldn't know," Lacey said. "You're young enough to have always been the youngest everywhere you worked!"

Alexa looked down. "I've never had a real job," she admitted.

Lacey waved a hand. "Don't worry about it, it's not all it's cracked up to be."

"Okay, I'm only twenty-one, but I know what you mean," May said. "At my last job before coming here, I was managing literal teenagers."

Drew laughed at that, a rather unattractive chortle. "Weren't you a literal teenager too?"

May made a face. "I was *twenty*."

Lacey patted her on the shoulder. "When you get to be my age, you'll see that that's the same thing."

Sara raised an eyebrow. "You can't be that old."

Lacey shrugged and downed her glass. "That's for me to know and you to wonder."

"Lacey's our old lady," Drew said. Slurring her words a little as if she were drunk, but Sara was fairly certain she was not. "She's actually 75."

Everyone laughed, but the words made Sara frown. "Does it ever bother you that there's no one here over forty?"

Shrugs all around.

"I wouldn't be hanging out with people my parents' age anyway," May said.

But Sara pressed on. "I mean, if this is the future, what's the future look like past forty? Are we just supposed to *die*?"

Drew reached over and ruffled her hair. "Don't worry your pretty little head about that, dear," she said, affecting an old-lady voice.

The conversation drifted on and Sara tried to drop the thought, but it continued to bother her. Everyone here was screened for health before they could enter and she was sure they were all monitored continuously, their saliva swabbed invisibly from their water glasses, the sewage checked for viruses. But things could still go wrong. Would they just be cast out if they fell ill?

And aging out was an eventual certainty. To Alexa it might have seemed like an eternity until she turned forty, but Sara knew how quickly time passed. They could not stay like this forever.

Humanity could not stay like this forever, either. Here was a community devoid of a future, filled by other people's children growing up and passing through. Dumping the challenges of life on a messy, disintegrating world outside its borders and taking only the easy decades of people's lives. This couldn't expand to encompass all of the world. The things they ran away from were required for the survival of this place.

The perfection and cleanliness and safety of this town were as fake as the wine they drank or the jobs they worked.

"Do you ever miss shopping?" Lacey was saying.

Sara didn't understand how her friends could continue on with such inanities in the face of their lie of an existence.

"What's to miss?" Drew asked. "Everything here is free and it's all that I want."

"I thought I'd miss scrolling forever, looking for the exact right thing," May said, apparently forgetting that anything was purchased in the physical world outside the town, "but I really don't. It's so much more convenient not to have to wait for delivery."

Lacey sighed dramatically. "I *mean*," she said, "bargain hunting. Searching for something you don't even have in mind. Trying to get the best possible deal."

"Is that really how you lived?" Alexa asked. "Sounds tedious."

Lacey met Drew's eyes and sighed again. "Children."

They both laughed and Sara felt like she should be laughing along with them, but she failed to see the humor in consumption as a source of entertainment.

"What I miss," May said, "is warm ocean water. Once when we were kids my parents took my brother and me to the Bahamas, and it was incredible."

"I hear you," Drew said. "The ocean here is nice and all, but it's only, like, half functional if you can't jump in it."

"I want to go back to the Bahamas," May said.

"Didn't you hear?" Lacey asked. "They're gone!"

They found this funny, too, and Sara had to admit that there was a kind of dark humor in it. Having a mental image of the possibilities of the world that had been made obsolete and inaccurate.

"I'd like to swim here," Sara said.

But no one seemed to hear her. The conversation drifted onward, someone asking May about her brother and then everyone talking about siblings and how annoying they were and how much they missed them. Sara offered some anecdote about Emily (her heart breaking at the thought of where Emily might be), mentioned how funny it was that she was now friends with girls even younger than her baby sister, and Lacey doubled down on teasing May and Alexa for their youth.

They were too many blocks from the shore for the ocean to be anything more than an idea, but Sara was comforted by its nearness. She imagined swimming in it now, wondering if she had been serious when she said that she would like to.

A brief flash in her mind's eye of the towering blue tank, glowing sunlight stretching tendrils down to where she stood three floors beneath the surface, orange-tinged kelp waving hypnotically and silver schools of fish dancing above her.

She *would* swim here, she thought. She realized she'd dreamt of it a thousand times. Sara wondered if something in the ocean's calling to her had been what brought her here in the first place, as opposed to the several dozen other intentional communities that had sprung up around the country. Maybe it hadn't all been Bea.

Her eyes closed, thinking of the gentle waves washing over her, trying to imagine the weight of all that ocean pressing down upon her, wondering if it would be terrifying or comforting to know that the world was winning over humanity. How small such a thing made her feel, more than the sky or the stars or a storm far out at sea. The ocean didn't care about her at all.

She didn't matter, and that was freeing, just like Everest said. Since nothing mattered, truly *nothing* mattered: she could be freed from not just the constant exhaustion of striving for achievement but also her next breath. The ocean could drown her—and it would be fine.

All her life, the only way forward had been to grab hold of fleeting metrics of success, let them trigger a tiny dopamine rush to keep her breathing. She could instead tether her identity to this new meaninglessness, compete with herself to be smaller and simpler, and learn to call that happiness. To assume everyone was doing the same, because they could not possibly be so disconnected from the world to truly believe any of it.

The conversation must have tracked her internal dialogue, or maybe she said something aloud, because just as she thought this Lacey's cackle broke through the depths of the ocean surrounding her.

"Imagine all those generations of progress," she said, her voice thick with irony or sadness or something else Sara couldn't identify. "Lucky us to see the peak!"

All eyes on her, some confused, some knowing exactly where she was going with this. Lacey raised her glass in the air and laughed again.

"It's all downhill from here, baby!"

64

THE NEXT MORNING, SARA STOPPED AT THE BUILDING WHERE BEA
went to her discussion group. Typically, they made arrangements for their
next meetup before parting ways, and they weren't scheduled to see each
other for several more days. But after dinner with her new friends, Sara felt
like she needed time with someone who actually knew her. There was an
appeal to them because they included her, but she didn't understand them
well enough to relax. Had things ever been so difficult with Bea? She couldn't
remember such a time.

The building was all white walls and floor-to-ceiling windows, reflective
and modern, with vibrant red furniture and severe architecture. Nothing unusual for the Community, but more than she had expected from a place styled
as so different from the rest of it.

A woman sat behind a black and red desk, looking at something on a
screen. Sara assumed she was a receptionist and approached.

"Can I help you?" the woman asked, before Sara had even reached the desk.

"I'm, um, looking for Beatrice Kim?" she asked. Her voice sounded reedy
and thin to her ears. Pathetic.

The woman nodded, her eyes flitting in the telltale way that meant she
was looking at something on her contacts. Sara wondered what the screen
was for, given the contacts' usefulness. "She's not here right now. Can I take
a message?"

Sara didn't want a stranger getting in the middle of her conversation with
her best friend so instead she said, "Do you know when she'll be in?"

The woman just stared at her blankly.

"I'm a friend," Sara offered.

"We don't share anyone's schedule," the woman said.

Sara nodded and turned slightly, taking in the room. There was a bench
over by the window, black and red like everything else, and she nodded toward it. "Can I sit and wait?"

The woman looked exasperated. "I can't stop you."

Sara crossed the shiny black floor and perched on the bench, which
hadn't looked comfortable and was even less so than it appeared. The woman
watched her for a moment, then shrugged and went back to her screen.

Hard at work on something. How strange, Sara thought. This place felt more corporate and modern and *real* than anywhere else she'd been within the Community.

She caught herself tapping her toe against the stone floor, making a sound that surely bothered the receptionist, though she didn't say anything. Sara rubbed her hands along the textured fabric of the bench. Pressed the back of her head against the window. Anything to keep herself entertained.

She resisted the urge to watch the minutes tick by on the clock in her peripheral vision. Every minute seemed longer than the last.

Why was she doing this, again?

It was a bit ridiculous, she thought, just how much slower time seemed to pass when you were waiting instead of doing nothing at all. She did nothing most days, for much of the day, but it was never quite so tedious as this. She should have brought a book.

Eventually the woman at the desk stood, stretched, and walked away.

No one else passed through the lobby the whole time Sara sat there, and according to her clock it was more than two hours. Maybe Bea wasn't going to show up.

Now without an audience, Sara returned to fidgeting, drumming her fingers against the bench and tapping her toes with gusto. Better than nothing.

She considered getting up and crossing the room to check the screen behind the desk, wondering what could possibly be on it, but didn't want to be caught doing something so clearly improper. There were not many rules here, but that was one thing she knew would be a major transgression. You didn't look at someone else's computer screen.

The woman returned after twenty minutes. "You're still here?"

Sara just shrugged.

She didn't have to work that afternoon, so she really had nowhere whatsoever to be. Before the Community she would never have waited for anything this long. She never would have needed to.

Everything was neatly automated and calibrated and monitored: you knew your plane was late before arriving at the airport or that your doctor was running behind while you still had time to stop for coffee.

Waiting was an example of inefficiency, that cardinal sin of the modern world. Time spent waiting was time poorly spent.

But if she was honest, she wasn't nearly as miserable as she should have been. Somehow it was pleasant; she was on a bench—not as uncomfortable as it first seemed—in a new room she could observe, with nothing stressful bearing down on her. She could relax. When was that ever true in her old life?

She was staring at the floor, trying to see a pattern in the subtle whorls on the surface of the tile that she suspected did not exist, when a familiar voice said, "Sara?"

She looked up abruptly and smiled. "Bea!"

"What're you doing here?" Bea crossed to her and gave her a perfunctory smile. The receptionist was observing them mildly.

Sara ran her hand through Bea's hair, which was waist-length now and a lovely ombre from violet to pink. "I love the hair."

Bea tossed her head and grinned. "It's my favorite I've had in a while. You're letting yours grow out?"

Sara fiddled with a strand of her own hair self-consciously. "It seems like the thing to do here."

Bea scowled momentarily and then smiled again. "Perks of living on the margins."

"That's what I wanted to talk to you about, actually," Sara started to say.

"You're defecting?" Bea's eyes went wide.

Sara shook her head quickly. "No, no, I just want to learn more. About your life."

Bea nodded slowly, thinking. "Well, I can't really talk right now," she said, nodding toward the interior of the building. "A meeting, you know. But you could come over for dinner tonight?"

"Sure!" Sara said. "But, um, where?"

Bea laughed. "It's so funny how no one *knows*."

"Why is that funny?"

"Eh, you know, the company fosters this terribly myopic world-view," Bea said vaguely. "You see what they want you to see."

"Right," Sara said, not understanding at all.

"Anyway, it's easy to find," Bea went on. "Follow the coast to the other side of town, then go up the hill. There's a trail, you can't miss it."

Sara had run a loop around the town at least two dozen times by then and never noticed a trail near where Bea said there should be one, but she didn't protest. "Okay."

"We usually eat around seven, so show up by then?"

She nodded. That was in only a few hours. "Sure, see you then!"

Bea grinned, waved, and blew a kiss as she walked off into the dark bowels of the building.

65

One year before the Community

SARA STEPPED INTO THE CHILLY, DARK OFFICE FROM THE POURING rain and immediately wished she hadn't come.

That morning when Zach left the apartment he'd been in a good mood, all things considered, but that seemed to have evaporated along with the customers and funding. He was blasting classic rock, which he knew she hated—so basic and masculine, universally admired by people who did not think about it enough—and singing along obnoxiously, and from the looks of the place he'd barely started packing.

She stepped around a pile of extension cords and took off her dripping raincoat—old enough now that it didn't really keep her dry—and approached him cautiously. "No one else showed up today?"

Zach paused in the middle of a poorly choreographed air guitar solo to shake his head. "Nope, because they're all assholes, apparently."

"Attention, volume down!" Sara shouted, and the speaker complied.

"I was listening to that," Zach snapped, little energy behind his protest.

"I know," Sara replied, crossing to the kitchen and opening the cabinets. They were still full of snacks and supplies, as if hungry engineers would arrive at any moment. "No one was obligated to come in, you know. They don't work for you anymore."

Zach slumped to a seat in a wayward office chair. "I can't forget."

She walked back over toward him to retrieve a cardboard box. "It'll be okay."

He looked up at her and she realized just how despondent he looked. Such an expression on his bullish, eternally confident face looked wrong.

"Will it?"

Rather than take the box back to the kitchen to begin packing, she set it down and dragged over another chair, sitting down knee-to-knee. She leaned forward and put a hand on his thigh. "Of course it will. Everyone fails in Silicon Valley."

Her words were empty, and they both knew it, but she had to say something.

He stared down at her hand, breathing unsteadily, then looked up sharply. "You're right. This is a rite of passage."

She patted his knee and got up, collecting the box and heading for the kitchen again. "There's so much money sloshing around the Valley. I'm sure you'll have something new and exciting to work on soon."

"Actually…"

She looked over her shoulder at him, still sitting in the chair. He was twirling in a slow circle.

"I was thinking of becoming an artist."

"An artist?" she asked, trying not to let the skepticism into her voice.

"Yeah!" He sounded a bit more energetic now. He spun the chair faster. "You know how many pottery classes I took in college?"

"You dropped out after sophomore year."

"But up until then it was all computer science and ceramics!"

She fought the urge to laugh. "Is ceramics really what you should be doing now?"

"It's not really more of a risk than another startup," he said.

She looked up from the half-packed box of snacks and dishes. "I'm not sure if that's true."

He stuck out a foot to stop the spinning. "Don't you support me?"

She frowned. "Is that a trick question?"

"Whatever," he said, pushing himself out of the chair. "We have a lot to do. You got these boxes?"

Before she could reply, he turned the music back up and walked away toward the server closet, leaving her with a mess and a headache.

66

THAT EVENING SARA WANDERED THROUGH TOWN TO THE HILL BEA
had mentioned, for some reason feeling like she should avoid looking suspicious. No one had ever actually said that spending time with the people who
lived on the periphery was disallowed, but the groups did not mingle. It felt
like an unspoken taboo that she didn't want to have to explain breaking.

Of course, this didn't involve being actually sneaky, as that would
surely count as suspicious, but rather an affected nonchalant meandering,
moving through town in the proper direction over the course of an hour.
Anything but direct.

As she neared the hill and had to search out the trail, she let the charade fall. She could not hold herself apart from the task when it required
actual effort, and, despite Bea's assurances, the path was not obvious. At least
not to Sara.

This hill was near the one she had ascended for the game of tag and was
its twin in all respects, imposing and ephemeral and cast in a delicate blanket
of low foliage, like lace stretched across the sand. She did not see a house.

After some deliberation she began trekking directly over the salt grass
and succulents, grateful for substantial shoes to guard against the prickly
plants, apologetic for stepping on them. A wry smile—begging her pardon
for trampling across the Earth seemed appropriate and necessary.

She could see it from atop the hill, a house with wood siding and glowing
yellow windows, looking old and rundown but also warm and safe against the
falling night. It was almost seven now, she saw. Time to arrive.

She rushed down the hill, kicking up trails of sand behind her, then stood
awkwardly on the porch, unsure whether she should knock or call out or go
right in. She had never arrived at a friend's house without the ability to text
them that she was outside.

She might have been a thousand miles or a hundred years away from the
world she knew, both the old world outside the Community or the village of
perfect apartments on the other side of the hill. Once again she found herself
without context or the guardrails of society, though these people belonged to
the same world she did.

Bea rescued her by opening the door and giving her a quick hug as she
ushered her inside. "So glad you could make it!"

Sara smiled and let herself be embraced by the warmth of the building, heated to a cozier temperature than her apartment back in town. A pleasant shiver ran down her spine as the warmth washed over her.

They passed through a hall—overrun with discarded jackets and shoes—and into a dining room that adjoined a kitchen from which delicious smells wafted. The place looked worn, with peeling paint and raw wood floorboards that Sara suspected might give splinters if you went barefoot. Some of the bulbs in the overhead lights had burnt out.

Bea rushed through introductions to a half-dozen people crowded around the rickety table and a few more people hard at work in the kitchen, who stuck their heads into the dining room to greet her. She couldn't keep up with the names even as Bea hurled them at her, and didn't intend to even try to remember them as the evening wore on.

"Everyone, be nice to Sara—she's one of my oldest friends," Bea was saying.

"Not *old*," Sara protested, trying to be funny.

The group chuckled dutifully, though it was a tired joke.

A young man wearing an ugly vest and ill-fitting pants and a thirty-something woman in an out-of-season yellow sundress brought the food from the kitchen: mashed potatoes and roasted brussels sprouts and a green salad and hard-boiled eggs, all fresh and brilliantly hued but, Sara discovered, somewhat under-seasoned.

The conversation among the eight roommates flowed comfortably and Sara mostly sat in silence, listening, watching how Bea thrived in this new life. But then, of course she did. This was exactly her kind of place and these were her ideal sort of people. Very comfortable with themselves, laughing a little louder and smiling a little wider than Sara was used to; dressing in clothes that looked a little ridiculous but not caring at all; content amid the chaos of this ramshackle house and all the noise of so many people in such close proximity. Bea, with her harsh black outfit and bright hair, stood out among the earth tones, but she clearly wanted it that way.

Once the food had all been eaten, Bea and one of the men sitting across from them stood and began clearing the table. Sara half rose to help but Bea shook her head, mouthing, "Don't worry about it," and left Sara to sit amid the roommates alone.

"So, you live in town?" asked a man with a beard that was impossible to ignore.

Sara nodded.

"How do you like it?"

She shrugged.

"A silent type, eh?" a pretty, red-haired woman asked, laughing.

"It's not really a place to like or not like," Sara said instead of defending herself.

Nods all around. "I'm so glad I was rejected," the bearded man said. "I go there a few times a week to do repairs and maintenance," he explained to her. "And every time I'm so ready to leave."

"It's not that bad," Sara said.

The group laughed, led by the redhead. Sara shot her a dark look when she knew she wasn't looking. How did someone get to a place where they could laugh like that, head back and eyes closed, as if nothing else mattered? Especially at the expense of another person. Sara would never understand.

"Let's stop interrogating her, guys," another woman said, rejoining the table from another room. "What'd y'all do today?"

"I was gardening," the redhead said. "Beautiful day for it."

A chorus of agreements, but Sara could only be grateful they were no longer talking to or about her and didn't much care to chat about soil types or how much to water various plants. The conversation moved on without her.

Before long Bea dipped back in. "Hey, Sara, let's head up to my room."

Relieved, she told everyone how nice it was to meet them and retreated into the dark of the hallway, following Bea toward the stairs.

"How'd that go?" Bea asked. "Sorry I abandoned you for a minute."

"It was fine," Sara replied. "I really could've helped."

"I didn't want to make a guest work," Bea said.

Sara rolled her eyes and they began trudging upward.

"So you met everyone," Bea said.

"They're interesting," Sara replied. "More than people in town, honestly."

But not enough to make her want to defect and join them. What did that say about her?

"I love it here," Bea said. "I've never been surrounded by so many people who know their own minds before."

"Not even in college?"

Bea shrugged. "People just thought they understood themselves back then."

Sara snorted.

"Aaaannd here we are," Bea said, flinging open a door. "Ta da!"

Bea had to cross into the room to turn the lights on, so Sara's first impression of the place was of vague gray shapes in the darkness. Far too many lumps to be normal furniture, she thought, and indeed it was revealed to be a rather insane assortment of chairs and boxes, the bed a pile of blankets in the corner. Part of a couch, very clearly sawed in half, sat against a window. A desk made out of an old door covered the other wall.

"This is really…something."

Bea laughed. "It's hilarious, right?"

"I guess. Where'd you get all this stuff?"

Bea shrugged. "Previous resident. I imagine this has all been piling up for years."

So the house was older than the Community. That was interesting, but made sense—it certainly showed its age.

Sara walked tentatively across the floor, suddenly worried it might collapse beneath her, and settled on a wooden chair. Giving that couch a wide berth.

Bea collapsed onto a beanbag and looked up at the ceiling. "I want to paint stars up there," she said.

Sara looked up. The ceiling was white. "You'll have to paint it black first."

"And won't that be great?"

Sara felt herself smiling, Bea's enthusiasm contagious. "I've missed you."

"Oh, I've missed you, too," Bea said. "Every day, when we're doing cool things here, I wish you could be here too."

"It's so lonely in there," Sara said.

"With all those people?"

Sara shrugged. "They're all so relieved to be there that they can't seem to talk about anything else."

Bea chuckled. "Typical."

"I'm sure it'll get better eventually, though."

"Maybe," Bea said. "Or maybe you'll just get so used to it that you don't care anymore."

Sara affected a shudder. "I better not."

Bea laughed. "So you're not happy?"

Sara sighed, fiddled with a scarf draped over the back of the chair. She didn't want to accidentally lie, and honestly didn't know the answer until she thought about it. "I'm content, but I'm uncomfortable."

"Go on."

"It's such a relief to be there, but I'm not sure how to make it feel real," she tried to explain. "I feel like I'm on an indefinite vacation and that doesn't feel as good as it sounds like it would."

"Well, it sounds awful."

Sara looked at her skeptically. "You *would* say that."

"What? It's true! What would I want with a forever vacation? Sounds like hell. So boring."

"But fundamentally, I *am* happy," Sara said, redirecting the conversation and not admitting that she'd once had a similar thought about the place. "I can spend my days eating good food and reading books and contributing to the innovations of the future, even if not quite how I imagined."

Bea rolled her eyes. "Don't tell me you believe that."

"Of course I do!"

Bea shook her head. "No, you don't. You just know you're supposed to. Look at me here—I don't belong to anything, I'm not amounting to anything, I'm sure if my parents knew what I was up to they would be ashamed. But, hell, at least I'm not a cog in some giant machine like *you* are!"

Sara blanched. "I wasn't trying to say that you're not…"

Bea waved a hand. "I know what I am. I don't know that you do."

Sara laughed a little, but it was forced. She thought Bea didn't know, either, no matter what she said. "Of course I don't."

"Do you remember how hard we tried not to work for the giant tech companies after college?"

"How hilarious to think that we actually had to try," Sara said dryly.

"I know, it seems absurd," Bea agreed. "But remember, this is exactly what we didn't want for our lives."

"I didn't imagine this future at all," Sara said. "Nothing like this seemed possible."

Bea considered. "I saw it coming."

"Oh, *sure* you did," Sara scoffed.

"I did!" Bea sat up and pointed at Sara. "Well, maybe not *exactly* this, but something like it. The takeover by our corporate overlords, erosion of democracy, impossibility of making a career like we'd imagined, the insecurity of an ecosystem crumbling around us."

"Is it totally dumb that it blindsided me?" Sara asked.

"Nah, I think you're just an optimist."

Sara laughed for real. "I am the furthest thing."

"How can you work on software for a decade without being an optimist?"

"A decade including school," Sara said. "And also, I have no idea what you mean."

"It implies believing in a future and believing you can help get there. Believing it can be built with ones and zeros instead of, like, water filters and gardens, which I think is more likely."

"That's exactly my problem lately," Sara said. "If we're not going to code our way out of this, what have I been *doing*?"

"You thought we could, once."

Sara grimaced. "I think I've just been selfish."

"I'm giving you the most charitable possible way out here, my dear," Bea said.

"And I'm refusing to take it," Sara replied. "But thanks."

They sat with their thoughts for a moment, smiling despite the subject, and then Bea said, "You feel ungrounded because the parameters have all fallen away, that's all."

Sara frowned.

"It's been all about survival for, like, all of human history. And then for a bit we broke free into trying to, I don't know, *actualize* ourselves, and it led to us destroying the planet. Descending back into survival mode is much harder than emerging from it, but it feels great once you give in."

"My friend Lacey said almost the same thing," Sara said, trying to digest Bea's words.

Bea shrugged. "Maybe the people in town aren't so different."

Sara smiled, looking toward the window and the night outside. "People are never very different." She paused, turned back to Bea, and her smile turned into a grin. "That's what makes them so *boring*."

"I thought you were about to say something profound."

"You know me better than that!"

They both laughed.

"You know, it's funny," Sara said. "I think there's fundamentally two ways of living and I've never felt great with either one."

"Oh yeah?" Bea asked. "And what are those?"

"Like, perfect crisp edges or a kind of ragged mess," Sara said.

Bea grinned. "You calling me a ragged mess?"

Sara gestured at the room around them, which could be more aptly called a ragged mess than almost anything else.

"I know what you mean, though," Bea said. "But what people always forget is that this ragged mess isn't any less modern than your new-build apartments and augmented reality."

"There are much further things from modernity than this place," Sara said, nodding toward the tablet charging on the desk. "But yeah, you're right."

"I'm not sure I agree, though," Bea said. "I really don't want to divide humanity into two broad groups."

Sara groaned. "All this egalitarian nonsense again."

They had had this conversation many times. Bea insisted on imagining the world as it should be, full of perfectly equal people. Sara agreed that would be nice but wanted to see how things truly were. It did not help anyone to lie and say that everyone was equal, even if they should have been.

Bea giggled. "I had to."

Sara let this hover in the air a moment and then said, "What would you do if nothing else mattered?"

Bea considered for just a moment before replying, "Well, nothing matters. So, this, I guess."

Sara scowled. "And isn't that sad?"

67

SARA AND EVEREST WERE WALKING ALONG THE EDGE OF THE COM-
munity, nearing her building at the end of the next day, when she caught
sight of the message column out of the corner of her eye. She had felt uncomfortable around him all day, reminded by her evening with Bea of her real
personality and what if felt like to truly relax.

"Have you ever sent a message with that?" she asked him.

Everest glanced over his shoulder at it, tucked among the plants. "No."

"You don't have anyone on the outside you want to message?"

He shrugged. "It wasn't here when I got here," he explained. "At first, they
let us keep our phones, with basic cell plans. Texts only."

Sara's eyes went wide. "When did that change?"

"You want to know when, not why?"

She frowned, surprised at her own question. "I guess I figure no one really
knows *why*."

"Sure we do," he said. "They decided it wasn't useful for their tests."

"Like personal music players."

"Oh, that was because they wanted to force people out of their rooms," he
said. "That one's easy."

Sara raised her eyebrows. "Is *that* why? Just like the food options are all
out here." She gestured across the courtyard, the bank of little shops selling
smoothies and salads and sandwiches.

"You said 'no one *on the outside*'," Everest said.

"What?"

"You asked if I had anyone on the outside that I wanted to contact."

"Oh." Sara hesitated. "Yeah, I mean, the only people it will let me message
are people not in the Community."

"You've tried?"

"You're asking if I've messaged *you*," she said, smiling and nudging
his shoulder.

He laughed. "I'm just wondering!"

"It's strange, though, now that I think about it," she said. "Early on, I tried
to message my friend Bea, and it wouldn't let me—with the message that she
was a Community member. But she isn't."

"Maybe you just haven't seen her. This is a big place."

"No, she's—" Sara grimaced. "She's one of the marginal people. Whatever you call them."

Everest nodded knowingly. "Well, they must be part of the Community, then." He widened his eyes slightly, the way he did when he was almost lecturing her.

"They're not, though," Sara protested. "They live in a house out on the dunes and they…"

Everest smiled. "And they what?"

"Bea would never have actually been happy here," Sara said, thinking aloud. "But she can be very happy *there*."

"Our benevolent employers have found a place for everyone."

Except Zach, Sara thought. Except Emily.

"But why do they live like that?" Sara asked. "Besides that it lets them feel like a counterculture?"

"You're asking about the supposed sex work."

Sara snorted. "Among other things. They do menial tasks. I don't know what all they do, honestly, but I figured it was things the Community needed but the company didn't approve of."

"People need a little rebellion. And some people expect that they'll have to fall back on rough ways of getting by. So why not let them?"

Sara shivered. "Bleak."

"Realistic," Everest offered. "Honest." He paused and looked out at the water, gray to the horizon under an equally gray sky. "Freeing."

Organized chaos.

68

Four months before the Community

WHEN SARA RETURNED HOME FROM YET ANOTHER FAILED JOB IN-
terview, this one for a position labeling images of cars by brand, Zach was
lying on the couch with VR glasses on, watching a movie projected into the
empty space in the middle of the living room.

"Have you moved all day?" she asked.

He lifted the glasses off his face. "I got the mail."

She rolled her eyes and leafed through the pile of ads and coupons he'd
placed on the counter. "You could've put this straight in the recycling."

"I figured you'd want to look at it."

"Why?" she asked, shoving him into a sitting position so she could sit
beside him on the couch.

He placed the glasses back on. "Want to join?"

She shrugged and curled up beside him, watching him flick his wrists to
resume the movie. The audio came through a bone conduction earbud and
the visuals only appeared when you looked at the glasses at the right angle, so
she couldn't even tell what he was watching.

They kept the apartment very close to the outdoor temperature, so it was
chilly. She tucked her feet up beneath her and pulled a blanket around them.

"Don't bump me!" he protested.

She ignored him and pulled her phone from her pocket, flipping through
notifications. A snowstorm in Texas, a flood somewhere in South Asia,
an IPO by a startup she turned down when she joined One. Her mouth
tasted bitter.

"Did you pay the rent yet?" she asked.

He groaned. "Why do I have to do everything?"

She snorted but didn't engage. It was like he was goading her. "Could you
please? It's your turn this month."

"I *will*! What are you, my mother?"

"Excuse me?"

She turned to face him, but he stared through her, still engaged in his stupid show.

She snatched the glasses off his face.

"Hey!"

"Can we please have a conversation?" she asked, keeping her voice as flat and reasonable as she could.

"Aren't we having a conversation?" he replied, reaching for the glasses. She gripped them tightly in her hand, but he deftly uncurled her fingers and took them back. She didn't fight very hard to hang onto them; the point had been made. "Just let me finish this, okay? Then we can talk."

"You've been watching all day, haven't you?"

He sighed and set the glasses down on the coffee table. "I should've gotten the contacts instead."

She made a sound of indignation. "Oh, is that the problem here?"

"I don't know, Sara, what is the problem here?"

His voice dripped with condescension and it was almost too much for her.

"The problem is that you don't do anything, ever since One folded! What are you doing with your life?"

"I'm devoted to my art, Sara! Creativity takes time!"

"You're making ugly lumps of clay for like five hours a week and putting no effort into actually selling them!"

"Art isn't about sales, it's about expression! Fulfillment!"

They glowered at each other. He seemed like a child to her then.

Her words seemed to take several heartbeats to reach him. "And did you call my sculptures *ugly*?"

She looked away. "Maybe not ugly, but certainly not…beautiful."

She realized she was just digging herself a deeper hole.

"Look, I'm sorry," she said. "But creative expression and fulfillment don't pay the bills!"

"Neither does whatever you're doing, interviewing all the time!"

She jumped up from the couch, sending the blanket flying. He'd touched a nerve. "At least I'm trying!"

"And I'm not?"

"All you do is play some dumb game and complain! Are you depressed or something?"

As soon as she said it, she realized that he probably was—his whole life had been tied up in that startup, in what it said about him as a man in their mad-rush society that he could raise funds and *innovate* and play on all those buzzwords and win. What did he have now?

His face melted from anger to hurt and then back to anger. "Fuck you, Sara. Fuck you."

She rolled her eyes. "Use your fucking words, Zach."

"Fuck. You."

She stood there, daring him to do—something. His face turned slowly redder.

She remembered how scared of him she had been at first, this giant of a man with college-varsity-athlete muscles and such clout in the industry, and then thought of how pathetic he'd turned out to be. She was not scared of him anymore.

Once, he had seemed so much grander than anyone else she knew, full of big ideas and the gumption to follow them through. Such bluster had driven her crazy, but it had always been interesting. Inspiring. It turned out he was just like everyone else.

He got slowly to his feet, towering over her, and she raised one eyebrow, wondering what he might do. Their eyes met for a heated moment, then he walked past her and out the door without another word.

She breathed heavily for a moment, heart pounding, veins rushing with adrenaline, then collected her nerves, pulled out her laptop, and resumed her search through job postings.

Either he'd come back or he wouldn't. She didn't care anymore.

69

SARA KNEW THAT IT WAS A SATURDAY, SO SHE WAITED A COUPLE
hours and met Lacey for brunch instead of having breakfast with Alexa.

"How're things?" Sara asked, joining her friend at the table.

Lacey had apparently been there a while already because she had a most-
ly-drunk mimosa in front of her along with an untouched plate of fruit.

"Have some of this fruit salad," she said. "I felt like I had to order something, but I don't want it."

Sara nodded and lifted a fork. "Have a good Friday night?"

Lacey shrugged. "It all feels like a bit of a wash, really."

"How's that?"

"I've been very much enjoying the general mood here," she said. "Everyone unattached, no one looking for a real relationship."

"But?" Sara asked around a bite of melon.

"I really thought the exhibitionist thrill of knowing you're constantly
watched would give it a little more zing."

Sara considered this. "I feel like there's another *but* coming."

Lacey laughed. "But it's just not the same when you know it's only computers watching you!"

Sara rolled her eyes but laughed, too. "I had not thought of it that way. I
have to say, I think that's kind of comforting."

Lacey shook her head. "You're missing out if you haven't embraced it yet,"
she insisted. "Makes sex feel as exciting as it did in high school, knowing you
might get caught."

"I see," Sara said. Of course she had thought that too. "So the problem is
that this takes away the fear of getting caught?"

"Yeah, I guess that, too. You just keep making it worse."

Sara smiled. "If it's any consolation, I'm sure people monitor the feeds all
the time."

"What makes you say that?"

"To make sure the algorithms are behaving," Sara said. "Gotta check
up on them."

"Lest they go rogue à la Skynet?" Lacey said dryly.

"Not necessarily," Sara said, laughing again. "Just that unobserved, computers care about different things than humans do."

"Like?"

"Well, for example, a program could be designed to tell apart day from night based on how bright it is in an image might just figure out that there's a clock in the frame, or something," Sara said. "And cheat."

Lacey snorted. "Sounds like a shortcut, maybe, but not cheating."

"But then what if someone takes away the clock? It falls apart."

"So you're saying someone might check in on me to be sure the computer isn't confusing sex with a nightmare just because it's dark in there and there's thrashing around."

"I don't know about your sex or your nightmares, but sure."

"How do you know all this?"

Sara hesitated before replying. "I was a software engineer."

Lacey practically recoiled, but Sara quickly realized it was for comedic effect. "And that couldn't keep you out of here?" she said. "What're you doing in here with all of us?"

Sara shrugged. "The fruit salad is just divine. How could I stay away?"

70

SHE MET UP WITH EVEREST THAT EVENING FOR DINNER, STEAMING bowls of pho and fresh salads in the dark back corner of a restaurant. The place clamored with people chatting and slurping.

"You know my mom said she'd never had Vietnamese food until college?" Sara said. "Can you *imagine?*"

He shrugged. "I think my grandparents didn't even try real Italian food until adulthood," he replied. "The world used to be very small."

"I mourn for them," she said.

He chuckled. "Is this your favorite then?"

She drank a careful spoonful of the broth while she thought. "That would probably be Japanese, actually. Nothing beats miso black cod."

"Decadent."

"Endangered."

"True," he said, nodding. "Was it hard to give up meat, coming here?"

She shook her head. "I've been vegetarian for a couple years, actually. It's cheaper."

"And the least we can do."

"Well, I still drove a combustion car up until the day I arrived, so I'm a major sinner."

"I guess it's all your fault, huh?"

She laughed. "Unfortunately."

"I ate meat before I joined," he said. "I think that was the hardest part."

"But the burgers are so realistic! What could you miss?"

"A solid steak," he replied. "They can't make that in a lab yet."

"Such a red-blooded American man," she teased.

"And look what I've been reduced to," he said. "Vegetables and tofu."

"Positively withering away."

They laughed and the conversation died down a bit while they ate, taking turns at the giant bowl of soup and the pile of cabbage and onions and papaya. When the food was mostly gone, he said, "Speaking of America..."

"Always a dangerous start," she commented.

He grinned but went on. "Do you ever feel like we've betrayed the American idea a little, living like this?"

"Do you mean twenty-first century excess in general or this community in particular?"

"What do you think I mean?"

She frowned. "You're very cryptic."

"No, I'm just curious."

She sighed dramatically, leaned back from the table a little and looked up at the ceiling. Wooden slats, probably bamboo.

"I've thought a bit about that concept of choosing between freedom and safety," she admitted.

"Those who would give up freedom for temporary safety deserve neither?"

"Exactly, but in more archaic English."

"What of it?"

"Isn't that exactly what we've done here?" she asked. "It's certainly safer and less free."

He shrugged. "We don't owe anything to a 300-year-old dead guy."

"Not to put too fine a point on it."

"But for real, idealism is ridiculous," he said. "Live your life. Don't let old philosophy by misogynistic slaveholders who had no idea what they were talking about get you down."

She shook her head, clearing it, and let herself laugh a little. "Thanks, I really needed to hear that."

"I find that my lectures are very well received in general."

"More of a rant than a lecture."

"Whatever you want to call it."

"Or an excuse, maybe?" she said, raising an eyebrow.

He raised a hand. "Not that."

They both laughed again.

"Shall we go?" he asked, nodding toward the mostly empty plates.

"Sure," she said, getting up and shrugging into her jacket. "It always feels weird leaving food."

"The lack of to-go boxes gets to you, but driving a gas-guzzling car up until the last minute was fine?" he asked, reaching for her hand.

"I never said I was rational," she replied.

"None of us are," he said. "None of us."

They wound between the tables and out of the crowded restaurant into the chill of the evening. As soon as the sun went down the warmth of the day bled out of the air, and Sara shivered.

"I'd offer my jacket," Everest said. "But you in fact have one and I do not."

"I would just say such a gesture is antiquated and regressive," she replied. "So do you want mine?"

He just shook his head, laughing.

"We headed back to your room again?" she asked after a moment.

He looked down at her. "Eager, are we?"

She scowled and said, "Or we could talk about my ongoing existential crisis."

"Oh, do tell."

"You know it all already," she said. "What are we even testing here? Who is the market for whatever it is?"

"That's for the market to figure out."

Sara scowled. "Don't be obtuse. Just, really…is the whole future just going to be like this, forever?"

"Nothing is ever the same forever," he said.

"Great, real helpful."

"What are you really asking?"

"I don't know. What's the point?"

He pulled his hand from hers and wrapped his arm around her shoulders instead. "You're getting awfully close to breaking the rules," he whispered into her hair.

She turned her head, looking up at him. "Are there rules, now?"

He raised an eyebrow. "There are always rules."

"I just never know what they are." That was always the problem, wasn't it? She spent her whole life guessing, trying to stay rigidly within lines that she couldn't really see.

He let that hang in the air for a moment, then said, "I think we better get you back to my apartment and cheer you up."

She laughed and let the subject drop.

71

One month before the Community

THE BLARING OF HER PHONE'S EMERGENCY ALERT JOLTED SARA OUT of sleep and into confusion. It wasn't an alarm she'd heard before and it took her an embarrassingly long minute to realize where the noise was coming from. When she did, her stomach sank and her head felt light as she realized with horror that this was it: the moment she'd somehow known was coming but had never acknowledged.

She shook Zach awake—he had somehow slept through the alarm—and he held his own phone above his face, blearily trying to read the tiny words.

"Evacuation notice?"

"It's the fire," she breathed. "It's here?"

For a shocked moment they stared at each other, trying to decide if it was real. Because it couldn't have reached them, right? Disasters happened to other people.

But then she had the presence of mind to go to the window and look out, peeling back the curtain to the thick air of the late night, the smoke heavier than she'd ever seen it. She lifted the window open to let it in, all its choking glory, and felt the unnatural heat and heard the roar and felt some instinct kick in that overrode the numbing panic.

"We have to go," she said, voice steady.

Zach was already struggling into jeans. She moved in a daze as the smoke continued filling the room, pulled a hoodie over her head, slipped on her running shoes and wetted down several towels to press over their faces, then pulled her emergency bag out of the closet and looked around the apartment one last time. Would it still be here when they returned?

Would they return?

"Come on," Zach said, gripping her arm harder than he ever had before and pulling her out of the room.

It happened so fast. It had been happening for decades.

They ran out into the hallway, pounded on their neighbors' doors and didn't wait for anyone to answer. Hoping they would get themselves out. Was it too late already?

Her phone was still blaring in her pocket. How to turn the damn thing off?

A neighbor burst into the hall before them, bizarrely wearing pajamas and a winter jacket. "Do you have a car?" he cried, sounding justifiably terrified. "Can you give us a ride?"

Zach nodded wordlessly and Sara beckoned the man to follow, but they did not slow down.

They ran, the two of them and their neighbors, a middle-aged gay couple they'd met only on the day they moved in. They ran and the air grew hotter and harder to breathe and the car seemed impossibly far away.

Sara was struck by the unlikely but horrifying thought that the car had been stolen. What if?

But then it emerged out of the haze in the parking lot, the taillights flashing and the horn honking as Sara repeatedly pressed the unlock button, desperate for the assurance that it was there.

They piled in and Sara threw her bag at Zach, shouting, "Find my glasses!"

He dug madly through the backpack as she started the ignition, blinking furiously against the smoke. She fumbled the glasses onto her face, pressing down on the accelerator, but the car wasn't picking up speed. The engine whined.

"Parking brake!" one of the neighbors called from the back. Sara cursed, released the brake, and they were off.

Her emergency-kit glasses were from an old prescription and so the world was full of starbursts and smears. She couldn't be sure that was just the glasses and not the fire racing toward them.

"Are you good to drive?" Zach whispered, or maybe shouted, as she sped away from the complex.

"I have to be!" she replied. Her voice sounded so normal in such an absurd moment. How could her voice sound the same as always?

They careened down the street toward the main thoroughfare, but where were they even going?

Zach studied his phone, looking for indication of where to go, but no one had thought to share such vital information.

"My uncle," the neighbor said, voice shuddering. "My uncle has a house in San Jose. If it's…"

She knew what he was saying. If a house deep in the city was at risk from this blaze, they faced problems on a scale they could probably not survive.

She turned right, winding as fast as she dared through the hills with the emergency flashers on, the grass around them blackened where the fire had already passed. Not able to catch her breath, gasping, heart jumping.

Her mind kept flashing to Bea, and she kept pushing it away. Bea lived up the ridge even further. She could not help her, could not waste a moment to even try to contact her. She just had to trust that Bea had gotten herself out.

The opposite ridge flared and caught, horrifically red and glowing, smoldering and inflaming in turns, like an image straight out of hell. She could feel the heat on her face through the windshield, though it was at least a hundred feet away.

A hundred feet was nothing.

They descended toward the lights of a suburban downtown below them, Christmas lights wound around palm trees and neon signs lit up like it was any other day. So close.

Zach's hands clenched on the dashboard, the neighbors murmured in fearful whispers in the backseat, and Sara tried so hard to remain calm, unhappy and uncomfortable in her role as savior. Her head pounded; what time was it? She always felt awful when she didn't get enough sleep.

Did she feel nauseated from lack of sleep or the panic or the smoke?

They reached the bottom of the hill and faced a stoplight, an absurdly human barrier between them and safety. The red of the burning hills behind them drowned out the red of the stoplight before them, a cosmic joke. She barely slowed before racing through the intersection against the light.

It was three in the morning, the dashboard told her. There would be no cross traffic.

The air did not clear, but the wind calmed and the temperature fell to something approximating normal and she let out her breath, trying again to calm her racing heart and almost succeeding this time.

"San Jose?" she asked, signaling to get on the freeway.

"I'll give directions," the neighbor said, his voice steady now, assured.

How odd it was that he sounded calmer just when she was giving into her fear.

Her arms felt shaky and weak and she could barely keep them on the steering wheel, her head spinning wildly as the adrenaline released her, but she followed his instructions and headed south, fifteen miles away from the conflagration, her mind stuck back where everything she owned was surely being devoured.

The annual California lottery that no one thought they would ever lose.

Tonight they had lost.

Getting off the freeway and turning onto slow neighborhood streets always felt surreal to her, brought her back to her childhood in the backseat while her father drove and she pretended to sleep in the hopes he would carry her into the house. When voices fell silent and lights dimmed and everything slowed down, you could almost believe something magical was happening.

That was especially true this time, as they slowed to a near crawl, creeping along streets made strange by the smoke through a community left whole. Her neighbor tried to guess at the appropriate turns to take. He'd been there many times, he kept saying, but he couldn't remember the address, and his uncle wasn't picking up the phone.

Were the phones even working?

She knew emergencies could overwhelm the network. Maybe emergency services had commandeered everything so they could push out alerts, or maybe they were using everyone's numbers for their own purposes, coordinating a response. That could happen, right? Wasn't that how things worked?

She realized she had no idea.

It seemed impossible that these people in these big houses would get to go on living as if nothing had happened, as if people just a few towns over hadn't lost everything that night, and she realized it was no stranger than every other year.

The smoke made each streetlight nearly ineffective. The whole of San Jose seemed to be one great yellow haze, almost poisonous. They swam through it.

And then the lights went out.

It took her a moment to realize what had happened, since the glow had been so sickly and unsettling to begin with; it was almost better this way, the white of her headlights the only light cutting through the smoke.

But the implications of the blackout shook her. Was the utility trying to prevent further burns, or had the fire destroyed transmission lines? The mystery of the night thickened, growing more ominous. Their refuge felt impossibly far away.

72

SARA AWOKE IN THE MIDDLE OF THE NIGHT AND HAD TO PEE.

This was one of the most frustrating parts of staying over, she thought: having to extricate yourself from someone else's bed without waking them so you could make your way to an unfamiliar bathroom in the dark. They had fallen asleep with her closer to the wall, too, which made it even worse.

She slithered out of the bed and tiptoed through the dark room, squinting and trying to avoid stubbing her toes on anything. The only light came in the window from a streetlamp outside, a neutral white that she was sure had been carefully engineered to minimize light pollution or modulate mood effects. Or maybe it was just moonlight.

Her eyes didn't really want to be open, anyway, so the lack of light was welcome.

His bathroom was small and far tidier than she expected for a man who lived alone, but then, she only had Zach as a comparison, and he was very messy. She was so glad to be rid of him.

She laughed to herself silently, alone in the dark bathroom, as she reflected on how much happier she was to be about to climb back in bed with Everest instead of her boyfriend of four years. What had she ever seen in Zach? She couldn't remember at all.

She washed her hands and returned to the bedroom, already craving the warmth and comfort of the bed that awaited her. This time she wouldn't let herself be sandwiched by the wall, though.

But there was something sitting on the desk under the window that she hadn't seen there earlier. To her half-asleep eyes, and in the darkness, it looked like a phone, that familiar rectangle of glass that had gone everywhere with her since childhood. But that couldn't be right. There were no phones here.

Rather than make a beeline for the bed, she crossed the room to the desk, the presence of the unknown object prompting a curiosity so strong she knew she wouldn't be able to sleep until she satisfied it.

The hairs on the back of her neck stood up. Something felt wrong.

She lowered her hand toward it, and it looked so much like a phone now that she couldn't convince herself otherwise.

And then she was holding it, the shape and weight in her palm as familiar as a pair of well-worn shoes, and she realized with a horrified start that it was not just a phone. It was *her* phone, the one she had tucked away in her backpack all those months ago, the pattern of cracks and chips its screen had accumulated over their three years together recognizable even in the dark.

She gasped audibly. Sara had the unmistakable feeling that someone was watching her. It could only be Everest, but suddenly that knowledge was not comforting.

"What're you doing up?" he asked, voice scratchy with sleep.

She just shook her head, unable to decide what to say.

"Come back to bed."

She lifted the phone to her face, hoping it wouldn't recognize her but knowing that it would. It had unlocked as soon as she picked it up, she knew, identifying her touch immediately, but when it sensed her looking at it, the screen would wake up too—if it was indeed her own.

The screen brightened, casting her face in blue light.

Light that, behind her, Everest could also see.

"Oh," he said, his voice heavy.

Sara turned slowly, holding the phone tight in two hands, not daring to look away. A stream of notifications flowed past, but not as many as she would have expected in almost two months away.

He didn't say anything.

Finally, she looked up. "Where did you get this?"

At first he just shrugged, looking far guiltier than she liked. She wanted him to hurl excuses at her, offer some reasonable explanation that she could hold onto, instead of this dreadful dead silence that she couldn't hope to understand. Her mind reeled. Trying desperately to construct a story that fit this piece of her past sitting here, in his room, but not able to come up with anything.

She advanced toward the bed, holding the phone aloft, accusatory. Like a weapon.

Noting finally that the oldest unread notifications were from only a few days before.

"Why do you have this?" she demanded.

Fully awake now, Everest sighed and sat up the rest of the way. "It's not what it looks like."

Sara felt like screaming in frustration. "I don't even know what it looks like!"

"I…"

"What does it look like, Everest?"

Her voice was low and tense, not shrieky like she had expected. Even to her own ears she sounded almost threatening.

"I'm not…well, I'm not supposed to tell you this," he said, stumbling over words. "But I'm not a Community member, like you."

She froze. Not sure what he was saying, liking this even less than whatever vague explanation she had expected.

"I work for the company like you do, but I have a different role."

A hundred old questions about him came flooding back. Why was he so blasé about everything? Why did he live alone? What did he know?

As she had wondered: who was he before he came here?

Who was he now?

"Go on," she said.

He let out a long, slow breath, like his words pained him. "My job is to help people adjust. They point me in the direction of people who are having difficulty integrating."

Sara scoffed, surprising herself that her only reaction was annoyance. Of course, she thought. Things made much more sense now. Of *course* she would be that person.

"So what now?" she demanded.

He looked somewhere over her shoulder, unable to meet her eyes. "I'm supposed to escort you out now."

It took her a moment to understand. "But…"

"We can't have people knowing that the company interferes like this."

Why not? she wondered but didn't say.

They stared at each other in silence.

"Why was my phone where I could find it?" she said, voice flat and low, her suspicion and sudden fear solid enough to keep herself under control.

"I—" Everest seemed to choke on his words. He scrubbed a hand over his face and then attempted a joke. "I guess I'm bad at my job?"

She wanted to throw the phone across the room at him.

A very large part of her ached to climb back in the bed beside him, her exhaustion hitting her all at once. Longing for the comfort and companionship she had felt so recently.

"This is the part where you tell me it wasn't all a lie," she said with a nod toward the bed. Starting to edge toward the door even as the conversation went on.

As she said the words, she meant the relationship. But in the beat before he replied, she realized that she also meant all of their shared skepticism, all the times he had sounded just as critical of the company as she felt.

"That's immaterial," he said. "And there's no reason to lie to you."

"Was I going to pass, anyway?" she asked.

Where else was there for her to go?

A shrug. "Not up to me to decide."

There was no reason for her heart to feel like it was breaking, but it did.

He was still in the bed. She was nearing the door.

She decided not to wait any longer to see what he would do and sprinted the rest of the way, ducking into the hall before his feet hit the ground. Not sure what she was doing but knowing, for that moment at least, that she wasn't going to go just because he said she had to, or stay because he said she could. He hadn't actually told her what he was going to do, and she was not going to wait for him to decide.

He may have been there much longer, but she ran around the town every morning. She knew the streets and the routes through them, she knew the way to Bea's house in the hills, and she knew that was the only place she could go.

73

One month before the Community

"TURN HERE," THE NEIGHBOR SAID SUDDENLY. "LEFT! SORRY."

Already halfway through the intersection, but the traffic lights were out and the streets were empty, so it didn't matter.

The street was lush and tree-lined and somehow felt even darker than the one they'd left. She was probably only going fifteen miles per hour but it felt very fast in the gloom.

"Here," the neighbor said. "The white one."

The house—or what could be seen in the glow of the headlights, anyway—was laid out on a grand scale, taking up most of the lot, with fresh white paint and expensive landscaping. She pulled into the empty driveway.

"Are they home?" Zach asked.

"No, I'd know if they were in town," the neighbor said. "His wife is some international business big-wig. They're usually in New York or London or Shanghai. I think they have like eight houses all around the world."

His voice sounded more awed than bitter.

The neighbor led the way through the yard, along an artful path between native plants and a fountain that was turned off. Or maybe it had stopped when the power failed.

Standing on the porch, he considered the keypad. "It's either their daughter's birthday or their cat's," he said, tapping away. The door unlocked on the second try, and they stepped gratefully into the sweet indoor air.

"How long do you think it'll stay this nice inside without power?" the other neighbor asked.

"A while, if we keep it locked up tight," Sara replied, closing the door against the smoke. A house this nice would be sealed well, possibly even equipped with passive filtering.

"What're your names, anyway?" Zach asked, shining his phone flashlight around the entry hall. Green tile beneath their feet, graceful glass sculptures on pedestals on either side of the door.

The one who'd guided them here snickered. "I'm Nick, and he's Nicholas."

Sara laughed a little, in spite of the horror of the night. "Really?"

Nicholas shrugged. "It was the '90s. Everyone named their kid Nicholas."

"Did you always go by, uh…" she started to ask.

Nick flipped the light switch, as if it might work. "No, we were both Nick when we met. But that would've been confusing."

They continued through the house, into a living room with a massive leather couch, then a grand dining room—the table could easily seat a dozen people—and finally a kitchen, too clean to ever really be used. A cat bowl sat on a cute mat in the corner. A rack of wine was displayed artfully against the far wall.

"A fucking chandelier," Zach said, gesturing toward the ceiling.

Sara hadn't even noticed it, but indeed there was one, modern and delicate instead of baroque and flamboyant, but decidedly a chandelier. She didn't think she'd ever seen a chandelier in someone's house, let alone in the kitchen.

"Have you reached them yet?" Nicholas was asking Nick.

Nick held his phone up, studying the screen. "No bars."

Sara checked her phone. "I have a signal, supposedly." She lifted the phone to her mouth and said, "Call Beatrice."

It took a long time to connect, longer than she'd ever experienced, and while it rang her heart pounded. Bea lived just a couple blocks away from her, but that had been in the direction of the flames. Going back for her would have been suicide, but…

Finally, Bea's face appeared on the screen, looming out of the darkness, and Sara was flooded with relief. "Sara!" she said, her voice gravelly.

"Where are you?" Sara asked quickly. "Are you safe?"

Bea glanced around. "A library in…Hey, what city are we in?"

A voice from offscreen replied, "Menlo Park."

Bea nodded and turned back to Sara. "Menlo Park, apparently. You?"

"A very fancy house in San Jose. Can you…you could come here, if you want."

She probably should have asked, but Nick was nodding as she made the suggestion.

"I'll have to bring someone with a car," Bea said. "But yeah, anywhere's probably better than here."

"Great," Sara said, handing the phone to Nick. "Give her directions, then call your uncle."

74

BEA WAS ASTONISHED TO FIND SARA OUTSIDE HER HOUSE AT FOUR IN the morning, throwing rocks up at the window like a cliche. She quickly ran to the front door to let her in.

"What are you doing here?"

Sara was out of breath and panting. Though he had chased her halfway through the town, she realized now that Everest probably didn't pose any real threat to her. Her mind kept jumping back to the moment when she spotted the trail to Bea's house, so stark and clear on the hillside, inexplicably obvious when it had been impossible to find before.

"It's a long story," Sara said. "Can I tell you in the morning?"

But her heart was pounding too hard to sleep and her mind was racing, trying to figure out where she would go and what she would do.

She removed the contacts that she had almost forgotten about, studying them with eyes that ached against the air, raw and naked now, unable to see any of the circuitry in the tiny cups of plastic but knowing it had to be there. Wanting nothing to do with it anymore.

Curled up beside Bea in the mess of a bed, staring at Bea's poster-clad ceiling and listening to her best friend's slumbering breath, Sara might have been ten years old at a sleepover. But back then she wouldn't have felt so lost.

Eventually the sun slit through the window, bathing the messy room in creamy morning light. Bea roused sometime after that, sitting up without an alarm and nudging Sara to see if she was sleeping.

"I never fell asleep," Sara said.

"Yeah, I can see that," Bea said, pointing to the dark circles under her own eyes.

Sara rolled her eyes. "Can always count on you for honesty."

"Speaking of which, are you gonna tell me what's up?"

Sara did, or tried to. In the morning light and over a cup of milky coffee in Bea's kitchen, nothing seemed as extreme or worrisome as it had the night before. She had nowhere to go, of course, and the betrayal of a fake relationship that she quite enjoyed stung, but there were worse fates than being cast aside.

Nothing matters, remember? So *nothing* matters.

Not even that feeling that you will never be good enough. Not even the questioning of a roof over your head or a meal in your belly. Not even…

"You really do look exhausted," Bea said.

"So you've said."

"You can take a nap in my room, if you want."

"And also maybe stay here forever?" Sara asked.

"I wasn't gonna offer, but since you asked."

Sara snorted. "I won't, though. I can't."

Bea nodded, though Sara didn't think she could possibly understand. "Are you okay?"

Sara shrugged. "No," she said after a beat. "How could I be?"

Bea pouted comically, trying to make a jest of it all. "Boy troubles."

"That's not it," Sara said. "I just…I want to understand, and I don't. What is this place, really?"

Bea looked down into her empty coffee mug. "Want to know what I think?"

"Always."

"They've seen how things are going. In the world. And they're scared." Sara didn't need to ask who Bea meant. "But this?" she asked.

"Some venture capitalist's idea of peace," Bea said. "They're trying to solve the same problem philosophers have long contemplated, I think. How little do people need to be happy?"

"So much of what they provided was fake, you know," Sara replied, thinking this over. "All augmented reality and cheaper than it seems."

"Of course," Bea said. She was smiling and nodding, warming to her ideas. "And they'll ratchet it down even more over time."

"It explains the really good food," Sara mused. "And lack of alcohol." And so much else.

"Right! Exactly! Alcohol just makes everything more…inflammatory."

"What? I was just thinking it was more expensive."

"That too," Bea agreed. "But they want to keep away the restive mobs."

Sara snorted a laugh. "The restive mobs?"

"Like I said." Bea shrugged. "They're scared."

"Of the people in the Community?"

"Of the people in general!"

Sara was not convinced. "They take us only when we're young and healthy. It's all about cost."

"Or you can look at it differently. After all, the youth have led every revolution in history."

Sara shivered. She wasn't sure whether that was true, but it was plausible.

"Give enough people a safe shelter for a while," Bea said, "make them feel warmth toward your brand in the most thorough possible way, and maybe when the masses come for the oligarchs, they'll spare you."

"That's horrifying."

"But it makes more sense than the idea that it's all about product trials."

Sara sighed.

An idea was forming in her mind, and she felt lighter for it. She didn't know what good it would do or even what the point of it really was, but it felt so obvious now. Forever would always be precarious. The world was falling down around her. How selfish to have ever imagined she could escape.

75

One month before the Community

NICK'S UNCLE WAS IN SHENZHEN WALKING HOME FROM DINNER WHEN they reached him. He hadn't heard of the fires but was glad they were safe at his house.

"Eat whatever you want, especially what's in the freezer," he said. "Who knows when the power will come back. The solar panels are wired to hit the lights and air conditioner first, probably not enough for the fridge."

The four of them were crowded around the phone on the couch, faces illuminated in the glow. His uncle looked maybe sixty, well dressed, face unlined despite his age.

"Thanks," Nick said. "Do you have flashlights? A lantern?"

"Under the sink," he said. "And listen, we won't be back until at least March. Stay as long as you want."

March was six months away. It was generous, but Sara doubted their neighborhood would be rebuilt by then.

"Thanks so much," Nick said.

"Okay, I've gotta go," his uncle said, looking at something off screen. "Take care of yourself, Nicky."

And the phone went black.

"I thought you said you were both Nick when you met?" Zach teased. "*Nicky?*"

Nick shrugged. "Family, you know."

At that, Sara realized she should call her parents. They hadn't been calling her, which meant they probably didn't know about the fire. It was not yet five in the morning, after all. They had to be asleep.

Nick went off to find light and she clicked off the flashlight on her phone. Sara's battery was almost full—it would last four or five days, probably, even if she used it more heavily than usual—but she wanted to conserve the battery anyway. As a matter of principle.

"You okay?" Zach asked, sitting next to her in the dark.

Her throat ached and she felt a kind of exhaustion that had nothing to do with how little sleep she'd gotten. She leaned against him, curling up as small as she could make herself. His presence was less comforting than she would have liked; she couldn't wait for Bea to get there.

"All things considered, yeah," she said finally.

"We can't stay here until March," Zach whispered.

Sara nodded. He was right; no matter what Nick's uncle had said, the offer did not really extend to them, perfect strangers. Some social niceties remained even amid disaster.

"Water?" Nicholas offered, coming in with a plastic jug in one hand and a stack of glasses in the other.

They gratefully accepted the drink and then Nick brought in a lantern. The four of them sat there in silence, staring at the LED faux-flame as it flickered, waiting for morning.

76

SARA SPENT THE DAY MOPING AROUND BEA'S HOUSE, SLEEPING FOR A few hours and staring at her phone for many more.

The house looked different without the contacts. The changes were subtle, things she wouldn't have necessarily noticed without her desire to seek out each detail. And she was sure she didn't notice everything, since she wasn't about to put them back in to compare. But she caught far more logos in the artifacts it housed than she recalled from her previous visit, and far fewer cobwebs in the corners. It was generally more modern and well-kept than she thought it had been, which made sense: the company would want to make it look as unappealing as possible to any members who made it there.

Usually, the phone remained charged without issue because she carried it with her everywhere, recharging the battery through the kinetic energy of motion, but Everest had evidently left it on the desk. It was almost dead. As a result, Sara found herself shuffling slowly through the chaotic house in Bea's old slippers, blindly dodging piles of laundry and stacks of old musty books and scavenged furniture.

She flicked through the recent notifications first, news alerts about a refugee crisis and a cyclone and some floods, junk email clogging an inbox she hadn't really used since high school, pings on social media accounts that she hadn't missed at all. She had missed calls from her parents and about a dozen texts, mostly from her family and a few from Zach. Nothing worth replying to, nothing she didn't already know. Nothing from Emily. Her broken heart cracked further.

She stared for a long time at the last message from her mother, an exact copy of the one she had sent through the company's message service telling her of their departure. Wondering where they were now, if they were okay, if they had time to think of her. She was still too afraid to ask.

Mostly, she scrolled through news feeds, devouring whatever information she could grasp from the outside world, a place she had already begun to categorize as separate from her own world. How quickly that happened. The events, good and bad alike, felt very far away. They were, as always, mostly bad.

The ongoing saga of Central Americans piling up on the border with Mexico, and Americans clamoring in parallel to be let into Canada. Canada had not yet commented.

Scandinavia and Germany forming their own economic union after a decade of threatening to end subsidies to the rest of Europe. Angry retorts by the French, but what else was new? Spain and Greece blaming Britain for everything. Switzerland bartering their glacial meltwater for continued prominence, unscathed as always.

Continued coverage of the war in the South China Sea, but she couldn't bring herself to care about that. After a decade of fighting, it hardly seemed urgent anymore.

Tales of degradation in Washington, exploding budgets and incapable politicians and a corrupt Supreme Court that hadn't issued a ruling worth writing about in five years. FEMA had collapsed and the Postal Service budget was being turned over to them. It was a wonder it hadn't happened sooner. She always figured it would be the National Park Service that was the first to go, but she didn't see anything in the headlines about that.

The Vice President had cried during a news conference, heartbroken that she could not do anything to help those affected by the floods, and the press alternately lambasted and praised her. It happened three weeks ago, but still dominated the headlines.

Leaks from the VA reported euthanasia of bankrupt veterans, what some called mercy killings and others murder and others a vicious rumor that should not be repeated. One editorial even boldly advocated expanding the policy.

When Bea returned from the Community, Sara was grateful for the distraction.

"It feels like the world picked these two months to fall apart," Sara said.

Bea shrugged. "Only because it's hitting you all at once."

They chopped vegetables and boiled pasta and sang along to songs Sara hadn't heard since entering the Community, songs she chose herself. It felt more luxurious than anything she had experienced.

Normally it would have made her feel more like herself again, but it just increased her sense of disassociation; she was unable to reconcile the two people she felt she had become. Trying to confront the depressing reality while still living for the moment as if everything was okay. And failing.

All day, in between reading articles about war and famine and disaster, her mind flitted back to Everest and his bewildered and guilty expression the night before, how ridiculous his reaction had been, how stupid.

Berating herself for letting herself ever feel anything for him, for not seeing through the charade. Hating that she had slept with someone she barely knew, and also, belatedly, that she had never actually broken up with Zach. What kind of person did that?

But she kept pulling herself back, diving into terrible stories of places far away, refusing to engage with her own complicity or idiocy.

So over bowls of noodles and fresh tomatoes and garlic, she laughed with Bea and pretended things were fine. The world was not melting down and neither was she.

Mercifully, Bea's menagerie of roommates kept their distance.

Sara tried to find the words to describe how she felt, not to tell Bea, but to narrate to herself. That felt important.

Afraid, maybe. Relieved, certainly. Disconnected. Grateful, that she was here with her best friend and not anyone else. Dreading what might come next but also excited to see it.

But she trusted Bea. Bea knew what she was doing.

Which was, in itself, strange. Who was this girl, so confident in this liminal life? Had this been Bea all along and Sara just too blind to see it?

They washed their dishes and the conversation drifted on, turning nostalgic, reminiscing about college and their big dreams.

"Remember that guy, what was his name, who liked you so much sophomore year?" Bea asked.

Sara shrugged. "I'm not sure..."

Bea laughed. "Right, you have guys falling all over you all the time!"

"David?" Sara offered.

"Yes! David!" Bea said, snapping her fingers.

"What about him?"

"Did you hear he IPOed?" Bea asked. "Made a cool billion last week."

They were back in Bea's room now. This news prompted Sara to flop onto Bea's pile-of-blankets bed and harrumph. "That's the worst news I've heard yet today."

"Sorry you turned him down?"

Sara rolled over to look up at Bea and considered before replying. "No," she said. "Because he was just *so boring.*"

Bea laughed. "I'm so glad not everyone's a gold digger."

"Why, you'd go for it?" Sara asked.

"Love, my whole life is about getting by," she said. "I'm just disappointed none of the guys I've dated for money are billionaires."

Sara chuckled and leaned back to stare at the ceiling. "Do you want to go outside?"

Sara hadn't spent an entire day inside since she entered the Community. Four walls for a full day felt impossibly claustrophobic.

"We could, I guess," Bea replied, reaching for a jacket. She paused. "Do you even have shoes?"

"I can't believe I forgot."

Bea shook her head, laughing. "You can borrow mine, but please don't wear those slippers outside."

Sara followed Bea out into the night like a shadow, wearing Bea's sneakers and sweatshirt to complete the effect.

Bea glanced over at her in the moonlight. "Did you want to talk about something?"

Sara shrugged and said nothing. Bea seemed to accept this.

They trudged across the dunes, walking over plant life that was invisible in the darkness. Sara mourned each crushed leaf but didn't stop.

Instead, she looked away, to the ocean, which always drew her eyes. A flat, silver plain from this angle, immense and expansive and all those massive words that didn't really mean anything. So calm from this far up, its irregularities and angry spots and tumult hidden by distance.

Like people, she thought. From too far away everything that makes them interesting disappears.

"I think I pity him," she said.

"Everest?"

"I might be deluding myself," Sara said slowly, "but I think he's as conflicted about this place as I am. And far more stuck here."

"What makes you think that?"

"He's not stupid," she said. "He left my phone out on purpose."

"Like a cheater who wants to be caught."

Sara chuckled. "Like someone who just wants it to be over."

"If you were standing here telling me how you really think he did love you, I might think you were deluding yourself," Bea said.

Sara raised an eyebrow. "Thanks?"

Bea laughed. "I'm saying I think you're right! I have no idea how he feels. Or how you feel, honestly?"

Sara shrugged. "Me neither." That wasn't quite true, but she did know that her feelings for Everest, whatever they were, mattered a lot less than her feelings about Bea, and about life.

"But I would not be surprised if he's doubting how great it is to be chosen. I'm sure many of you lucky few feel that way eventually."

"You were chosen too, Bea." Sara whispered the words, so quiet she feared the wind would steal them.

And for a moment she thought maybe it had. It took Bea a very long time to reply. "I have wondered about that."

Sara reached for her fingers and squeezed, then let her hand drop. "It doesn't matter. It's just what a tech giant thinks of us. Chosen or not, we hate them, remember?"

It was very similar to something Bea had said to her years before, when Sara did not get a prestigious internship offer that she'd longed for.

"You really have a thing for guys you work with, don't you?" Bea asked, trying to lighten the conversation.

Sara laughed and nudged her with her elbow. "I think we both need to work on avoiding that power dynamic."

"Start a company. Hire someone and sleep with him."

"I wouldn't go *that* far."

They were both laughing, then, and though Sara knew nothing was all right, she was glad she could at least experience one more perfect night. The full moon dipped toward the waves, so bright and sharp, just like the night of the museum party when she had wanted to walk out upon the path it drew. It called to her still.

77

One month before the Community

BEA ARRIVED SHORTLY AFTER DAWN, TWO OTHER TWENTY-SOME-thing women in tow. They had a tiny, three-seater electric car, the kind with a ten-thousand-mile range designed for people with nowhere to charge them, which fit in the driveway behind Sara's old minivan and made it look ridiculous.

Once inside, Sara and Bea embraced and the two new women introduced themselves as Cleo and Priya, roommates from the apartment across the hall from Bea.

Everyone gathered in the kitchen, where people always end up.

The stove was gas-powered, but they hadn't been able to heat anything up yet because they couldn't light it. Nick had been looking for matches for the past hour.

"Oh, I have a lighter," Priya said, when she took stock of the situation.

Soon they were heating frozen fried rice and boiling water for tea. With daylight streaming in the window, things almost felt normal.

The lights clicked on suddenly sometime around eight in the morning. Their appearance made Sara jump.

"We don't really need these during the day," Nick said.

With light emanating from it, the chandelier looked even more ridiculous.

"Does your car work as a house stabilizer?" Sara asked Priya.

"Oh, yeah, does this house not have one?" she asked, looking surprised. "I mean, I just assumed…"

"Silly, the things people forget," Nicholas said.

While Sara and Priya shuffled the cars and searched for the connection in the garage, Nick wandered the house turning off all the lights.

Nicholas studied the circuit breaker and electricity meter, tapping at the screen and confirming a few changes. "They had it set to sell back to the grid."

Sara rolled her eyes. "Greedy bastards."

Priya laughed. "Rich people, man."

"But you fixed it?" Sara asked.

Nicholas nodded, and they headed back inside. The solar panels would now back up the electricity they made into the car's battery and they could turn the lights on after dark.

At some point they slept, sprawled across the couch and guest rooms. At some point they woke up again. Sara called her parents and her sister, displaced by a different fire not even twelve hours after she fled her apartment. They were stuck in a shelter in the North Bay. She marked herself safe on social media, and finally fell into a kind of exhausted daze.

That evening, social media started blowing up with warnings that a right-wing militia was prowling the streets of newly abandoned neighborhoods, telling people to either leave or give over their valuables. Like pirates, which were much scarier in reality than in the movies. No one could be sure what was real and what was invention, but rumors like this had been springing up after every disaster for more than a decade, and more often than not, they were based on some manner of truth.

"You think we're safe here?" Sara asked Zach, showing him a post about it.

He frowned deeply, thinking about it longer than she liked. "Sounds like they're in the neighborhoods under evacuation orders."

The implication was clear: it would be a while until they reached towns left fully standing, like where they were. But it still terrified her.

They received another notification sometime around dinner that their neighborhood had been mostly razed and that the fire was now sixty percent contained, but that they were not to return yet.

Nick and Priya scavenged through the kitchen, searching for ingredients to make a reasonable meal when the notification came in, singing along to throwback songs from Nick's middle school years, which Sara only vaguely knew. The blare of the emergency notification cut through some emo male voice crying about a breakup.

Nick glanced at his phone, silenced the notification, and went right back to emptying the freezer out onto the counter. Apparently unfazed.

Sara exchanged a glance with Nicholas.

"He's always like this," he said. "Steady, calm. Useful characteristics these days."

They were sitting on stools at the kitchen counters, working their way through a bottle of pinot noir. Zach was in the living room, talking to each of his panicked parents in turn in Hawaii, and Bea and Cleo were both still napping.

"What are we going to do, though?" Sara asked.

Nicholas shrugged. Took a sip of his wine. Stared at the deep red liquid, like blood in the glass. "This kind of feels like the last straw, you know?"

Sara nodded. "Our startup folded a year ago," she said. "Zach and I have barely worked since."

"Nick worked in finance between the recessions, but now he mostly does app errands. It's depressing."

"What about you?" she asked.

He shrugged. "I graduated with a physics PhD in 2018. Dumb idea, but we thought science funding would come back."

She nodded. Everyone had the same story.

"I'm working on a physics PhD right now!" Priya shouted over the music. Sara was surprised she'd been able to hear them.

Nicholas laughed. "Good luck with that."

Priya did a little half dance and said in a sing-song voice, "I'll need it!"

Nick started frying some veggie patties.

Bea walked into the room then, blinking tiredly. "Something smells good."

"Trying," Nick said. "Can't promise it'll taste good, though."

Bea poured herself a glass of wine then jumped up to sit on the counter since there weren't any more stools.

"So, listen," she said. "I'm thinking we should head to Monterey."

Sara frowned. "What's there?"

Last she'd heard about it was several years before, when the historic downtown was abandoned as the sea level rose. She never did hear what happened to the place, but when your entire economy depended on tourism and the neighborhood that attracted tourists went away, it couldn't be good.

"New city of the future bullshit," Bea said. "They're calling it the Community."

"The *Community?*" Nick asked. "How very euphemistic."

Bea shrugged. "Sounds better than the one in Napa focused on quote-un-quote *wellness.*"

"Doesn't sound all that different to me, honestly," Sara said.

"Selection criteria includes acceptance to college, though you don't actu-ally have to graduate, and you must be under forty. I was just reading about it."

"Well, that counts us out," Nicholas said. "Too old."

"We should really go check on my parents, anyway," Nick said pointedly, and Nicholas nodded.

But Sara wasn't really listening to them. She was trying to see if Bea was serious, and it seemed like she was. "This could be a terrible idea, Bea."

Bea downed her glass of wine. "You got a better one?"

78

SARA SLIPPED OUT OF BEA'S HOUSE BEFORE ANYONE ELSE AWOKE. SHE had planned to set out without even a water bottle, stripped bare by the experience of her life here in all ways, but on her way through the kitchen to the door she saw a pot of coffee sitting cold on the counter, brewed the night before, and couldn't leave it there unwanted. After a minute's pause while it spun in the microwave, she hiked out over the dunes with a thermos in one hand.

She still wore Bea's sweatshirt and sneakers, and now also her pajamas, too. Her hair was tied back in a messy bun and she squinted into the predawn air, wishing for a flashlight but also glad to be invisible without one.

For once she was as anonymous as she now understood she had always been and would always be. She trekked onward, sand melting around her feet, a breeze twirling around her legs. She opened her mouth to taste the ocean on the wind.

She was, like everyone else alive, both a tragedy and a miracle.

With every step, she used some sense she did not control to keep upright in a marvel of engineering she couldn't hope to understand, obliterating an entire community of microorganisms and insects that she would never consider.

A tragedy and a miracle.

She sipped her coffee and stumbled through the night. The moon was long gone and the sun still half an hour away, according to the weather app on her phone.

The horizon began to glow gray, then blue, and she increased her pace, not wanting to miss the sunrise. Plants and sand and soil passed fluidly beneath her.

She reached the hill she had come to think of as her own, where she had run on that early day during that first game of twisted tag. She paused at its base, staring up at the muddy slopes and tangled vines, forcing herself to exist in the single moment of insignificance below it before beginning the arduous climb.

She made herself feel each scrape against rock, each straining muscle a miniscule atonement for the sins of her species.

She made herself feel very alive, the breath coursing through her, the air brisk against her face, the blood pumping through her limbs and the thoughts flitting through her brain.

She let herself search for them.

When each human takes up so much space, is living a betrayal of what matters?

If one is any less worthy than that which they might destroy, then perhaps.

She scrambled upward, the balance difficult to maintain.

Applied properly, you are not a threat. You are entirely meaningless, remember?

Not in the sense that you're worth destroying. In the sense that the universe would not even notice if you disappeared tomorrow, would not even care.

The sky to the east bled orange and pink along the timid coastal mountains, the sun glowing brilliant against the underside of scattered clouds stretched thin across the blue above. Not silver linings, but something grander. Gold.

Viewed from the scale of the universe or the ants, the suffering one human causes without notice is tremendous but unimportant, she thought, as she scrambled on and dislodged lichen that had grown for a hundred years.

The top of the hill drew near and so did the sun. Sara lowered herself to sit on a long-dead fallen tree and watch the ocean and the sky, muscles aching from the exertion and the cold.

Sara remembered being wary of the cliff before, but now she could not remember why. It was not much of a cliff—not a fall that could kill her, or even injure her, most likely—and she could see a plausible path through the shrubbery to the damp sand below. She drank the last of the coffee and set the thermos between a rock and a tuft of seagrass, checking it to be sure it was clearly left there on purpose rather than littered, and then set off toward the waves.

The descent went better than she expected, her feet and fingers finding purchase on the disintegrating dune without difficulty. Downclimbing felt good, like giving up.

Too soon, her feet reached the beach. She turned away from the dunes and out to the water, breathing slowly and forcing her mind to quiet. The ocean seemed to glow rich blue in the predawn light, lapping with the gentle insistence of a receding tide. Above her head, the sky had just begun to stretch from black to red to daylight, but had yet to commit to a full sunrise. It was a perfect in-between moment.

She sighed and bent to remove her shoes, relishing the feeling of the sand between her toes once she stepped free. Why did people ever wear shoes? The sand caressed her, rough and soft in equal measure, exactly what she needed.

She realized she had almost ceased to smell the salt air rising off the water, so used to it had she become. Another small tragedy.

Would it be easier in her clothes? She didn't know how cold the water was, didn't much want to ruin Bea's pajamas or be pulled down by their wet weight, but couldn't quite stomach stripping naked there in the exposed light of breaking day. She was not quite so bold.

Compromising with herself, she removed the outer layers and stood shivering in a t-shirt and underwear, the hairs on her arms rising atop goosebumps. Before she could lose her nerve, she broke into a run and dashed out into the frigid Pacific.

This was not the balmy ocean of so many California dreamers, but the more honest, sharp winter water of the north, still cold even in the warming world. She gasped as it reached her knees, had to force herself onward with all of her willpower, and sucked in another urgent breath when it crested past her delicate stomach. Too cold. So cold.

She kept going, breath sharp and challenging as the gentle waves crushed in around her. Why had she thought this a good idea?

But it was, she told herself. It was the only idea.

Up to her chest now, she pressed herself off the seafloor like a ballerina going up on her toes, letting the strength of the saltwater carry her. It was easier than she had expected it to be.

And then she started to swim. Without looking back over her shoulder, she knew the sun rose behind her; it was far too chilly on that winter morning for any warmth to reach her there amid the waves, but she could still feel it, the imperceptible shift into day from night. She swam away from it as forcefully as she could.

She cut broad breaststrokes through the soft waves and kicked in time with her arms, pulling herself through the bay the same way she had pulled herself up the hill. The water ceased to chill her anymore. The cold seeped deep into her body; her fingers went numb. Her mind went numb, as she wanted.

Somewhere behind her, a voice.

Sara did not turn, but kept forward, out toward the fleeing night in the water. The Pacific for once living up to its name, so calm she could feel how her every stroke disrupted its peace.

Even she did not know where she was going, or how long she could possibly swim. Even she did not know why, just that it was all she could do. Someday she would return to the shore. Somehow.

The voice lifted toward her on the wind and she turned, languidly, not even meaning to. Her feet dropped down below her, dangling into the darkness. She marveled at just how far she had swum. She wondered how deep the water was beneath her, how distant the seafloor.

There was a figure on the beach, all alone. Shouting something, but she was so far away already and water filled her ears.

Sara treaded in place, letting the waves hold her, letting the cold reach even deeper into her. Fear and despair seemed silly when there was so much unknown around her. Someone once told her the depths of the ocean were as unknown as the expanse of space. She hoped that was true.

She pushed up onto her back, floating there, staring skyward. The bleeding sunrise stretched its greedy fingers into the fast-departing night. As it always did, the darkness was losing. But she could still see the last proud stars.

The person on the beach shouted again and this time she recognized the word as her name. Almost sadly, she let her curiosity tip her forward, let some emotion fill her again as she turned back toward the beach. The person was Everest. Of course it was.

Her moment of solitude broke and her reverence shattered.

Was he coming to apologize? To kick her out? To beg her to stay?

She turned away slightly, looking instead to the rising sun far behind him. Ignoring his voice in favor of the whispering waves which she could almost understand as words.

She had tried to flee that sun, chasing the night out into the waves, but the daylight was so very beautiful. Casting the landscape in a multicolored morning, making the windows of the Community's buildings glitter as if they were something to cherish rather than fear.

She could keep swimming away. She could just stay where she was and let the ocean decide what to do with her.

She couldn't remember a time when the ocean did not seem to hold all the answers, but she also had always known it would never share them. It cradled her there, in its silver hands so far from where she belonged, keeping her safe but also pulling the life from her slowly, so slowly. Her limbs spun in the water, holding her body aloft even as she felt herself fading.

She could not swim forever. Had she ever meant to?

It would be so easy to give in, to let the waves pull her away. It would be so easy to sink beneath the surface, feel the water pressing into her closed eyes, let it swallow her whole. The ocean would not care.

That's what it meant not to matter, she thought. She was meaningless, immeasurable, a tiny blip. Something the waves could caress or condemn so easily.

She still had her hands, though, and her legs, kicking and keeping afloat. She did not have to rely on the waves alone.

The waves would be waiting when next she needed them. The fires could not take them away, even if they could take everything else.

She decided she should return, try again, see what the daylight might bring.

She leaned toward the shore and came in against the retreating tide.

Acknowledgments

FIRST OFF—THANK YOU TO THE (UNNAMED) PUBLISHER THAT OF-
fered me a contract for another book which I later declined. Without you,
I might never have reached out to my network and found All She Wrote
Productions to bring *Platformed* into the world.

Thanks, of course, to Thea Chard with All She Wrote and all the editors,
designers, and publicists who helped make this a book and not just a story. I
had some idea how much extra work there was beyond writing the thing, but
now I know I couldn't have done this alone.

A big thank you to Lulu Miller, who responded to her Twitter DMs and then
graciously agreed to let me use an excerpt from her wonderful book *Why Fish
Don't Exist* as an epigraph.

Thank you to the friends who inspired Bea: Grace Oh, Maggie Ford, and
Sierra Alef (in no particular order).

Thank you to Roman Decca for reading an early draft and coming up with
the title. And also for the "surface dwellers" line, said entirely in earnest.

Thank you to the friends who encourage me and cheer me on. You know
who you are.

Thank you to the not-quite-friends who gave me the ideas for some of the
less flattering Silicon Valley characters. You probably don't know who you
are, but some of our mutual acquaintances will.

Thanks to those who love me and who I love. Those who always agree to read
my drafts no matter how messy they might be: my parents Kim and Marty
Josund, my grandparents Bill and Liz Hawkins, and my partner Gawan Fiore
and his mom Morgan Buckli. And to my sister, Anika, who I know better
than to bother with a rough early draft.

Thanks to the city of Seattle for nurturing my love of the environment and particularly the ocean, and to Silicon Valley for being a weird, intense place full of real people, not just algorithms and giant corporations. Thanks to Stanford University for immersing me in this strange world, and thanks to the wonderful startups I've worked for that are nothing like One.

About the Author

KELSEY JOSUND IS A SOFTWARE ENGINEER AND AUTHOR OF SCI-FI, cli-fi, fantasy, and new and young adult fiction, including a series of forthcoming feminist retellings of classic fairy tales.

Originally from Seattle, Kelsey loves getting outdoors and living in places that allow her to escape to the mountains on the weekends. She cares deeply about the ecosystems that humans impact and that impact them in return. Her writing explores these themes through the prism of the traditional coming-of-age arcs of science fiction and fantasy. Kelsey is particularly interested in stories and characters that complicate the traditional and familiar, leading her to rediscover old tales from new and unexpected angles.

With a passion for storytelling in all its forms, Kelsey approaches writing fiction the same way she approaches writing code: she likes to know where it's going, but wants to figure out the details as she goes. She believes good software is a lot like a good story—full of neat and clever solutions to tricky problems, beautiful at a granular level but also from a distance.

Kelsey lives and works in Silicon Valley, California with her partner and their cat. She holds a bachelor's and master's degree in computer science from

Stanford University, and is currently plotting her return to the Pacific North-west and working on her next novel.

For more information, visit www.KelseyJosund.com.

Other books by Kelsey Josund

Pretty Deadly

Book Club Reading Guide

1.   How would this story change if told from the perspective of another character, such as Everest or Bea?

2.   What motivates Sara's changing opinions of the Community, herself and her loved ones over the course of the book?

3.   Do you think it was the author's intent to make a statement about science and technology, its effect on the modern world, and its role in forging our future—and if so, what do you think that statement is?

4.   Why do you think Sara chose to enter the Community at the beginning of the book? Would you make the same choice, under the same circumstances and if given the opportunity? Why, or why not?

5.   How does Sara change as a result of her time in the Community? What about the other residents—do they change, and if so, in what ways?

6.   What predictions about our world does this book make? How plausible do they feel to you?

7.   Is this book optimistic, or does it serve as a warning?

8.   What could you do today to prevent a future like this from occurring?

9.   Though written in 2018, the themes prevalent in *Platformed* are quite prescient of some of the shared experiences felt around the world in 2020 and 2021—which themes resonated the most with your personal experience, and why?

10. What similarities, if any, does *Platformed* share with other recent science fiction stories in the media today? What makes it different?

Thank You for Reading!

Did you enjoy *Platformed*? Consider leaving a review with your preferred retailer or favorite bookish organization to help other readers who might enjoy *Platformed* find it!

All reader reviews are greatly appreciated, however reviews on the following platforms are particularly helpful in connecting new and independent authors with new readers:

Amazon
BookBub
Goodreads
Your Indie Bookseller of Choice...

Thank you & happy reading!